SUMMERTIME

WILLOW ASTER

Annabel —

So lovely to
meet you!

Xo,

Willow Aster

Nate, Greyley & Kira, and Indigo, my favorites of all time,
I love you.

You know me best and love me best and I'm so grateful for all
of you.

1

HELLO, HOLLYWOOD

Everyone hopes for the best summer ever. At least I don't think that's just something you outgrow. My mom hasn't. And this year, newly graduated from the University of North Carolina, I have built my hopes up to otherworldly status.

I am *counting* on the best summer ever.

After a lifetime of sporadic visits to see my director father in Hollywood, occasional phone calls from his crazy set locations, and incredible presents for all the holidays but a lack of presence, you might say...I am headed to California to spend the entire summer with my father. Sounds completely normal, right?

Somehow, I'm not feeling the normalcy quite yet.

Last week, I went to the grocery store and saw my dad's face on the cover of *TIME Magazine* with the title: **Cole Winters, the Most Influential Director of All Time.** *Insert eye roll here.* I'm proud of him and even inspired that he's followed his dreams, but I'd probably be more so if I saw him on a regular basis and if I'd watched more of his movies. But that's part of why I'm here—to get to know him better.

For this girl from Charlotte, where I live a simple life with my mama, our dog Jericho, and my sister Autumn, I don't quite know what to expect.

What I do not expect is the sexy-ass driver that picks me up at the airport in place of my dad. It's hard to be disappointed that Dad's not here when this chiseled god with dark wavy hair that's slightly too long says, "Summer Winters?"

You can imagine the jokes I've heard all my life about the name. It wasn't my mom's finest move. And then she went and did it again with my sister. But hey, my dad had already bailed double by then, so I cut her some slack for giving us the dumbest combo in the history of names.

But this guy, he says it in this husky rasp that makes chill bumps pop out across my skin and I shiver.

"Present," I say, lifting my hand like I'm in school.

The hell is wrong with me?

He nods and his features don't move in a smile or a frown, he just sort of pleasantly takes my luggage and puts it in the trunk before opening the back door for me. My messy updo and leggings suddenly feel like they're not my best look. In fact, I'm certain they're not. I really wish I'd made more of an effort, but how was I to know I'd be facing this hottie? It was the crack of crack when I left for the airport this morning and a five-hour flight.

Once I'm in the car and we're driving out of the airport, I'm always shocked that there really are so many palm trees. And also, that LA isn't super pretty. I mean, I've seen it enough now to know both of these things, but it still seems to catch me by surprise.

"You haven't told me your name. How do I know you aren't kidnapping me and holding me for a ridiculously high ransom?"

He looks at me from the rearview mirror, eyes still giving nothing away. "You should have asked that before you got in the car, Summer Winters. Little late now." At the light, he looks back and smirks. "Hudson Callihan at your service."

"Well, that's a distinguished name. So, you drive for my dad?"

"You could say that."

"Is he nice to work for?"

"Most days."

I like that he's not sugarcoating it for me. "And when he's not?"

"Then everyone stays out of his way."

"Noted."

His eyes meet mine in the mirror again. "It's been a long time since you visited your dad?"

"A few years. I haven't been to the Malibu house yet."

"Ahh. You'll like it."

"Do you know what my dad's doing today that he couldn't be interrupted to come pick me up at the airport?"

"You noticed that, huh."

I snort and then cringe. Snorting is so not Hollywood.

"He had a last-minute guest come through town. He

asked you to meet him for dinner. It'll give you time to rest a bit, change, do whatever you want to do for a couple of hours."

"How nice," I say under my breath.

I can't say I'm surprised that I'm already disappointed, but when my dad asked me to come for the summer, I thought maybe we would have the opportunity to—you know what? I'm not even going to finish that thought. I'm here. I need to give him a chance. Take him as he is, all that. Fresh start, yada, yada.

Hudson is quiet and as much as I want to get to know him better and stare at the way his hair curls around his ear on the one side and the way his tanned arms look against the steering wheel, being in the back seat with the sun shining on my face is making me so sleepy. I close my eyes for just a minute and I guess I fall asleep because the next thing I know, Hudson's hand is on my shoulder, leaning over me with concern.

I jump and he pulls back, standing up.

"I'm sorry. You weren't waking up."

"I was dreaming." I stare at him and see the whole picture in front of me. "We were on the beach and a jellyfish walked out and stung both of us."

Hudson laughs for the first time and I stare at him, stunned. Holy crabcake over a campfire, he is a sight to behold.

"Do you just say whatever you're thinking at all times?" he asks, still grinning.

I step out of the car and shrug. "Most of the time." I pride myself on being upfront about things, but I have to keep *some* things private. Such as the fact that I wouldn't mind ripping his clothes off right now.

His light eyes twinkle and his white teeth do that little

twinkle thing that teeth commercials do, I swear it. And by the way he smirks at me as he pulls my luggage out of the car, I think maybe my face gives away what I haven't said.

My hopes for the best summer are looking up. About six feet, two inches up, to be exact.

2

HOME, SWEET, SO NOT HOME

I STRETCH ONCE I'M OUT OF THE CAR AND TURN SLOWLY TO face the house. Or mansion. Geez, Dad. Overcompensating for something? The circular drive is impressive and the mansion gazing down at me is even more so. I can smell the salty air and would wager a guess that the ocean is just right over there in the backyard.

Five of my house in Charlotte would fit in this one.

The yard is spacious. A couple acres maybe, which is like a jillion in California. Even I know that much.

"A couple horses that way." He points to his left. "Tennis courts past that. Pool in the back, can't miss the ocean…"

"Who'd he have to kill to get this place?" I ask Hudson, and again with his smirk. It is a dang cute smirk.

"Have you watched your dad's movies?" he asks.

"Most of them. Usually a little blast-happy for my taste. I did really enjoy *Midnight* though."

"Really?" He sounds pleased at that and I glance over at him. We walk to the front door and he opens it without knocking. "I would've pegged you as more of a rom-com kind of girl."

"Oh, I love rom-coms, but my favorite are the *bittersweet, cry in your sleeve at the sadness while being amazed at how deep the dialogue is,* kind of movies. With a little laughter thrown in, so it's not too morose."

"Specific."

"I'm a writer, what can I say? I care about the words, not just watching things explode."

Hudson and I get locked in a stare and he looks like he wants to say something, but instead, he sets my luggage down.

I glance around the open floor plan. It really is beautiful. Cozy couches and fresh flowers, windows everywhere. Everything is white but the flowers and the hardwood floors, more white than I'd imagine in a bachelor pad, but then again, my dad could have twelve wives living here for all I know. They'd certainly fit.

The ocean is *right there.* Just walk outside and into the water.

Maybe I don't even need to connect with my dad, maybe it'll be enough that I am in this paradise for the next few months.

"I can show you to your room, if you'd like."

"That would be great."

He grabs my luggage again, even though I've tried every time to take it myself, and we walk down the hall past the kitchen.

"This is my favorite side of the house. You get the best view of the water." He opens a door and it's hard not to gasp.

The walls are white, the bed linens are white, the couch is white, but there are walls of glass and the room is literally suspended over the water. It's the most beautiful thing I've ever seen.

"Wow," I whisper.

"Think you can be comfortable here?"

I look back at him and feel sad that he's probably going to leave as soon as I answer him. He can let my dad know I'm settled and wash his hands of me. Meanwhile, I feel like I want to hang onto the only person I know...even if it's only been an hour since I met him.

"I think so." It comes out sounding sadder than I intended and I try to smile to lighten it up.

"I'm in the room next to you, so if you need anything and I'm around, just knock."

Well, that perks me right up. "You live here?"

"Yep. I can show you all the secret hiding spots." His words sound like he's joking, but he doesn't smile, just says it in that sexy low-key way that makes me wonder what in the world he's thinking. He reaches in his pocket and holds out a card. "Your dad wanted me to give you this." He seems embarrassed to say it, but I can't hold it against him that my dad is an asshole for giving me his business card. Correction: Having *someone else* give me his business card. "I put my number on the back, and you can text me whenever. I work an insane amount of hours, but I'll do whatever I can to help when you need it."

"I bet that's what you say to all the girls," I try to joke, but it comes out weak. I can't pull off that sexy rasp like he can.

"Your dad will be back in a couple of hours. Get some rest, or check out the horses. Bertha and Milly are sweet. Swim if you like."

I suddenly feel exhausted by the day. And all of it. The grandeur of this place, the expectations, all of it catches up with me.

"I don't need to be entertained, Hudson." It's sharp and it catches him off guard. He goes still and looks at me warily. "Thanks for everything. I'll see to myself from here on."

He nods and doesn't say anything as he leaves the room, shutting the door behind him.

I fall back on my bed and stare out the window. It's instantly calming. I felt like crying just moments ago, but when I stare out at the endless water, it makes me feel like my hurt feelings aren't so big after all.

Instead of sleeping, I FaceTime my mom to let her know I'm okay. I show her and Autumn the view and they are sufficiently impressed. Autumn has been doing college abroad, so she wanted to spend the summer with Mama instead of coming here. I don't blame her, but I wish she was with me.

"What are you doing tonight?" Mama asks.

"I think we're having dinner in an hour and a half."

"That sounds nice. Enjoy yourself, honey. Okay? And rest. You've worked your tail off the past four years getting your bachelor's and keeping up your schedule at work. You deserve this time there in that beautiful setting. Enjoy every minute."

"You deserve a break too," I tell her, my eyes filling with tears.

My mom owns a group home for adults with disabilities.

I've worked with her there for as long as I can remember, and I'm really going to miss some of the residents. Not Hank with the wandering hands and the foul mouth...or Ellen, who was like a dark thundercloud on the sunniest day...but everyone else.

"My time will come." She smiles. "This is your time now. Enjoy it."

I think of Hudson and how just looking at him is enjoyable. I grin back at her, partly because I want her to know I'm going to be okay, and also because I'm excited to see Hudson again. He lives *here*! I think that just sunk in. And I was rude to him before. Gah. I need to settle that so I can at least have one friend around here.

3

SURFER COMPETITION

I HUSTLE INTO THE GINORMOUS SHOWER WHEN I GET OFF OF the video chat. It's also overlooking the water and I'm glad no ships are passing by with sailors and binoculars. It's like I'm bathing outside in the open air with all this glass. Weird but oddly freeing, I guess.

I feel better after talking to my mom and sister. As long as we talk often, I shouldn't get too homesick. The summer will fly by and I'll be home in August to have a couple of weeks with Autumn before she starts her senior year of college. Yes, we have the same dad. No, he wasn't around for her birth either. Let's just say my parents were high school sweethearts, but my dad had big Hollywood dreams that my mom didn't seem to fit into. He was also a smooth talker and apparently didn't know the meaning of using a condom.

Mama never has a bad thing to say about my dad though. She blames herself for two back-to-back pregnancies with a guy she knew was more committed to chasing his career than he could ever be to her. With Autumn, she was taking the pill, but that whole antibiotic thing was a slap in the face when she found out that nullified the pill. The rest is history, and I'm so grateful to have my sister.

Dad thought he could handle papahood for about a minute when Autumn came along and then said something like *nope, meant it the first time, I'm out.* Mama says she doesn't regret a thing. Yes, he broke her heart. Twice. But she has two amazing gifts to show for it. She really is the best mom in the world.

I open my suitcase and shake out a cute dress I bought before I came. I should've hung it up when I got here. Oh well. I open the closet and gasp yet again. This closet already has clothes. *Nice clothes.* I check them out to see if they belong to someone. Does he have another daughter I don't know about? I'd say it's entirely possible. But the clothes all have tags on them and are my size.

Hell yeah, now we're talking. I hang up my dress next to these far more fashionable clothes. The dress I brought looks like something the little old ladies in Charlotte would call precious. Their way of saying sweet but kind of pitiful.

I slip on an ivory mesh mini dress that's so beachy and sweet yet sexy I can hardly take it. I look in the full-length mirror and the back is whoa, an open back, lots of skin, low neckline too. How it manages to look sort of innocent still is beyond me. Maybe these clothes are for someone else, but I'm going with it until I'm told otherwise.

I let my hair air-dry and spray it with my favorite wave enhancer. Too lazy to smooth out my waves tonight with a flat iron and they're cooperating better than they usually do in the Charlotte heat anyway. I take my time applying my makeup, playing up the eyes. I put on a matte lipstick in blush nude and press my lips together. I wonder if Hudson will be at dinner...and who else might be there?

I slip on my rose gold platform sandals and my mixture of gold and silver and rose gold bracelets, feeling a little more like home when I put them on. Autumn gave me these from London before I left.

At exactly six thirty, I step out of my room and make my way down the hall toward the living room and dining area. Two women are in the kitchen and they smile at me.

"Everyone's outside already," the taller one says. "I'm Bella, and this is my cousin, Monique."

Monique smiles and picks up a tray of hors d'oeuvres to carry outside. Both women are beautiful and seem comfortable here. Bella picks up a glass of wine and motions for me to follow her.

"That dress looks beautiful on you," she whispers with a wink. "I knew it would."

"You picked out those clothes? And they're for sure for me?" I whisper back, just as I hear my dad calling out, "Summer!"

Bella laughs. "All for you." And gives my back a little nudge, pointing out where my dad is sitting.

I turn and walk toward him and he stands up and comes toward me, arms outstretched. I'm always struck by how handsome he is when I first see him, and this time is no different. He can hold his own in this town where everyone is beautiful, that's for sure. And somehow, he's managed to look younger than he did when I saw him a year and a half ago.

"Sweetheart," he says, hugging me. "You look beautiful. Wow. I think you're taller than when I saw you last. So good to see you." He leans back and smiles at me.

"It's good to see you too."

He motions to the side of him and a tall blond surfer-looking guy steps closer, his eyes trailing down my body in slow motion. He's a pretty boy all right, that long hair on top and tanned skin, the blue-green eyes and pouty smile that probably makes every girl do his bidding. I lift an eyebrow when his eyes finally reach mine and he grins, his eyes crinkling in an adorable way. Damn. Are there any hideous boys in California?

"Liam Taylor," he says, holding out his hand.

I take it and my dad finishes the introductions for us. "I'm sure Liam needs no introduction, right? He's probably the first one you recognized around here." My dad grins and one eyebrow lifts like we're in on a joke together, but I'm not following.

I study Liam and force myself to let go of his hand. It's a very nice hand. Warm, firm, with just the right amount of— I force myself to come back to the conversation and not drown in Liam's stunningness.

If that's even a word.

All I recognize is someone entirely too hot for his own good.

"This is my daughter, Summer." Dad puts his hand on my shoulder and smiles at Liam. "She'll be helping you for the next couple of months in place of Wendy."

"Sweet," Liam says.

"What am I helping with?" I look back and forth between the two. I missed whatever memo they put out.

"Liam is the lead role for the movie I'm working on now," Dad says like I should know. "You'll be his assistant this summer."

My mouth kind of falls open and Liam looks at me, eyes doing that crinkly grin thing again. *Liam's assistant? What?*

"Fuck yeah," he says, his eyes doing another stroll down my body.

I snap my fingers. "Eyes up here."

"You tell him."

I feel warmth skate across my skin and look up to see Hudson staring Liam down. He glances at me and barely gives any acknowledgment, which is a disappointment to my ego, but just knowing he's here has kicked my adrenaline up a few notches.

Liam puts his arm around my shoulder and I flick it off with my hand. "Need a cocktail?" he asks. "Right over here."

Hudson steps in place on the other side of me. "Don't let this douchebag get to you, Summer. He'll be quick to move on."

My eyes widen at the open hostility bouncing around between the two of these guys.

"Hudson's just jealous I get all the action," Liam says, motioning for me to step ahead of him to the bar. "Even when it comes to his mentor."

"You just made it sound like you're sleeping with her dad." Hudson laughs.

I shudder because I don't want to hear about anyone sleeping with my dad. Liam shudders too, for different reasons.

"Not that there's anything wrong with that, but I do not swing that way," he says for my benefit.

"I need to speak to my dad. I didn't sign up to be anyone's assistant this summer."

"You're breaking my heart," Liam sings after me.

I lift my hand and keep walking. Daddy Dearest and I need to have a chat.

4

ONE BIG HAPPY FAMILY

I WAS SO DISTRACTED WHEN I CAME OUTSIDE LOOKING FOR MY dad, I failed to see how gorgeous it is out here. The twinkle lights, the tables topped with white linens and colorful flowers, the long banquet tables overflowing with food and a bar close by. Music is playing and everyone seems like they've had at least two glasses already. I regret not snatching a glass of something while I was over there, but I search for my dad instead. He's talking to a tall man that looks somewhat familiar. Everyone kind of does here. Being in school for so long, I've read more than I've watched movies, and I make it a point to not follow my dad on any kind of social media, so I feel clueless about most of these people, but I could swear I've seen this guy before. Bella and Monique are standing there too, and a blonde girl that has to be a model or an actress. Ultra-thin and a formidable resting bitch face. I wonder if she's nice underneath, but I don't really want to find out. She looks bored by the whole affair and Bella and Monique try to engage her in conversation, but she's not having it.

"Are you a Winslet Barry fan?" the girl next to me asks.

I look over and a girl who could be an actress herself with her girl-next-door looks is smiling at me and then glances back at the blonde.

"I don't think I've ever seen anything of hers," I admit.

She puts her hand over her mouth in a mock gasp. "Don't let her hear you say that." She turns to face me and holds out her hand. "But I think it makes me like you a little more than I already intended to." She grins so big I can't help but grin back.

"She's that bad, huh?"

She holds up her hand. "I have said too much. The two of you might end up being besties." She shakes her head to negate her last words and I laugh. "Hannah Donovan."

"I'm Summer. It's nice to meet you."

"Oh, I know who you are. We've been so excited for you to get here. Have you met everyone yet?"

I wonder who she means by we because I'm kind of surprised she even knew I was coming. "Just you, Hudson, and Liam."

Her eyes twinkle when she smiles and she leans in closer. "I hope Liam was on his best behavior."

"Not sure what his best behavior looks like. Is he capable of reining it in?"

She laughs. "I knew I'd like you. And no, he's not. Watch out for him. He's slippery."

"I got the impression Liam and Hudson aren't too tight."

"Hell, no. Liam's lucky he can act and surf; otherwise, Hudson would've never agreed to have him in this movie."

I frown. "Hudson has a say about that?"

"Yeah, he's the assistant director. He's your dad's right hand—you didn't know that?"

"I don't know a lot." Not sure why I thought a driver would live on the premises, but I jumped to all kinds of conclusions with that one. Still don't know why he lives here, but that question can wait. "Didn't know this was a surfing movie even."

"I'm Liam's sister in the film." She puts her hand on her head and gets a faraway look in her eyes. "We have a tragic past and can only heal when we surf together. So it really sucks when *one* of us has an accident." She presses her lips together and pretends to be locking the key. "You tell that to the press and I'll have to kill you." She laughs again and I feel more at ease than I have since I got here. I like her.

"Trust me, I want to stay as far away from the press as I can. The photographers only bother with me when my dad is around, and that's more than enough for me. I prefer the background, thank you."

"What do you like to do for fun?" she asks.

"Read, write. I'm kind of boring, I guess."

"I love to read. What do you write?"

My mouth opens, but I'm hesitant—I don't tell too many people about all the screenplays and novels I've started. A couple that I've finished. I choose to be honest but downplay it. "I've started a novel...just for fun."

"That's awesome! I'd love to be able to write. Sometimes I need to get out all these feelings and acting is my only outlet. When the roles aren't pouring in, it's hard to know what to do with all of it."

"Don't tell me you guys are holed away over here all to yourselves!" Liam yells, putting his arms around both of us. "Where are your beverages?" He enunciates beverages to make it sound proper and I don't want to think so, but the guy is so stinking cute. I can tell he knows it, but even that comes across as charming on him.

"I'm getting to know Summer. Mind ya business," Hannah says, flicking Liam's arm off of her shoulder.

He pretends to be hurt but turns to me in the next second, pout gone. "I want to get to know Summer too." When he says it, it sounds dirty and a little bit hot.

"Summer!" my dad calls and motions for me to come over. I smile at Liam and Hannah and walk over to Dad.

"I don't believe you've ever met Billy. Billy Roberts." A tray of champagne is carried past and my dad grabs two, handing me one. "My oldest and dearest friend and the backer of all my movies." His laugh is hearty and so is Billy's.

Billy looks down at me and takes my hand in his. "You're even more beautiful than all your pictures. And all grown up."

"But way too young for you, Billy," my dad cuts in, laughing. I cringe but am glad it got my hand out from Billy's. The hold was going a little long. "And I wanted you to meet the other star of our film...Winslet Barry."

Winslet looks at me coolly and when she smiles, it looks like her teeth are being pried open with little pins. Painful. She holds her hand out to me and when I shake it, hers is limp. She pulls away from me like I'm a germ.

"Charmed," she says.

"Nice to meet you too."

"No, that's the movie you probably know me from. I looked a lot different for that role." She shrugs and I don't know what to say.

"Never saw it, sorry."

There's a slight lift to her eyebrows and then she goes even deeper into RBF. I wonder how she is able to play emotion on the big screen if everyday acting is so hard for her.

The party goes on and on and I try at different times to find Hudson, but he's always moving. He talks to everyone—everyone but me—laughing and chatting away in a much easier way than I've seen him. Like he's comfortable here, which seems odd. I wouldn't think he'd fit in with this crowd.

By midnight, I'm exhausted. And very few people have left. When people start milling into the house, I follow, relieved that someone is finally leaving. But Winslet disappears down the hallway toward my room, and Hannah lifts a hand to me.

"You look exhausted. You heading to bed?" she asks.

"I was trying to stay up for the whole thing, but I really am tired. I don't think I can tell everyone bye."

She gives me a funny look. "No need. Most of us live here, you know."

"What?"

"Yeah, your dad likes the immediate crew to live together while we're filming. One big happy family."

This summer just keeps getting crazier.

5

TOO HOT TO HANDLE

AN OBNOXIOUS ALARM SCREECHES NEXT TO MY BED AT SIX THE next morning. I sit up, holding my head and slamming the alarm, knocking it off the bedside table.

When it's finally off, I fall back on my pillow, holding my head again. The water sounds amazing outside and I'm sure I'll love going out and exploring this beautiful yard and beach and everything...much, much later.

My phone buzzes and I pick it up, certain that I'd turned off my ringer before I fell into bed.

It's my dad. I have him as an emergency contact so he

can get through at any time. I'll have to change that now that I'm here with him all summer.

Morning, Summer! I hope you slept well. You went to bed before I could discuss the day with you. We'll need you to pick up the Starbucks coffee order and be back here by seven. The key fob to the Audi is on the hook by the garage, and you're free to use it for errands this summer. Starbucks has our order, but I'll forward the list so you can double-check it. I've slipped the Starbucks card under your door, along with a credit card you can use for other necessities. So glad you're here! Love you.

I rub my eyes and read it again. And then again. Because I'm half asleep and this sounds like I have to get out of bed and go somewhere. What? I read it one more time and then force myself to get up and take a quick shower, hoping it gets my blood pumping. I'd wanted to ask my dad what he meant about assisting Liam at the party, but it got too hectic with everyone else around. I'm sure there will be other people around to help out. Bella and Monique seemed like they were pitching in last night. But I have no idea if they are employees or part of the movie? I'm so confused. And everyone just kind of talks to me like I should know who they are. Even Hannah, as nice as she was, didn't stop to explain much. I guess they think my dad and I are great communicators.

The next text comes through and the list is nothing short of ridiculous. It's a mile long and the specifications these people go to about their coffee is comical.

I throw on my favorite shorts and my softest long-sleeved T and go to the kitchen. No one is in sight except my dad and Hudson.

"There she is." My dad beams at me. "You got my texts, I

see. I was going to knock on your door in a few if you didn't respond."

"I got it." I have to tamp down the heat I'm feeling over this whole arrangement, but I don't want to have it out with my dad in front of Hudson. Plus, Hudson looks so delicious when he's sleepy, it's hard to hold on to any anger.

I'm gonna have to get the hormones in check if I'm living in a house with this guy. Not to mention the swoony actor who I have no intention of touching with a ten-foot pole, but that doesn't mean he doesn't awaken the girly bits.

God, it's too early to think, much less bring up the bits. Too early, and I should have coffee before I'm required to go pick up the coffee order from hell.

"I can drive you over, since you don't know the area yet," Hudson says. "You okay with that, Cole? We've covered all we're doing today?"

"Oh yeah, good idea," Dad says. "That way, you could just meet us at the set instead of back here." He nods at me and then at Hudson. "And yes, I think we're squared away."

"We won't be coming back here?" I maybe would've dressed differently if I'd known we weren't just hanging out here.

"No, no. Full day ahead. Hudson can tell you about it on the way."

Hudson nods and walks toward the back door. I follow because I haven't even been on this side of the house yet. Yesterday feels like another lifetime ago. He pulls the fob off the hook and we step out into the garage of the gods. Ten phenomenal cars line the temperature-controlled garage. All shiny, top-of-the-line beauties. I can only imagine what my mom's reaction would be about everything my dad owns. She's a firm believer that no one should be this wealthy, insisting that Autumn and I paid cash that we earned ourselves for our cars, and that we saved the money Dad sent us, but only after we'd shared a large portion of it with those less fortunate.

If you want to get my mom on a tangent, bring up entitlement...

I never felt I was lacking though, and I'm glad she taught me to be empathetic and generous, but I won't be complaining about the Audi, not in the slightest. It sure as hell trumps my 2012 Toyota Corolla, but it's the lightweight of the bunch. I'm glad he didn't tell me to drive the Bentley or Lamborghini...with coffee? I'm already a wreck thinking about how I'll get twenty orders in the car in one piece without wrecking the interior.

"Thank you for doing this. I'm a nervous driver when it's a place I don't know, and I can't imagine all these drinks and not spilling, it just—"

Hudson puts his hand on my shoulder and I realize he was stopping me from going past the Audi. My heart skipped away from me for a moment there thinking he was going to say he hadn't been able to stop thinking about me or something else equally as great.

"Breathe," he says.

Okay, I guess that's good too, but not exactly where my thoughts were headed.

"We have a spill and we'll get the car cleaned. And it's not a bad drive. I didn't want you to have to do it by yourself the first time, but you'll see it's easy. You'll be comfortable doing it next time for sure."

"Oh. Well, thank you. That's sweet."

We hop in the car and I keep my eyes on my side of the road. Barely glancing at Hudson at all.

"So, what did you think of everyone?" he asks.

"It was a lot to process. Hannah is really nice and Bella and Monique."

"I thought you and Hannah would hit it off." He nods.

"So, how many live in the house?"

"Usually between ten and twelve."

"Wow. Does that get old?"

"It does, which is why I've kept my place too. I just stay here while we're filming. Your dad likes it that way, says it builds a stronger movie if we're bonded the whole time we're making it. I don't mind it, but I couldn't do it without breaks from time to time."

"Makes sense."

We pull into Starbucks and I can't believe how close it was. I can totally do this. I glance at the text with the long list again and groan. He laughs.

"Don't worry, kiddo. They've got it down."

My heart swoons a little more every time he laughs and then he has to go and bring it to a screeching halt. *Kiddo?* How the hell old is he? Twenty-five? Twenty-eight at the most? I stalk in front of him, determined to show him I am fully capable of handling this on my own. Kiddo, my ass.

But I run into the guy coming out of the Starbucks with his coffees in a four-cup container. They pour out on the ground, and some on him, but mostly all of it lands on me.

Thank God, they're iced coffees. The hot coffee would've sent my already elevated heat to another level.

6

STAGE NAMES

Yesterday was the longest day known to man. Every time I turned around, someone was asking me to bring a coffee, a sandwich, rubber bands, a toothpick, mouthwash... I had to run to the store for wart remover, a green tea supplement, and a laxative. I didn't sit down the whole day.

Winslet does not have a winsome personality, let me tell you. She's a particular b-word with lots of backhanded, passive-aggressive hatred. Hatred might be a strong word. It's hard to tell if she's capable of feeling an emotion as strong as hatred.

My mama would be lighting into me for all the negative things I'm still thinking about Ms. Barry this morning. She certainly did last night when I took a nosedive while telling her the events of the day. By the time I'd told her everything, she was laughing and shaking her head at me, thinking I was overdramatizing the whole situation.

I might've cried a little too about my shock over being the errand girl who does the jobs no one else will do, when I thought I was coming for a potentially bonding vacation with my father, and she told me to talk to my dad.

"He doesn't know how to be a father," she said. "You might have to teach him. Talk to him. Tell him how you're feeling."

I'd gotten off the phone determined to talk to him today, but I'm doing second verse, same as the first—on my way to Starbucks for the mile-long order, only this time solo. My pal Hudson wasn't around this morning when it was time to go. And it's a freaking Sunday. Who's at Starbucks at seven on a Sunday morning?

A lot of people as it turns out.

As I pull into the Starbucks in my cushy ride on this gorgeous California day, I realize this isn't such a bad life to be living. Yeah, it wasn't how I thought it was going to be with one-on-one time with my dad, but who gets to say they assisted A-list stars on a Hollywood set?

Yeah, I did a little internet surfing last night instead of writing and turns out Liam, Winslet, and Hannah are the hottest of the hot shit. May have done a little investigating on Hudson too, and he's worked on six films with my dad. He has an impressive IMDB list. So I've slightly reined in my bitterness about him calling me kiddo since I probably do seem like a country bumpkin who is *so* unsophisticated compared to all these actors he's been around nonstop.

And here I thought he was my dad's driver.

Which would've been a lot less complicated.

I sag into the seat and unbuckle my seat belt. Still trying to get up the energy to do day two of this. There's a tap on my window and I jump.

Hudson.

That sexy wavy hair and his eyes that are swirling with so much mystery. I wish he'd give something away, but his emotions are locked up tight.

I get out of the car and put my hand over my eyes to block the sun.

"I thought I'd missed you this morning. Wanted to help you one more day. Tomorrow things will start getting hectic," he says.

"Yesterday wasn't hectic?"

He smirks. "That was nothing."

I groan.

"You'll be okay. With these egos, you just have to act like you know what you're doing and don't let them get under your skin. Your dad probably told you about everyone—and I've given you a heads-up about Liam."

"My dad hasn't told me about anything or anyone. I thought I was coming here for a vacation."

Hudson stares at me and bites the inside of his cheek. He puts his hand on his hip and looks away. Finally he just says, "Cole," and shakes his head.

I point toward the coffee shop. "I'm just gonna grab the coffees."

"Right."

We head inside, going straight to the pick-up side. The same guy is back there today and he grins when he sees me. He was chatty yesterday, but I was too tired to think straight.

"Summer Winters?"

"That's me."

"Great stage name. Clever." He winks.

The guy's cute, so I don't feel as snarky as I normally would. And he seems sincere, not like he's making fun.

"I can thank my mom for that," I say.

"No way, it's your real name?" He laughs. "That is smokin'."

Hudson snorts next to me and I nudge him with my foot.

"I'm Clyde Matthews. I'll be seeing you." He gives me a megawatt smile and points to the cup with my name on it. Below that is his name and number.

He grins at me again, and I lift my hand awkwardly in a wave.

"Subtle," Hudson says under his breath as we carry the boxes of coffee out.

"I thought he was cute," I say with a shrug, mostly to see what Hudson will say.

He does a shrug back, not giving anything away. Something tells me I'd be better off taking my crush elsewhere. This guy's a stone brick. And yet, he helps me get everything situated in my car and before he turns to go to his car, he pauses.

"Just breathe, Summer. You did great yesterday."

Now it's my turn to snort. "I only had multiple spills and caused Hannah to trip before her scene."

He presses his lips together and oh my god, is he trying not to laugh? "You'll be the most memorable person on the set if you keep that up."

I roll my eyes and get in my car. He does laugh as he gets into his.

Little did I know that these few moments would be the most peaceful part of my day.

7

GLISTENING FACES AND HOT LIPS

TODAY WE'RE FILMING ON THE BEACH NOT TOO FAR DOWN from the house. Liam is showing off his skills as a surfer and there's a stunt double that's practicing side by side with him. It's weird seeing two guys with the same build, same coloring, and then they turn around and their faces are just different enough to be unsettling.

I want to watch, but Winslet has me holding a battery-operated fan in front of her face so she doesn't glisten. I so didn't sign up for this.

My dad is in his shorts and flip-flops, baseball cap on backwards, and grins from across the beach. It's not fair that even slightly grungy, he manages to look like Joe Manganiello on vacation.

"Thanks, love," he says, lifting his coffee.

I grin back. I can't help it. I like it when he calls me that, even when I'm mad at him.

Winslet chokes back a laugh and I look at her, surprised. I didn't know she was capable of laughter. Looking at her, it's impossible to tell she's laughing. Maybe I imagined it. There's an umbrella over her so the sun won't mar her porcelain white skin. Why Dad has her doing a beach movie is beyond me. Shouldn't she be tan?

"Looks like your dad thinks a lot of your skills—coffee duty and wiping someone else's butt all you're capable of?" She makes that sound again and her lips don't even tilt up at the edges.

"Yeah, he clearly is a disaster when it comes to the roles he gives people," I say, switching her fan off and moving away from her.

With the fan still in my hand.

"Hey, I wasn't done with that," she yells.

She's shushed because they're getting ready to film the next scene.

I grin at her and wave, moving toward Hannah and her double, Maddie. They're sighing over Liam and his double, Tanner.

"I'm not picky. I'd take either one of them." Maddie falls back into her chair and sighs. We're quiet for a few moments staring at their forms in the water. I'd expect Tanner to look better out there, but Liam is holding his own. It's obvious he spends a lot of time on the water and I have to confess, I'm drooling a bit myself. His body is—

"Summer!" I hear the screech and everyone turns to Winslet as she stands, hands on hips, her pale vampire skin turning mottled. "The fan, *now*."

"Geez. Sure. Why didn't you just ask?" I say as I'm walking toward her and chuckle when that seems to make her madder.

I turn the fan on her face as she shoots daggers at me and watch as Dad starts shooting the scene with first Tanner and then Liam in the water. Tanner does an impressive surf out and back and then Liam is in the shot when he's riding back in. They do multiple scenes and when they do the final cut, Liam goes out and catches his own wave.

He rides the thing all the way in and leaves his board in the sand, a huge grin on his face. I turn and look behind me because it looks like he's heading straight for...me.

He stops in front of me and puts his wet hands on my cheeks, lowers his face to mine, and gives me the longest, most passionate kiss I've ever been given. At first I just stand there, and then I kiss him back because what can I do?

This might be the hottest moment of my life.

I just thought it was hot when Eli Jarden showed up at work with flowers and kissed me. Or the kisses that caused me to lose my virginity to Jacob Salverson. Turns out that the kisses were the highlight there.

This far surpasses those kisses.

His hands tug me to him and even though his hands are cold, I feel the heat from my head to my toes. When we pull apart, he looks at me and grins.

"Hot damn, you taste as good as I knew you would."

"What was that?" I ask, putting my fingers to my lips.

He shakes his hands out and reaches for a towel just past me, putting it around his neck. "I get all this adrenaline after a scene like that and have to let it out somewhere." He leans in close and kisses my nose. "Thanks for being there."

I'm too stunned to say anything and when he walks away, I take a look around. Hudson is the first one I see. He's standing close, like he was on his way over here, but stopped due to the shock waves. He does not look happy.

Neither does my dad.

Fingers snap in front of my face, and I turn to see who's being so obnoxious. It's Winslet and she doesn't look happy either. She points to the ground and the fan is lying there broken. I guess I dropped it in all the kiss excitement.

Hudson stalks back over to my dad, and Liam is chatting up Tanner and another actor that I haven't met yet. Yeah, no big. An actor just kissed me for funsies. Okay, moving right along. Except I feel slightly woozy.

My dad motions for me to come to him and Hudson is right here too but doesn't look at me.

"It's a little soon to start a relationship, don't you think?" Dad asks.

"Uh, I'm not in a relationship with anyone. That little display took me by surprise as much as it did you, I promise you that."

He looks uncertain, which annoys me.

"Well, I'd rather you take your time," he says. "You've barely been here any time, and if you start kissing the first guy you see and it doesn't work out, which with Liam, that would be doubtful...it would make it really awkward around the set and at home."

That also annoys me. Like I see red and don't know if I can keep it together without yelling a little bit.

And maybe I *want* to kiss the first guy I saw...Hudson! But the way he's glaring at the floor in front of him, I don't see that happening any time soon.

"Maybe we can talk about a few things later tonight," I say under my breath.

Dad nods.

And I go look for a replacement fan to hold over Winslet's face for the next six hours.

8

OBLIVIOUS

I'M THE LAST ONE OUT ON THE SAND; EVERYONE ELSE LEFT A while ago. I'm trying not to be bitter about it as I clean up after them. Even craft services has gone in for the night. I try to carry too many things at once and drop them and want to drop myself and cry on the sand.

Feeling foolish and sweaty, I get a better grip and start dragging back what I can. The house isn't far, but it feels like it with all this stuff. I'm just getting started when I see Hudson walking back toward me.

"Thought maybe you could use some help," he says gruffly. Still doesn't look at me.

"Thanks. That's so nice of you. Next time I need to bring a little cart or something to carry all these things."

He nods. "Your dad has permission to drive on this beach during filming, so tomorrow you should bring the 4x4 out. The crew drove most of it out this morning before you got here."

"Nice of him to let me know," I mutter.

"A talk with him would be a good idea," he says.

I keep my mouth shut and focus on not dropping anything as we both haul things back to the house.

"So, Liam, huh?" he says it right when we're rounding the gate to my dad's property.

I stop and look at him. "I have no idea what that was about."

He smirks, his eyes cutting over to me. "Didn't look like you minded."

I roll my eyes. It was a good kiss. Weird. And also super obnoxious. I don't like how everyone else is acting about it though. It's not like I did anything to make Liam think I wanted that...besides not shoving him off of me. I smile and Hudson's eyes narrow on mine. He turns toward me and pauses like he wants to say something more and then turns and stalks off.

"Thanks for helping me get all this back," I tell his back.

"You're welcome. Talk to your dad," he says.

I want nothing more than to shower and go to bed, but once I set everything down, I go searching for my dad. He's not in the living room or the kitchen, and when I look down both hallways of bedrooms, I have no idea which one is his. Wandering down the hall toward the back of the house that

I haven't been down yet, I find his office. And when I see him sitting at his desk, the door slightly cracked, I knock.

He holds up his hand and I freeze.

"Why don't you come out tomorrow and hang out with us on set? We'll be in your neighborhood." He laughs and it's only then that I realize he's on the phone. I've rarely seen him laugh since I got here and it looks good on him. I don't recognize myself in him—nothing about him feels familiar to me except his love for movies. He has brown hair and brown eyes, a significant nose that only adds to his charm, and dimples. I take after my mom with long blonde hair and blue eyes, down to the shape of our small noses and slightly too-big lips. He's extroverted, and I'm so introverted it isn't funny. I back away when he keeps talking, not wanting to eavesdrop, and decide to go for that shower after all.

When I reach my side of the house and walk toward my room, I pause when I hear someone's laughter and it's coming from Hudson's room. A girl's laugh. My heart sinks and I shove that feeling down as quickly as I can. Of course, he has a girlfriend.

I take a shower and stare out the window for a long time as the water pours over me. The view is incredible, endless turquoise and navy blue ocean in front of me and cliffs to each side. I'm exhausted, but I feel better when I get out. I find my favorite sweats, the really old ones that are so soft they're almost falling apart, and put them on, feeling slightly comforted by them right away. I flop back on my bed to FaceTime Mom and Autumn when I get a text from my dad.

I'm done with my phone call. Why don't you meet me in the dining room? Dinner will be ready in about five minutes.

Now that I'm in my room, the last thing I want to do is go back out there, but my stomach grumbles. I can't remember the last time I ate today.

I type **Sure** back and throw a hoodie on over my tank top. My hair is still dripping, so I towel dry it a little more and don't look at myself too long in the mirror or I'll be putting makeup on and I don't have the energy for that.

I listen for voices or laughter from Hudson's room when I step out, but it's quiet. Not sure that makes me feel any better, but I have to get over this little idea I'm carrying around about Hudson and me. A summer fling with Hudson is not happening.

When I get to the dining room, it's full. I want to turn around and go back to my room. Winslet and Hannah are sitting on either side of Hudson, and Maddie is sitting next to Tanner and Liam. Monique and Bella are sitting next to what I assume is my dad's seat, and they're piling food onto their plates. Monique scoots over and pats the seat where she was just sitting.

"Here, sit here. Your dad will be here in a sec."

Before I sit down, Liam says, "Over here, Summer. Sit by me." He pats his lap and grins, and I roll my eyes and sit down by my dad's seat. Directly across from Hudson and Winslet. I wonder if that's who was laughing in his room.

I'm still not sure she knows how to laugh, but she's turned on the charm tonight. And it's all for Hudson.

My dad walks in and sits down by me. He smiles at me but doesn't say anything. He starts eating and I don't know how to talk to him with all these people around. I'm not great at it when it's just the two of us.

I fill my plate with chicken enchiladas and a taco and look up to see Winslet staring at me with disgust. I put a big bite on my fork and lift it up to her, waving it and then stuffing it in my mouth. She looks down at her plate that has lettuce and tomatoes and shuffles it around on her plate. No wonder she's so mean.

"Do you think we can talk later?" I ask my dad.

"Let's talk here. What's up?"

"Well, just wondering if this is what the summer is going to be like."

He grins. "Pretty great, right?"

"Uh, I can see where it would be great for you, yeah."

He nods and tucks into his food.

"It's just not what I was expecting at all," I say quietly. Hoping that the chatter around the table is covering up our conversation.

"I can get you an itinerary, if that would help," he says.

I eat a few bites, trying to rein my temper in, then set my fork down. "You could have told me I was only here because Wendy quit, or better yet, asked me if I *wanted* to work here this summer. I could've made the choice whether I wanted to blow someone's face with a fan all day or to do something else a little more meaningful, or...I don't know...*fun*."

He looks at me then as if he's finally hearing what I'm saying. And the rest of the table goes quiet all of a sudden.

It's an awkward pause that feels like forever but is probably only a few seconds.

Hudson says something to Hannah and conversation picks up again.

"I thought you'd enjoy the experience," my dad says quietly.

"I came to get to know you." I try to take another bite, but the lump in my throat is growing.

"This is me," he says.

I get up quickly because I'm afraid I'm going to cry if I sit here a minute longer.

"I'm out of wine." Winslet holds up her glass for me to fill it.

I keep walking and don't stop until I've reached the water.

9

SPINNING TOPS AND HOBBIES

THE TEARS START ONCE I FLOP DOWN ON THE SAND. I HATE crying and try to put it off for as long as possible, but it seems like when I'm mad, I cry more than when I'm sad. It's so annoying.

I'm out there for a few minutes feeling sorry for myself, when someone clears their throat. I look up and Hudson is standing there with my plate.

"Thought you might want to finish eating," he says.

"Are you a nice guy?" I ask.

"Do I seem nice?"

"Most of the time."

"What about the rest of the time?"

"Like maybe you regretted when you were nice before."

He laughs and sits down next to me. I take a bite of the enchilada and even though it's cooled down a lot, it's still delicious.

"Your dad was excited about you coming," he says.

I just keep eating. I don't really want to think about my dad right now.

"He's not the best communicator," he adds.

"Oh, you think?" I glare at him and again with his laugh. It's a really nice laugh. I wish he didn't maybe have a girlfriend.

"Do you regret coming?" he asks.

And I have to think long and hard about that, because even though this is not what I signed up for and I can think of a lot of other things I'd rather be doing back home, when I look out at this ocean and have Hudson sitting here beside me, this feels pretty great. It's all the moments in-between that have made it difficult. The Winslet moments being high on that list.

"I wish I could have mentally prepared before coming." I look at him then and he nods. He looks so perfect with the dusk light across his face. His dark wavy hair makes me want to run my fingers through it and bring his mouth to mine.

Hold up. Not going there.

I don't kiss two boys on the same day even if I'm not with either one of them. *Especially* if I'm not with either one of them. Some people have boundaries, and it's official: This is mine.

But sitting out here right now, it's kind of perfect.

I hear something behind me and Dad is walking toward

us. Hudson turns back to look and when he sees him, he stands up. I've finished eating and he holds out his hand to take the plate. He nods at my dad and makes his way back toward the house.

My dad sits down next to me. "We've got beach chairs right there." He points down a few yards where there are white chairs with umbrellas facing the water.

"Next time," I say.

"I wanted to clear up something you said," he starts, clearing his throat. "About only being here because Wendy quit. It's not like that at all, but I can see where it could seem that way since I didn't go in-depth about what this summer might be like. I'm so glad you're here, Summer." He puts his hand on my arm and I look at him. His eyes are sincere. This is what makes it so hard with my dad—he usually does seem sincere when we're talking, but then I don't hear from him for months. "I should've seen if you'd be okay with working while you're here, but with your interest in writing and specifically for movies, I thought you'd love the chance to work your way up from the ground floor. This gets your foot in the door the organic way."

"I just wish you'd told me all of this. It's felt like you are avoiding spending any real time with me and that this summer will be all about work. Not what I thought I was coming for...and you haven't even asked about Autumn. Don't you wonder how she's doing at all?"

"I thought if she wanted to see me, she would've come. I'm still hoping she'll come at some point this summer."

"That would be great, but she needs time with Mom too after being gone for so long. Still, it would be nice if you'd call her, invite her to come later in the summer—just let her know ahead of time if you're going to put her to work once she gets here." I roll my eyes, but I'm smiling now. My mom told me I needed to teach him how to be a dad, which feels really shitty as his daughter honestly, but I think she might be onto something.

"Noted. I'm really sorry I suck so bad at this fatherhood gig."

And when he says things like that, I want to forgive him for everything. He puts his arm around my shoulder and I lean into him for just a second. Too long and I'll get teary again. That would really send him running.

"Remember the time I got sick when we had the hot dog competition on our weekend together in Oklahoma? You were filming there and it was hot dogs or brisket and I was scared they'd killed one of the cows I'd just petted to make the brisket?"

He laughs and squeezes my shoulder. "You said you were so hungry you could eat six hot dogs, so I dared you to." He shook his head. "Your mom killed me when I took you home and you were still throwing up. I don't blame her. She's always known exactly what to do with you girls."

"She's a good mom, that's for sure."

"Look, I know I'm not gonna get it right, probably a thousand times more, but know that I want you and your sister in my life. I love having you on the set with me and in the house...just having you here makes me feel better even when we're not together at the moment. I'll try to do better, I swear it." His hand drops off of my shoulder and he leans back with his elbows on the sand. "California gets in your blood." He winks at me. "I'm hoping it'll get in yours while you're here and that you'll never want to leave. Are you still writing?"

I sit up a little straighter and nod. My dad has never seemed to take my writing very seriously, but after the things he's said tonight, I'm wondering if maybe he does more than I thought. "I had to focus on wrapping up school for a while there, but yeah, I've been writing a ton on the weekends. I need to get into a schedule while I'm here."

"Good. I know it's been a helpful outlet for you."

And my spirits go whomp-whomp back into the sand like a top spinning and fizzling out at the end. He thinks writing is a hobby for me, while I'm imagining myself writing the next great American novel that will hopefully one day become an award-winning movie.

10

LET IT OUT

The Impasse
By Summer Winters

Life had always been about choices, and even now, Charli found herself in an impossible situation. In the past, she was shuffled between two parents, and now, she was shuffled between two men. Why did it always feel like she had to choose?

Her mom loved her, took care of her. Kissed her when she

scraped her knees and held her up when her first boyfriend broke her heart.

Her dad provided for her. Paid for college tuition and bought her a reliable car when the cheap one she'd bought broke down.

David loved her. There was no question. David knew her like no one else did. He was a steady comfort and calming presence in her life. He lived to make her happy.

But she loved Micah. Try as she might, she could not resist the draw to him. He was the spark that lit her fire no matter how she tried to resist. And he cared for her too.

Just not like David.

It took one of them being murdered to—

There's a knock on my door and I turn from my laptop, tempted to ignore it while I'm on the beginning of a roll with writing after a few weeks' hiatus. But there's another knock, this time louder, and I yell, "Come in."

Hudson peeks in the door and looks away quickly when he sees my skimpy outfit. I threw on a tank crop top and tiny shorts when I got back to my room, certain I was done peopleing for the night.

"I just wanted to make sure you got the itinerary." He waves it and places it on my bed.

"Thanks."

"The next few days will be intense. We've got to be out on the beach before daylight, so it'll be early mornings all week. I wasn't sure if you'd heard about that yet..."

I shake my head and he makes a face.

"Okay, so clearly, we're not all on the same page yet." He picks up the paper again. "This will help so much." He points at a line on the page. "If you could place an order at this email for our coffee to be delivered, that would be perfect. It needs to happen soon though."

"Why doesn't craft services provide the coffee and tea too?"

"They do, it's just that most prefer Starbucks."

I make a face. "It's nothing like Smelly Cat back home."

"Smelly Cat? Do I even want to know?"

"Only has the best coffee in Charlotte."

"I'll have to take your word for it." He smiles. And my heart skips a few beats. I look away so I don't make it too obvious that I just want to stare at him all night long.

"Thanks for your help today. With everything." I look at him again then and he's still smiling.

"Anytime. It'll get better. You're doing a great job, and I really think knowing what to expect will help."

We both know it's something my dad should have done. Why Hudson is being so nice to me when he has so many other responsibilities, I have no idea.

"Goodnight, Summer," he says.

"Night."

I turn back to my laptop and read what I just wrote. Ugh. I delete *It took one of them being murdered to*—and I sit there for a few moments and think about where I really want this book to go. I think I want it to be more about the feelings and emotions than a thriller/suspense novel/movie.

It's ridiculous that I'm even starting something new. I'm avoiding working on my manuscript. It's at that seventy percent mark that I struggle so much with and I need to just bite the bullet and finish the thing.

I keep typing instead.

.   .   .

David looked at me with those sweet eyes. "Why are you afraid to let me in?" he asked.

I put my hand on his cheek and sighed. He closed his eyes and leaned into my hand.

"I don't want to hurt you again," I whispered.

"Loving you hurts, but losing you will kill me," he said.

I tried to blink away the tears, but one dropped down my cheek and he wiped it away. He put his forehead against mine and then kissed me one last time. My heart did not pound, but I felt a deep sadness over that realization.

He backed away and brushed my cheek with the back of his hand.

"I hope you find what you're looking for," he said.

I didn't tell him I'd already found it, because he knew about Micah. He knew it was like the two of us only backwards—that I felt for Micah what David felt for me. He didn't believe Micah and I would make it.

But I had to choose.

And I chose to follow my heart.

I sit back and read what I've written and nearly delete the whole thing. What kind of crap nonsense is this pouring out of me? And what the hell does Micah have over David? I want to yell at her for not giving David another chance because he sure seems like a nice guy.

But Charli and I have a little something in common with our history of not dating the nice guys. I don't know why that mysterious—not even bad boy per se, but the challenge of getting someone who doesn't fall for anyone ever—just seems to do it for me. Autumn says it's our daddy issues screaming to be acknowledged.

I think she's probably exactly right.

I remember that I need to place the coffee order, so I do that and close my laptop. If I'm going to be worth anything tomorrow, I need to sleep. I set my alarm for four and turn off the light.

My dreams are a mash-up of Hudson, Micah, David, Liam, and even the cute guy from Starbucks, Clyde. When my alarm goes off, I want to throw it across the room and go back to sleep, back to my dreams.

11

IMPROMPTU GETAWAY

I'M IN THE KITCHEN BY 4:25 AND MY DAD IS ALREADY instructing the camera crew out on the patio. I step outside and listen as he tells them exactly where to go. It's a little closer to the house than yesterday.

Hudson walks up.

"Morning, sleepyhead," he whispers, nudging me with his elbow. His voice sounds like sleepy, gravelly heaven.

Liam comes in and bumps me with his hip. I must have a *Hit Me* sticker on me somewhere.

"It's not right to look so good this early," Liam says, his

eyes roaming over my body. I roll my eyes. I know I look like I got dragged out of bed far before it was time. He looks perfect, of course. All A-list Hollywood star with the messy blond hair and his chiseled tan muscles on display.

He's right, it's too early to look so good.

"Why don't you head outside, loverboy, and see where you'll be this morning," Hudson says. It's a little growly, but I think it must just be his morning voice.

Liam smirks. "Okay, *loverboy*. Will do."

We all end up outside and my dad has already moved down the beach. Bright lights lead our way and when we get there, my dad is agitated. He's waving his arms all around, motioning this way and that to the camera crew.

"Hey, Summer," a voice says behind me.

I turn and it's Clyde with a big cart of coffee and all the things anyone might want to add to their cup. I even see chocolate sprinkles. I flush and am grateful that it's dark. My dreams rush back to me with him smiling at me and acting flirty, and I almost expect to see David and Micah here somewhere.

"You didn't call," he pouts.

I laugh awkwardly and pour myself a cup of coffee. I need it more than usual. "Sorry. Good to see you. Didn't know you'd be bringing the coffee."

"Pretty sweet, right? It's not every day that I get to hang around a movie set."

I smile at him and back away to let others get to the coffee.

I hear my dad then and go over by him.

"I don't like how the waves are looking. It was supposed to be a bigger swell than this by now, and by the time we get the light...I still don't think it will be enough." He looks at Hudson. "Check out the waves at other beaches, Hawaii, if you have to. We've gotta get something in the next few days. Preferably today."

Hudson taps away on his phone. "The waves are perfect in Oahu. We'd need to leave quickly, if we want to do anything today."

My dad nods and takes off toward the house. I look at Hudson for answers about what that means for the rest of us, and he follows after my dad.

Hannah is at the coffee cart now with a robe over her bathing suit. She motions for me to come over.

"You okay? You left in a hurry last night," she says.

"Yeah. I just-yeah, I'm good."

"I'm glad. Because I could use at least one sane person around here. Besides Hudson." She smiles.

"Are you and Hudson close?"

"Yeah, we're really good friends. We've worked on two other movies with your dad. Have you really not watched your dad's movies?"

"He's told me not to watch a few of them." We laugh. "So yeah, I've seen most but not all."

"And you listened to him? I'm so impressed." She grins.

Bella rushes up to us, out of breath. "Your dad needs the two of you back at the house right away."

Hannah nods and I glance at Clyde before heading to the house.

When we get there, Hudson is waiting for us.

"Get a bag of all your essentials. We're going to Oahu."

"What? Today?" I ask. Hannah is already rushing to her room.

"Yeah. Just grab what you want—we can take care of anything you might need once we get there."

"You're coming too?"

He grins. "Yep. Hustle. Your dad is impatient to get there."

"I can see that."

———

We're on the plane before the sun has even come up. My dad, Hudson, Liam, Tanner, Hannah, Maddie, and me. I lean back in my seat beaming because *Winslet is not on this little trip.*

"You look extremely happy right now," Hannah whispers.

"I've never been to Hawaii and I'm really glad my first time won't be with Winslet Barry."

Hannah giggles. "It is the best thing ever, isn't it? I'd heard she was difficult to work with, but I had no idea."

"This might be a short trip, but I'm going to enjoy every second away from her." I close my eyes and fall asleep.

The flight is over five hours, so when I wake up we still have a couple hours left, but I feel better. Hannah passes me a breakfast sandwich and Hudson holds up a carafe of coffee. I've been on my dad's plane before and always enjoy the experience. But this morning feels especially nice. I nod and he stands up, bringing the coffee and grabbing a mug from the table he's sitting at with my dad.

He pours the coffee and asks if I'd like cream or sugar.

I say yes and he smiles again.

My dad clears his throat and it seems to snap Hudson out of it. He presses his lips together and walks back for the cream and sugar. When he places it in front of me, he doesn't make eye contact. I'm in too good of a mood for it to bother me.

He goes back to sit down and he and my dad spend the

next couple of hours discussing logistics with our new location. Apparently there's a camera crew there getting lined up already. It amazes me how money can make things move so much quicker.

Liam is stretched out on the couch and he opens his eyes and sees me watching him. He winks and I look away. The ego on that one.

When we're landing, everyone gets buckled up, and I stare out the window until we're on the ground. The water is such a beautiful blue-green color. We step off the plane, and it's three hours earlier than California, just past eight, but already toasty.

One of my dad's friends is there to meet us in a massive SUV and I somehow end up wedged between Hudson and Liam. They both turn to look at me and I stare straight ahead, feeling the heat in more ways than one.

12

WHOLE NINE YARDS

My tasks seem so much more manageable without Winslet in the picture. I go over the menu with craft services and make sure Liam and Tanner are where they're supposed to be for every scene. Hannah and Maddie cooperate and stay put when it's almost time for their scenes, but Liam needs a wrangler most of the time.

"It's time for you to oil me up, Summer," Liam says, wiggling his eyebrows.

"Has anyone ever told you you're supremely annoying?"

I ask, as I take the sunscreen from him and start rubbing it on his back.

"Hmm, supremely annoying? Don't think I've heard that one. Supremely hot, yes. Supremely good in bed, I've heard that a lot."

"Shut up and let me get your chest."

He turns around, that grin still in place, the one that I've now heard makes girls scream when he comes on the screen in the theater. I apply the sunscreen as carefully as possible, making sure I don't miss any spots. Wouldn't want our star to get a spotty burn.

"Aren't there people who do this for you? Makeup people or someone like that?" I ask.

"Usually," he says, his voice all husky.

I glance up and his eyes are getting all dazed as he looks at my mouth. "Stop," I whisper.

"What?"

"Stop looking at me like that."

His dimple pops out. "Can't help it. You're a beautiful girl. The sweetest lips."

"You tell all girls that. Your voodoo magic won't work on me."

He leans in. "So, you think I've got magic. Good to know."

"Back off."

"But this is so fun," he says. He pushes my hair away from my face and my hand goes still on his chest. "Your eyes are the color of this water."

His are too, but I don't tell him that. I take a deep breath and step back. "All done," I whisper.

"But you didn't do my legs yet."

"You can do your legs." I walk away to the sound of him laughing. The guy thinks everything is a joke and I'm sure

I'm his new target. But he stays focused the rest of the day and the footage is incredible. The waves are higher than I've ever seen and both Tanner and Liam blow my mind with their surfing skills. And there's one emotional scene with Liam that's so powerful, I pretend I'm busy with something else and didn't see it right before the scene cuts so Liam doesn't see how transfixed I am.

It's seven before we stop for the night. We load up in the SUV and head to the house my dad has rented for us. I still have no idea how long we'll be here, what the plan is for tomorrow, or what's necessarily expected of me, but for the first time on this little summer adventure, I am all in.

The house is gorgeous—I shouldn't have expected anything less, but I'm still blown away when I step inside. My dad has a house type: lots of windows, neutral furniture, and surrounded by ocean. It's smaller than his house in Malibu, but it reminds me of it.

"We are being treated to a luau in about an hour. A little something special to thank all of you for going with the flow at the crack of dawn this morning," my dad says. "I'm gonna go get cleaned up, and I'll see you out there." He points to the gorgeous backyard overlooking the beach.

I go to the first empty room I see and pull out a few clothes that I threw in a bag this morning. One is a cute red, sleeveless boho dress. I give it a good shake and decide to carry it into the bathroom with me to get a few more wrinkles out while I shower.

When I look in the mirror, I realize I got more sun than I meant to. All my watching out for Liam and I'm not sure I ever reapplied. Yikes. I get in the shower and take a cool one. I didn't want to wash my hair again tonight, but after a long day in the sun, it needs it. When I get out, I wrap a towel around my head and one around my body. At home, my mama would fuss at me for using two towels. Am I getting spoiled to this life already? I grin at myself in the mirror and toss the towel off of my head.

The door flies open, just as the towel around my body drops to the floor. Hudson stands there, gaping for what feels like a solid minute. I'm too stunned to react at first and by the time I do, grabbing the towel and holding it in front of me, he's stuttering.

"I'm so sorry. I had put my stuff in here. I just thought—"

"What? Where?" I'm mortified. *Hudson just saw me naked! And it wasn't for good times.* And then I think of every cuss word in the book.

Hudson opens the closet door and grabs his bag. "I'll just take this."

"I'm so sorry. Didn't see that." I put my hand over my face and he backs out of the room.

"I can't exactly say the same," he says, grinning so big I want to throw something at him.

And then he says something else that makes me go hot all over.

"Don't think I'll find another view like this room." His eyes are twinkling as he closes the door, and I fall back on the bed and cover my face.

"I die," I whisper. "I'm dead. *Dead.*" I pinch my arm and yelp because I'm a little sunburned and that did not feel good.

"Okay, you're going to get up and get dressed and go out there like Hudson didn't just see you, full frontal." I'm talking out loud to myself now and groan as I go back into the bathroom.

The first guy who ever saw me naked (and only partially) was Jack Robbins. We didn't have sex, but we fooled around a lot. The aforementioned Jacob Salverson, who I should've just stuck to kissing. Then Henry Fremont saw the whole nine yards and we *did* the whole nine yards too. I broke up with him before my senior year at UNC because he couldn't stay faithful over the summer. It hurt, but he had started to act weird leading up to the breakup, and honestly it was a relief when it was finally over.

And now Hudson.

My body has had a little hiatus from being seen and my nerve endings are still on fire from those seconds with Hudson.

I can't imagine what would've happened if he'd touched me.

13

MOVIES AND LONG WALKS ON THE BEACH

I ALMOST PULL A NO-SHOW AT DINNER, BUT I'M TOO HUNGRY, and I'll have to face Hudson at some point anyway, so I just make sure I look really, *really* good. Every time I think about accidentally flashing him, the mortification nearly knocks me over, and I have a full-body flush all over again.

I take time with my hair and makeup and when I'm done, the effect is subtle but exactly what I was going for. Autumn FaceTimes while I'm giving myself a last glance in the mirror.

"You look like a beach babe," she squeals. "Who are you hoping to impress tonight? Hudson or Liam?"

I frown, about to tell her about showing Hudson full nips and then some, but also because she seems to think Liam is also someone worth impressing. She's watched all of his movies, so she's still on the swoony side of him. Freaking flipped when she found out he was on Dad's movie and that I didn't know who he was. I've tried to tell her Liam is obnoxious, but she doesn't seem to be hearing me.

"Myself," I say, as if I'm in deep meditation and it's a profound realization that I can impress myself. While my insides are chanting, "Hudson, Hudson, Hudson."

She rolls her eyes and grins. "Yeah, right. You only pull out the full makeup and big waves when you're dressing to make a move."

Now it's my turn to roll my eyes and I motion for her to shut her mouth.

"I've gotta go, but I'll call you tomorrow. I want to hear about your date last night."

"Oh, I can save you the time," she says. "But still call me tomorrow. The date sucked. The guy talked about sports the entire time, and not in a fun, let's talk about who we both like kind of way, but all about the baseball team he's on, period. He's obsessed."

"I guess it's cool he knows what he likes."

"Maybe if he could've been interested in one other thing during our two-hour dinner, I could see it that way, but nope, didn't happen even for a second. Well, except when he wanted to shove his tongue down my throat after dinner."

"Sorry, Auto. That sucks. He seemed promising."

"Okay, Season." She rolls her eyes without fail at my nickname for her. I've never cared for mine either. "Moving on. Don't forget to call me. I need the deets."

I hang up and don't hesitate to leave my room. If I keep putting it off, I'll talk myself into getting back into my pajamas and hiding.

I wander through the empty house, following my way to the music. When I step outside, the scent of tropical flowers and roasting meat hits my senses. The place has been transformed. I find a seat next to Hannah and enjoy the dancers and the men twirling fire. The firelight is our only light and the beat of the drum has all the intensity of Hudson walking in on me stirring up both my nerves and all the feelings. Heat floods through me—or embarrassment and humiliation, all sort of one and the same as far as I'm concerned—and I look around to find him, only to see him already staring at me. My skin gets even hotter and I smile at him before dragging my eyes away.

When I've eaten more than I should and still feel a bit restless, I decide to take a walk down the beach. The waves lap up to the shore and the sound eases some of the anxiousness.

"Mind if I join you?"

I glance up and Hudson is there next to me.

"Not at all. Just soaking in this beautiful ocean. I've always wanted to come here."

"I love it here," he says. He clears his throat. "Hey, I'm really sorry I walked in on you earlier."

"I'm the one who should apologize for being in your room. Where did you end up?"

"Just one down. No worries. So, you don't seem like you're into the party scene. Everyone's just getting started back there." He motions toward the house and I look back. The lights look so pretty against the sand and water.

"I like an occasional cocktail, but yeah, not really my

thing. Doesn't seem to be yours either...or is that just while you're on the job?"

"My mom is an alcoholic and that kind of cured me of wanting alcohol. I mean, I've enjoyed it in the past, but...she's in the best treatment center I can afford and this isn't her first time through. I think it's something my dad struggled with too, but only from what my mom has told me. She doesn't remember too much about it because they weren't sober for most of their time together. I guess I've always wondered if I could derail easily myself if that's in my blood."

I nod. "I like that you've put thought into this. Many people wouldn't think twice about just doing what they want to do." I glance at him then and it's getting dark from walking so far down the beach. "So, does it bother you to be around it so much? Even my dad seems to be able to put it away more than I knew and still be up so early in the morning."

"My escape has always been movies. From the time I was little and my mom would have what seemed like endless hangovers...I watched every movie I could, multiple times, each time trying to look for something new and to figure out how they pulled off every shot. I'm still that way."

I turn and face him and we pause before turning around and walking back toward the house. "Have you ever thought about making your own?"

"I used to all the time...until I met your dad. The experience I've gotten with him is more than I ever learned in college. We're a really good fit. I don't know though—if I ever found the right script, maybe I'd branch out."

"It feels like you're kind of running the show around here anyway."

He chuckles. "Nah, I'm just more of a planner than your

dad is. Someone has to be that way on the set. Seems like I come up short in other areas...like properly claiming a bedroom and not knocking before I enter."

I laugh and it's not as mortifying as it was before. So he saw me naked—oh god, yeah, I'm still not over it.

"So embarrassing," I say, covering my face.

"Believe me, you have *nothing* to be embarrassed about."

Damn. His voice sounds all husky and sinful when he says that. I'm fanning my face in the next second and trying to slow down my rapid pulse.

He stops and I do too. The air is thick with all my lustful thoughts, and from the look in his eyes, I'm hoping he's tracking right along with me. Although, it *is* pretty dark and the lights from the house are flickering, so it technically could just be faulty lighting making me *think* he wants to kiss me. But he moves closer to me, his head lowering slowly toward mine. My eyes flutter closed as his face inches forward, when a wave splashes on us, soaking us both.

14

PLAY PRETEND

"WHAT ARE YOU GUYS DOING OUT HERE?" TANNER PUTS HIS arm around me and Maddie shoots me an apologetic look. Hannah is on the other side of Maddie and she's looking between me and Hudson with a huge smile on her face.

"Just went for a walk," Hudson says. He glances at me with a sheepish expression, and as much as I like everyone else, I wish our moment hadn't been interrupted. And I really wish I knew what he was thinking right now.

"Summer, your dad is looking for you," Hannah says. She leans in closer to me. "Sorry to ruin whatever was happening out here." She winks and pulls away. "Last one to the house has to go to bed first," she yells before taking off toward the house.

"She says that like it's a punishment," I say, taking my time running back to the house.

Hudson jogs beside me. When he starts to go slower, I walk and then he goes even slower.

"You're trying to win. You ready for bed, Hudson?" I tease.

He fakes a yawn. "I'm so tired."

I inch along and when he realizes what I'm doing, he tries to slow down, but he's already by the house.

"You lost," I tell him. "Touch the house."

He shakes his head. "You touch the house."

My head falls back. "Oh my god, I didn't realize children were on this trip."

He's laughing and his eyes are twinkling and he looks so cute I can hardly take it. "I'll let you have it...since you're the newbie and all."

"Oh—thank you—"

"Summer." My dad steps out from the house and motions for me to come in. Liam is standing behind him and both look somber enough to make me take a step back.

"What's going on?" I ask. "Is Mom okay?"

Dad frowns. "What? Yeah, Jenna's fine." He rubs his hand on the back of his neck. "I need a moment with you."

"Okay." I glance at Hudson again and he gives me a reassuring squeeze on the shoulder before I follow my dad and Liam into the house. We walk all the way to the office my dad has taken over, no one saying a word. When we get there, my dad ushers us in and shuts the door behind us. I look at Liam for clues, but he's avoiding looking at me right now. That's a first.

There are a couple of magazines on the desk and Dad turns his laptop around for me to see the screen. It's a picture of me putting sunscreen on Liam's back. And then I glance down at the magazines. There are various shots of me with Liam, some looking more flirtatious and intimate than others, all of them more so than what was really happening.

I look up at my dad and he's looking at Liam, who clears his throat and finally glances at me.

"I've been on the phone with my agent for the past hour. She is *pissed* at me. I don't know if you heard about the girl I was seen with six weeks ago—" he pauses and I shake my head, waiting for him to continue.

When he doesn't right away, I wave my hand to hurry him along.

"It wasn't good. Catherine has been after me to clean up my image for a while, and that girl was the kicker. Catherine says I'm going to lose all credibility if I don't get my act together, so when she saw these pictures with you, someone new...she lost her shit."

"Well, did you tell her it was nothing? And that I'm working on the set?"

"Here's the deal. She really liked the idea of you."

"What do you mean?" I glance at my dad and he looks like he'd rather be anywhere but here.

"You've got that wholesome, sexy vibe. Sorry," he says to my dad, who rolls his eyes. "And if you could just pretend to be into me for like a month or two, six tops, it would really help me out."

"What? What do you mean pretend to be into you? Like fake date?"

He nods and I laugh. It dies down quickly when I'm the only one laughing.

"We'd just have to make a few appearances together. No big deal. Maybe a few dinners out together."

"Is this because you kissed me the other day? Did they see that too?"

I scan the pictures and sure enough, there's one of us kissing too.

"Sorry about that." He makes a face. "I think that's what started this whole deal and really made her see red. I've been seen kissing a different girl every time I'm photographed and Catherine is *not* pleased."

"Well, I'm not going to kiss you and let you grope me just so you can make Catherine happy," I tell him. I look at my dad again. His arms are folded and he's being awfully quiet. "Why aren't you saying anything, Dad?"

"Because it's not a bad idea. It would create interest in the film, if people find out Liam fell in love with the director's daughter while on this set..."

"Fell in love?" I spit out. "I thought it was just a few dinners or something."

"We wouldn't have to kiss," Liam says. "Just a little hand-holding, a little arm around your shoulder...a few laughs. No big. What do you say?"

My dad and I speak at once.

"I say this is a terrible idea."

"I think you should do it."

"What?" I turn to face my dad. "I can't believe this. I can't believe you're wanting me to do it."

"Liam's a good guy. It'll help him out, get your name out there more...that's what you're wanting, right?"

"I want to make my way as a writer in this town, not as a sidepiece." My eyes fill with tears and I turn to walk out.

"Please, Summer," Liam says. "I promise I'll be respectful. It doesn't have to be a big deal."

My head falls back as I glare at the ceiling. I have always struggled with telling people no. It's maybe my biggest fault ever, and I count it as a doozie, especially in this moment.

"One month," I tell him. "I'll give you a month."

He rushes toward me like he's going to hug me and pauses when he sees the look on my face. "Thank you," he says, smiling his pretty Hollywood smile that makes all the girls forget their names.

I nod and turn back toward the door.

"One more thing," he says, "please don't let anyone know we're pretending. Okay, Summer? Not a soul. Not even your mother. And no one on set."

"That would be for the best," Dad adds.

I turn and glare at both of them. Because all that's going through my mind right now is that moment with Hudson earlier...

Looks like that won't be happening again.

15

AGREEABLE AND FEISTY

I DON'T GET TO GO TO BED EARLY AT ALL. I'M GRILLED FOR hours about the ways we can make this relationship with Liam and me look as authentic as possible. It's ironic to me that the word authentic is actually used when it's a fake relationship from top to bottom.

As we've hashed out the details of how we'll let everyone know we're together the next day, Liam leans in close to me and grins.

"It'll be fun, I promise. Okay? I'll be on my best behavior. I won't be a jerk and grab your butt or anything like that...

or-or kiss you, I swear it." He looks longingly at my lips and I blink slowly.

This guy.

"And I won't—well, I can't promise I won't flirt with you because you're really hot, you know? But I'll make it as fun for you as I can. I'm really grateful," he adds at the end of his mini-rant.

"What did you do that was so bad with that girl?"

He looks embarrassed for about two seconds before grinning. "We got caught having sex on Space Mountain in Disney World."

"How is that even—?" Disturbing images of body parts, flashing lights, and dropping stomachs take over and make me shudder.

"We were supposed to be the only ones on the ride and it's honestly not as cool as it s—"

"Enough." Dad holds up a hand, pausing Liam. "I don't want to hear the details of this. Don't make me regret being agreeable to this little arrangement, Liam."

Liam emphatically nods like he couldn't agree more. "I will not, sir. I promise to treat our little Summer here like a queen."

"I'm not little," I snap.

"I think we should have nicknames, don't you?" Liam says.

I walk to the door. "I'm going to bed. Seems like the two of you have it all figured out. You can let me know if I'm Snookums or Sweet Pea tomorrow."

Liam frowns. "I don't really see you as a Snookums or a Sweet Pea."

I groan. What have I gotten myself into?

"Before you go, I'd like you to sign this contract, Summer." My dad has been quietly working on something the past half hour and now he slides the paper across the desk.

"I'll be compensated for this?" I point to the sum on the paper. It would be a nice sum of money to put away for a future film of my own, or to get my own house once I'm back in Charlotte.

"Does that seem like enough?" Dad asks. He glances at Liam, who nods.

"I'm good for it," Liam says. "You're really doing me a huge favor, Summer. I won't take it lightly."

I'm kind of touched by his earnestness and then remind myself that he's an actor. A damn good one. A damn good player too apparently, something that I would do well to remember.

"Thank you. I guess I can't say no."

Liam and my dad both sink back into their chairs and I make my escape.

I pause outside my door, looking toward Hudson's room. We had such a fun night before all this craziness started. It feels so long ago when the biggest thing I was worried about tonight was the fact that I flashed Hudson. And then wondering if he was going to kiss me.

Things can change in such a short amount of time.

What is he going to say about all of this? I hate that my dad doesn't want me to tell him.

———

I'm exhausted when I wake up the next morning and am running late. When I get to the kitchen, one of the sexier pictures of me lotioning Liam up is on the refrigerator and so is the one of us kissing. Liam walks in, holding his coffee cup, and Hudson is behind him. Liam puts his arms around my waist as I'm pouring coffee and nuzzles into my neck.

"Morning, Sunshine," he says. "I'm still thinking about last night."

I spill coffee on the counter and he rushes to wipe it up for me. I glance back at Hudson who is looking between the two of us with an indecipherable expression. I will him to look into my eyes, to see the truth there, but he never quite makes eye contact with me.

"Everyone's outside already. Waiting on you both," he says, walking out of the kitchen and leaving me alone with my new boyfriend.

"Did you have to lay it on so thick?" I say between my teeth.

Liam's eyes are wide. "I just thought we could use the practice before we take it out in the real world." He grins. "I think Sunshine fits you perfectly. Don't you?"

"No," I snap. "It doesn't."

Liam sticks his lips out, pouting. "Well, not if you're grumbling like that, but if you use your normal voice—"

I walk out before he can finish that sentence. It's going to be a long month. He falls into step beside me within seconds.

"I was thinking, we should probably have a romantic dinner together while we're here. Get things rolling with our Hawaiian lovefest."

"Fine," I say. "Just tell me when and I'll be ready."

He props his arm around my shoulder and beams down at me. "I love it when you're so agreeable."

I roll my eyes and he kisses the tip of my nose.

"And feisty," he adds.

"We said no kissing."

He holds up both hands. "I said we wouldn't *have* to kiss. I never agreed to not kissing your nose."

I stalk off and try to catch up with the morning tasks I'm already behind on.

My phone starts going bonkers within the next few hours. I have to turn off the sound because I'm getting texts every two seconds. My mom and Autumn most of all, but also friends from school, numbers I don't recognize, and a few guys I had dates with at UNC that I'd hoped had lost my number. The question everyone wants an answer to, and immediately, is: When did you start dating Liam Taylor?

Hudson hasn't spoken to me all day except to bark orders in my general direction. Hannah keeps trying to grill me about what's going on with Liam and me.

She finally says, "I thought the gruff, serious persona was more your type, but you do you, girl."

We finish filming for the night, and Liam links his fingers through mine as we're walking back toward the house. "Dinner with me tonight?" he asks.

16

OUT OF MY LEAGUE

I CHECK THE MIRROR ONE MORE TIME BEFORE LEAVING MY room. A short chiffon corseted dress with a flowy hemline. It's both sexy and sweet. I have two loose braids that complete the look, and my makeup is on point, if I do say so myself. If I'm going to be photographed, I hope I will at least look my best.

I shoot a quick text to my mom and Autumn because I've avoided them all day.

I promise I'll fill you in later! Going to dinner now and the days are so long. Love you.

Mom writes back first. **You better fill us in! :)**

And then Autumn quickly follows. **Giving you a break since you're dating a celebrity and must be SO BUSY, but if you forget about me, I'm cutting you.** I laugh and slide on my strappy heels.

When I step into the living room, everyone is in there and they all go quiet.

"Wow, Summer. You look gorgeous," Hannah is the first to say.

"Thank you." I smile at her and look for Hudson. He's looking out the wall of windows toward the beach.

Liam walks up to me and puts his hands on my waist. "Fucking amazing," he says.

"Watch that mouth near my daughter," Dad says, and everyone laughs. Well, I can't tell if Hudson laughs or not because he won't turn around. "Have fun, you two."

We walk hand in hand to the car and there's a driver already waiting. When we get in the back seat, I drop Liam's hand and he smiles at me.

"How do you feel about seafood?" he asks.

"I love it."

He sighs and leans back in the seat, still looking at me. "Whew." He acts like he's wiping sweat off his brow. "You look really gorgeous tonight."

"You don't have to say that."

"But it's true."

I whisper in his ear so the driver can't hear us. "When we're alone, you don't have to pretend with me. It'll be too stressful if we feel like we're always *on*."

"But I'm not pretending. You really are gorgeous," he whispers back in my ear.

I shiver when his lips brush against my ear and lean back, staring straight ahead.

He takes my hand in his and puts it to his lips. "Come on, Summer. Let's make the most of our time together, okay?" he says, still whispering.

I nod, but I don't look at him. His smiling eyes and quick charm would make it so easy to get confused during all of this, and I'm determined I won't let that happen. This is a game we're playing and I will play my part and bring home a nice sum of money. It's probably one hundred percent more than what I was going to make from being his lackey, since my dad hasn't mentioned me getting paid in any of our "communication" or lack thereof. The whole thing is bizarre. I feel bad for taking money from Liam, but he and my dad just acted like that was a given.

I should have argued the whole arrangement more than I did.

It's possible that I have issues. Huge issues. I already know what Autumn will say to me agreeing to this craziness, her starstruck ideas of Liam aside—she'll blame it on me wanting our dad's approval, and she's not entirely wrong.

The restaurant is romantic and sets the mood for seduction with the low lights, the pulsing soundtrack played just quietly enough to stir the blood. We're treated like royalty when we walk in, being seated at the best ocean-view table.

"You can order whatever you want, but there's a seven-course meal that they are specializing in tonight and it will be out of this world," Liam says, setting aside the menu.

"I can put away a lot, but I think I'll just stick to the mahi."

He smiles and leans in close. "So, is this going to mess you up with anyone at home, our little arrangement?"

"I don't have anyone at home, but pretty sure this is going to mess up any options I have for a while, yes."

Thinking of the way Hudson wouldn't look at me, I deflate into the seat.

He makes a face but is still smiling. I think it's his default button. Maybe he's naturally this happy and easygoing? Seems hard to maintain. He reaches out and takes my hand. "Well, I'm sorry for that. Feel free to use me for anything you might be missing—since I'll be in the same boat." He leans back as the waitress walks up, and my face is flaming because I think his "anything" includes sex.

I'm so out of my league here.

That's the most awkward part of the night, though. It does get better. Liam talks about the last set he was on with my dad and asks me about what my life is like back home. I tell him about my mom and Autumn. He has a brother and a sister, and they live on Nantucket.

"Really? I've never met anyone who lived there. Year-round?"

"Yep. Top coastal cuisine. We own a restaurant. I grew up working there and my brother and sister are still there. I'm the rebel of the group since I have no desire to take over the restaurant, now or ever." It's the only time his voice loses that teasing quality.

"I'm sure they're so proud of the success you've had..."

He makes a face. "My dad's words and I quote: 'We both know you don't have what it takes. Come home when this phase has run out. Preferably sooner than later.'"

"Ouch. I'm sorry, Liam. That's rough."

He shrugs and the lightheartedness is back. "I guess we all have something that motivates us," he says.

He glances over my shoulder and back at me, leaning closer and taking my hand again. Next thing I know, his hand is brushing the hair away from my face and he's staring into my eyes so intently, I think he's going to kiss me right here in the restaurant.

"You are so beautiful," he says. "I can't believe you're here with me."

That clues me in that he's acting for someone, but geez, the way he delivers his lines. He's a better actor than I realized.

And then he leans in even closer, his forehead against mine. "Any reason this can't be real?" he asks.

17

FIRST DATES AND SLIMY SNAKES

IS HE KIDDING ME RIGHT NOW? LIAM, WHO ACCORDING TO MY sister, is Hollywood's biggest IT guy right now, is asking if we can have a real relationship?

I feel like I'm leading a double life right now. My life in Charlotte seems so far away, and yet this one I'm in right now feels impossible.

This is why I prefer to stay behind the scenes. I'd rather know who the screenwriter is than the actor. I'd rather date the director's assistant than...

"Summer?" Liam says, smiling that cute twinkly-eyed smile he has.

"No. No chance," I tell him. "I prefer to keep my feet on the ground instead of whatever whirlwind you'd take me on, thank you very much."

"See, when you say it like that, it sounds like a compliment," he says, laughing.

"Only someone like you who has no insecurities whatsoever could take that as a compliment." But I'm grinning because his charm is infectious. Even when he's obnoxious, he's bubbling over with charisma.

"Who doesn't want to fly?"

"I've never been a huge fan of flying," I admit. "And I prefer to fictionalize the drama rather than living it."

Our waitress comes up before he can respond to that, but his eyes stay on me.

"Have you decided what you'd like?" he asks.

"I'll have the mahi-mahi with garlic-lime oil."

I have to give it to the waitress—she appears calm and professional as she looks at Liam for his order, but I see her hand shake slightly and realize she's just really good at her job.

How many people are playing a part all the time?

For some reason, it makes me think of Hudson and how easy it feels to be around him. But I don't really know him and he's already giving me the cold shoulder. I mean, who can blame him? He thinks I've fallen under Liam's spell.

I sigh and Liam leans forward, pouring a glass of chilled white wine into my glass. After he's poured his, he lifts his glass and motions for me to lift mine.

"To embracing flying," he says.

I roll my eyes but clink his glass and take a sip. The wine is crisp and smooth and I have no idea what notes are in it or all that wine jargon, but it tastes really good. Before long, Liam and I are trading stories about bicycle accidents and prom dates. The food is delicious and I've gotten through a dinner with Liam. When we step outside the restaurant a few hours later, there are a couple of photographers waiting. Nothing too intimidating, but they're persistent. We pause and pose for one or two and then walk hand-in-in hand to the waiting car. When I slide into the back seat, I want to sag against the cushion and catch my breath, but the cameras are still right there.

"Well done," Liam says. "You handled them like a pro."

"Do you ever get sick of it?"

"Of course, but it's just part of it. I knew that going in. But yeah, it's exhausting."

"You don't love having the constant attention on you?"

He grins as we're pulling out of the parking lot. "It's not all bad. If they're not paying attention, I'm probably on my way out."

We're quiet the rest of the short drive to the house and when we pull into our gated drive, Liam reaches over and takes my hand. "Thank you again for doing this, Summer. I hope it wasn't too much torture for you to be around me tonight?"

I laugh and squeeze his hand before letting go. "It wasn't bad at all."

He reaches out and flicks my knee and we're both laughing when we get out of the car. I walk toward the house and he reaches out and puts his arm around my shoulder, slowing me down.

"Just trying to make it look real," he whispers, pressing his lips to my shoulder.

"Is that really necessary at the house?"

"Only while we're still outside."

I look around, and even though there's no sign of any photographers around our spacious yard, after seeing all the shots they already had of the two of us, I know they have their ways. I turn and give him a hug before we reach the door.

And it's easy—I enjoyed my time with Liam tonight. It was actually really nice.

We step inside and I drop his hand. He grins at me but doesn't give me a hard time like I expect him to.

"Night," I whisper in the quiet house.

"Night."

I turn to go down the hall to my room just as Hudson steps out of his room. He pauses when he sees me and is about to walk past.

"Are you still ignoring me?" I ask.

He stops in front of me. "What?"

"You heard me."

"I'm not ignoring you."

"Well, good. That would be sad if you were. I kind of liked what we had going there." I grin up at him, but he doesn't smile back.

"Hudson, could you bring me a San Pellegrino?" Winslet peeks her head out of Hudson's room and when she sees me, her eyes narrow and a small smile plays around the edge of her lips.

All the blood inside me shrivels up and I feel the icy-hot combo like a jolt. *When did she get here?* And *what* is she doing in Hudson's room?

Hudson clears his throat. "Sure." His eyes have never left mine and I have so many questions, but he nods briskly and moves past me. "Night, Summer," he says.

"Night," I say to his back.

I look back and Winslet is still watching me. I imagine

inside she's roaring a Maleficent laugh right about now, but on the outside, she's calm as a creepy, evil cucumber. Calm and condescending and like she's won a game I didn't know we were playing.

Her fingers flutter in a wave and she slinks back into Hudson's room like an exotic snake.

18

OW

IT'S PAINFUL WHEN MY ALARM GOES OFF THE NEXT MORNING. I had the hardest time falling asleep. Winslet's eyes haunted me every time I closed mine. And my ears strained to hear any conversation from Hudson's room, or worse, a creak in his bed.

Nothing.

These damn walls are too insulated.

I guess I should be grateful.

But my brain has filled in all the blanks and then some.

I drag to the shower and put on a little makeup to hide

the dark circles under my eyes. Most are gone already when I get to the kitchen. Hudson and my dad are there, grabbing coffee and talking.

I flush when I see Hudson, knowing all my conflicting feelings about him are showing on my face.

"There you are," my dad says. "I was just about to see if you were awake."

"Sorry. Barely awake."

"It's okay. We've pushed out our start time about a half hour. Hopefully, the wind will calm down by then."

Hudson isn't looking at me again and I hate it. He moves toward the door and I follow, feeling like I'm forgetting a jillion things, but at the moment, I don't care.

"Hudson, do you have a second?"

He pauses. I can't tell if he's annoyed or just in a hurry to get outside. "Sure. Walk out with me? We don't have far to go today."

My dad is already out the door, so it's just the two of us. When we step outside and I see the expanse of ocean just right there, I'm blown away all over again that this is my summer. My dad's place and now Hawaii...despite any angsty thoughts I have about Hudson and that witch who was in his room last night, this summer has turned out to be pretty wonderful.

Hudson doesn't say anything and I realize that he's waiting for me to start whatever conversation we're going to have. I take a deep breath and stare straight ahead.

"I feel like you're mad at me," I finally say.

"Why would I be mad at you?"

"You tell me."

"I'm not mad. I'm a little...surprised by your choice of boyfriends, but you've done nothing wrong."

I feel his eyes on me and I turn, happy to be making eye contact once again. "Hudson, it's not—"

"I just don't want you to get hurt," he says. He stops and turns to face me. "Promise me you won't?"

I smile. "If my heart gets broken, I don't think it will be from Liam."

He stares at me for several long beats and my heart does that flippety-floppety thing.

And I open my mouth to tell him the truth, despite the fact that I signed a contract and that it's supposed to be under wraps so it's more believable...when Winslet sashays up to us and loops her arm through Hudson's.

What's worse is that Hudson seems happy to see her.

"Hey, studly," she says, ignoring me. "You kept me up way too late last night."

My face burns. My skin burns. My eyes burn.

Ow. Ow. Ow.

My heart burns.

Hudson chuckles and I can feel his eyes on me, but I stay laser-focused on the sandy beach ahead. I am walking with a purpose now. Anything to get away from this conversation.

"I didn't force you to watch the movie," he says.

I feel a little bit of hope. Maybe they didn't spend the night together.

"And miss falling asleep next to you?" she says.

And there go my hopes again, crashing to the ground.

We reach the location setup and my dad calls Winslet over. She walks away, but not before squeezing Hudson's hand and then giving me a pointed look as if to say, *back off, bitch, he's mine*.

Once she's gone, I look up at Hudson. "So, you and Winslet, huh?"

"We're friends. About like you and Liam, I guess." And with that, he walks away.

What am I supposed to make of that? For the rest of the day, I dissect what he meant. Does that mean he's dating her? Because he thinks I'm dating Liam. Or does that mean he knows the truth, and he and Winslet really are friends?

Gah. I get to work, which for today entails fulfilling every whim of Liam and Tanner. I do it halfheartedly, too tired and distracted to put much effort in and too happy to be helping them and not Winslet.

The day drags on forever and I just want to go to bed.

When I'm packing up for the day, Liam puts his arm around my shoulder.

"You okay?" he asks.

"I'm fine." I look around to see who's close to us and everyone is too preoccupied to be paying much attention. "What do you know about Hudson and Winslet?"

His eyes widen. "You mean, are they a couple?"

I nod, and his eyes widen more, a big grin stretching across his face.

"Do you like him?" he whispers.

"What? No," I snap. "I just don't see how anyone could be interested in her. She's mean."

We both turn and she's laughing at something Hudson has just said. I didn't think she was capable of joy. In fact, nothing about her looks mean in this moment.

"Hmm, well, maybe he brings out the best in her, the way you do with me." Liam shrugs and I roll my eyes.

"You've known me all of two minutes, Liam."

"You're right. Maybe it's their history that's working for them," he says, and then he starts laughing. He puts his arms around me and pulls me in for a hug. "I'm kidding, Summer. You should see your face. You look like your dog died. Come on, it'll be okay. You know what? He's looking over here right now and he looks like he wants to fucking hit me."

"He does?" I say hopefully.

Liam pulls back and bops my nose. "That stings, Winters."

But we're both grinning at each other and I miss it completely when Hudson and Winslet leave.

19

COCKBLOCK

THE NEXT DAY IS LONG AND TEDIOUS. WE START EARLY AND shoot for as long as we have daylight. I'm tired and grumpy by the time we're wrapping up.

Winslet has been beyond annoying all day long, asking to be fanned and to go find pancakes made with coconut flour but no eggs and no milk of any kind even almond, but the pancakes need to be fluffy and not dry...and with coconut syrup...but sugar-free, sweetened with only monk fruit made with allulose and topped with farm-fresh berries. And with vegan sausage.

#SpecificAF.

It takes a while, but I find it.

God bless this little bakery that has sugar-free treats and doesn't normally sell pancakes, but they're willing to do it for an extra twenty bucks. I don't find a close vegan restaurant, but I find a market that just so happens to have some wannabe sausage. I stop by the house and heat it up before taking it out to her.

When I get back to the set, grinning in triumph and holding up the container with her perfect pancakes, she rubs her nonexistent stomach and pokes her lips out.

"I couldn't wait any longer. You were taking forever and craft services had these black bean burgers." She waves her hand over the container of pancakes. "You enjoy those. I didn't need the calories anyway." She gives my body a long look and smirks. "You can always get back to your diet when you go home."

I wish I could spit on the pancakes and watch her eat them, but that's not happening.

I open the container and stare at her while I shove the entire sausage into my mouth.

She shudders. "You are so disgusting."

"That is *hot*," Liam says from across the sand.

Hudson looks back to see what's going on and my mouth is as full as a chipmunk's.

Great.

No one is happier than I am when her scenes are done and she whines her way back to the house, leaving the rest of us to finish the day more peacefully. Liam and Tanner head to the house, with Liam circling back around to kiss my cheek.

"See you later?" he says, glancing around to see if anyone is listening.

"I'm kind of tired. I'll probably go to bed early tonight."

He nods. "Sounds good. Night, Pooh Bear."

I shake my head. "Nope. Absolutely not Pooh Bear."

He grins and walks away, waving without turning around. "I think it suits you."

"Not answering to it, ever," I holler back.

"What are you not answering to?" Hudson asks, walking up with his hands full.

"How do you always get stuck with cleanup?" I ask.

"Everyone else expects it to just get done for them. I've been where you are and know what it's like to be the only one left with a mess."

I turn to him, overcome with the desire to hug him. "Thank you. I didn't realize you were doing all of this just to help me."

He looks away, a shy expression on his face. "It's for somewhat selfish reasons. I'd be the one called out if anything wasn't ready for tomorrow."

I grin. "Mm-hmm. Most would just blame the new girl, slash director's daughter."

He grins back and my heart picks up tempo in my chest. "You would make a good fall guy."

"Well, thanks for not putting me in that position. What's up for tomorrow?"

A crack of thunder makes me jump and I take three steps closer to Hudson, colliding with him.

"Come on, we better hurry." He shifts so everything is on his left side and holds out his hand. I take it and we run to the nearest shelter as the rain pounds down from out of nowhere.

We stop under a bar with a thatched roof that has been set up for our location, and it's just enough to keep us from getting more drenched than we already are. We're laughing as we drop our things and stand facing each other. It's suddenly harder to breathe, like all of the air has been whooshed out of my chest. I don't know if he's feeling the way I am, but he steps closer to me, our chests rising and falling, and his hand brushes my hair off of my face.

I take another step closer to him, unable to stop myself. It's a physical pull, and his hand lands on my waist.

This is happening, this is happening, my mind is chanting, and his face lowers to mine. My lips part and my eyes close, anticipating the feel of his lips on mine when another crash of thunder sounds, jolting us into each other. My arms are around him in the next moment and his are around me as I stare up at him, rivulets of water dripping down our faces and mingling with each other. I swear I can see how much he wants me, his face a combination of desire and confusion, and I close the distance between us, my lips barely brushing against his...

Honk, honk, HONNNNNK. The loudest honk ever known to man comes barreling toward us.

Hudson jumps back, his arms falling off of me, and I immediately feel the chill. He's not looking at me anymore but toward the Jeep that's pulling up by us. Tanner motions for us to hop in, and we grab our things, throwing them in the vehicle before we get in.

"Thanks, man. Appreciate you coming to get us," Hudson says.

Speak for yourself, I want to say, but I mumble my thanks instead like a decent human being.

"Thank Liam, he didn't want you left out here in the storm," Tanner says.

Then where is *he*? That's my first thought. And then I

remember he's a big-time actor who's just acting like he's my boyfriend and actually doesn't feel anything for me, but he still managed to ruin my spectacular first kiss with the guy I really want to be dating.

20

SNACKS OR KISSES?

THE IMPASSE
By Summer Winters

Life without David was both easier and harder than I anticipated. I didn't miss seeing the hurt expression on his face when I rebuffed his attempts to be intimate, but the loneliness I felt from not having his attention was a surprise.

Just because I'd left David for Micah didn't mean Micah was fully ready for more. Micah was like a tomcat that couldn't quite settle down at night. He came around for pets and scratches during the day and then disappeared when things got a little too chummy. And then he deep dived into work and seemed too busy to talk about anything beyond the surface chitchat.

This isn't always the way it was.

Before, when I was with David, Micah and I had these deep, soulful conversations that moved me so much that I knew David and I would never have anything close to that connection.

How did it all dwindle to nothing once I was available?

I determined today was the day I'd make progress with Micah. Decide once and for all if what I thought we had was anything real, anything worth salvaging.

Meet me at our beach? *I texted, hoping and praying he remembered the beach where we'd stayed up all night talking months ago.*

Sure. What time?

Half hour?

See you there.

Excitement kicked up inside me. This was it. I'd tell him how I really felt this time, no more dancing around the conversation as I had all along.

Giggling breaks me out of my writing fervor. My eyes narrow and I lean against the wall that separates me from Hudson. Is Winslet in his room again? How could he go from almost kissing me to hanging around Winslet again? And what could she possibly be giggling about? I glare at my computer screen, willing Hudson out of my mind. He'd stomped into the house without another glance my way after our almost kiss earlier. Well, we did kiss, it wasn't almost...it was just the lightest kiss ever. He might not have even felt it, it was so light.

I let out a ragged exhale and instead of crying like I want to, I focus on my story.

I pulled into the parking lot in front of the ocean and looked around to see if he was here yet. He was. He stood by the water, and instead of facing the water, he faced me. I couldn't tell if he'd seen me yet, but he was watching expectantly.

That had to be a good sign, right?

I sigh out loud and feel like a thousand pounds are hanging on my back. This story is depressing me. I want to get to the kiss already, and it's only chapter four. It's too soon for a kiss.

I hear giggling again and am sure that it's Winslet laughing extra loud just so I hear her. I start typing faster than Jim Carrey in *Bruce Almighty*.

I started walking toward him and he put his hand over his eyes, grinning when he noticed me. He walked toward me, meeting me halfway, and the air between us was supercharged with energy and sparks.

"Hey," I said. "You came."

"Well, yeah, you wouldn't expect me to stand you up, would you?"

I shrugged and he frowned slightly before reaching out and putting his hands on my waist. I soaked in the warmth, the salty damp air, but everything else was scorching hot.

"I've missed you," he said. "I've been thinking about you nonstop. What are we waiting for?" His head lowered toward mine...

· · ·

A loud shriek startles me and I jump out of my writing stupor. I shut my laptop and sag forward.

You're being ridiculous, Summer. He thinks you're dating someone. He's a free man. Even if he had kissed you earlier, he would still be a free man. You kissed Liam—well, he kissed you —but technically all Hudson knows is that you and Liam kissed, so why wouldn't he do whatever he wants?

I bang my head against my desk, weary of my thoughts and wishing I could shut off my brain for a while. I venture out into the hall and away from Hudson's giggling guest, and I stop in the kitchen. My dad is in there with Bella, and Hannah comes in behind me.

So much for raiding the refrigerator on the sly.

I grab a few snacks and make my escape, wishing I could grab ice cream too but not wanting to take the time to get it in front of everyone. I'm in such a hurry to get back to my room and hide that I collide into a hard, muscled body.

"What's your rush?" Hudson says.

You're my rush, I think. My stomach dips to the ground and then back to my throat in one split second.

His hands are still on me, steadying me from our collision, and I want to stay right here forever and ever.

"Want some snacks?" I ask. Lamest line ever when I really want to say, "Wanna make out?" but I've never claimed to be good at spur-of-the-moment sexy banter.

His eyes twinkle even though his mouth is a flat line, almost like he's trying not to laugh.

"I could do some snacking," he says.

I back into my room and he follows me, and I toss everything on the bed before closing the door. I lean against the door and he turns to face me.

"Beef jerky?" I ask.

Again with my stupid mouth before my brain.

He shakes his head and takes a closer step toward me.

"Wheat Thins and Cheese Whiz?"

It's like I have a disease.

He takes another step closer and our toes touch. I'm barefoot. So is he.

It's hot.

He reaches up and touches my cheek, the barest flutter across my skin and I shiver.

His head lowers and I feel lightheaded. I step on my tiptoes to meet him halfway. Our lips crash into each other. Finally. All of my awkward flies out the window, all of his hard-to-read mystery is gone too, and if I'd known we'd communicate so perfectly this way, I would've made sure we kissed a lot sooner.

21

DON'T GO

HUDSON'S LIPS ARE ROCKING MY WORLD AND HIS HANDS ON MY waist and in my hair are doing crazy things to my insides too. My body is crushed against his and I am here for all of it. So when someone pounds on the door, making me jump away from him like a woman on fire, I'm breathless and disoriented.

I glance at Hudson and his chest is rising and falling rapidly. His teeth reach out and slide across his bottom lip and I want to go right back to making out with him.

Pound, pound, pound.

I fling the door open and it's my dad.

Worst timing ever.

He points at Hudson. "Been looking all over for you. Just the man I wanted to see. I think we've got what we need here. I'm ready to fly out tonight and would like you to come with me, Hudson. We can get everything ready for the shoot day after tomorrow." It's like he just noticed that I'm here and he looks between me and then Hudson before he speaks again. "Liam was looking for you. You guys will fly back in the morning."

I cringe because I realize how it sounds to Hudson and I want to set it straight while my dad is here.

"Can't I fly back with you guys?"

Dad lifts his eyebrows. "It's not necessary. Everyone else will be flying back tomorrow and this will give you time to enjoy one last night in Hawaii." He looks at Hudson. "With Liam."

I glance at Hudson and his whole demeanor has changed in the few minutes my dad has been in the room. He looks like he wants to escape.

"We can tell Hudson the truth, Dad," I whisper.

Hudson looks at me then and there's a long, pregnant pause.

"Right," my dad says. "The truth is I don't need a front-row seat to my daughter's love life, so it'll be good if we go ahead and get out of the way."

My eyes narrow on my dad. I'm not sure what nonsense he's spewing, but this wasn't what I was expecting. Nothing about this summer has been.

"I mean the truth about me and Liam," I say between my gritted teeth.

"Contracts are a tricky business," my dad says quietly. "I wouldn't mess around with that if I were you."

This time I do roll my eyes and groan. But I find that I'm whispering like the walls are listening when I say my next sentence. "I'm going to be Liam's girlfriend on paper for a little while. Only on paper."

I wait for Hudson to say something, but his lips just twitch a little bit. Those lips that I wish my dad hadn't interrupted my time with...

"Well?" I can't stand his silence anymore. I can't tell if he's mad or jealous or—

He starts laughing and I laugh too because the sight of Hudson laughing is an instant aphrodisiac, and the last thing I want my dad to see is how turned on I am right now.

My dad stares between the two of us, confused. "What's so funny?"

And I wait for Hudson to answer because I want to know too. He's obviously not laughing for the same reason I am.

"Liam told me," Hudson says. He looks at me pointedly and I nearly melt into a puddle on the floor. "Right before I came in here tonight."

But why was Winslet giggling in your room? If it even was her for sure. I want to ask, but does it matter? He came over as soon as he knew and kissed my face off. My mouth breaks into the widest grin and Hudson's face matches it. My dad gives us both a strange look before gripping Hudson's shoulder.

"Can you be ready to leave within the hour?"

Hudson nods. "Sure."

My dad opens the door and pauses like he expects Hudson to walk out with him. Hudson puts his hand on the back of his neck and avoids looking at my dad. He looks nervous and it's cute as hell.

"See you tomorrow, kiddo," Dad says, kissing my forehead.

"Night, Dad. Safe travels."

He leaves, but the door is still open and I close it and turn to face Hudson. "So you knew."

He nods, his eyes still bright but his face as serious as stone. "I'm really glad you're not dating Liam Taylor."

I have to bite the inside of my cheek to keep from beaming again. It's so hard to be cool right now. "Yeah?"

He steps closer and puts his hands on my waist. "Yeah." He bends down and is so close our lips touch when he says, "Do me a favor. Come back tomorrow still single, okay? We'll see if we can pull off a date around your hot summer romance with Hollywood's It Boy."

I laugh. "When you put it that way, I sound terrible."

He kisses me, not even close to as long as I want him to, but enough to make me weak in the knees.

"There is nothing terrible about you," he says, pulling away. He moves toward the door and I lean on the desk to catch my breath. "I'm really glad we had this discussion."

We both laugh because so little was discussed and yet, everything that has needed to be said was finally covered with his brief visit tonight. And most of it was said without words.

I sigh as he opens the door. I really hate to see him go.

"I'll see you tomorrow," he says.

"Good night, Hudson. Sweet dreams."

His gaze heats my skin as he takes a long look. "I'll be dreaming wide awake."

22

UNFRIENDLY SKIES

I GO TO BED SMILING AND WAKE UP SMILING, TAKING MY TIME getting up since we don't have to do anything but fly home later. I should be using the time to sightsee a little bit on my last free day here, but I'm enjoying the slow morning too much for that. It's been nonstop *go, go, go* since I got to my dad's.

I check my phone and respond to my sister's texts. She's wanting more details about my relationship with Liam than I've been giving. I don't think I can keep it a secret from her. She's too smart to not see through me. I'm not sure how long this whole thing will go on anyway—I'm kind of hoping the hoopla will die down quickly and we can return to normal.

"Summer, want some coffee?" Liam knocks on my door.

"Yeah, come in." I sit up in bed and he opens the door, holding a big mug. He hands it to me and then tosses a magazine in my lap. A picture of us together is right there on the front cover.

"Wow, that was fast."

"It's working. Just got off the phone with Catherine and she's happier than she's been in months. Wants us to hit a couple of hot spots this weekend, amp up the PDA."

I crinkle my nose and he bops it. "I thought we wouldn't have to do all that. Just look cozy for the camera."

"Yeah, I thought so too, but she's been on all these online sites that are talking about it and they're into you. I don't think they've ever liked anyone for me before."

"Great," I say sarcastically.

"Hey, I did a solid for you last night. Told Hudson—"

I take a long sip of coffee and can't stop the smile from taking over my face. "Thanks for that."

He tilts his head and lifts an eyebrow. "What happened?"

"He came to see me after, and—"

"Spare me the details. The lovesick eyes and the cheesy grin are already more than I can take. Just play it cool when we get back, okay? You guys can screw around, do whatever you want, as long as the two of you are the only ones who know about it."

I make a face. "You make it sound so sleazy."

"Screwing around? No, that sounds like my kind of life. What I wish I could be doing right now instead of talking with you about it."

I throw a pillow at him and he falls back on the bed laughing.

"So, you and Hudson, huh?" he says. "Damn. I never stood a chance."

"I'm hopeful," I say. "Not sure how easy it'll be to date him when I already have a boyfriend."

Liam looks up at me and bats his eyelashes. "It's the least I can do, make things difficult for you guys. The only way I know to nurse my broken heart."

I roll my eyes. "As if your heart will ever be broken."

He sits up and looks back at me, grinning. "I cannot be contained...except by the unobtainable Summer Winters."

"So full of it. What time are we flying out?"

"Well, I was kind of hoping you'd be awake and we could head back sooner rather than later. We're shooting early in the morning and everyone wants to get on back to be ready for that. Joe said we could leave as soon as noon if everyone is ready."

I nod and take a few more sips of my coffee. "I'm good with that." Getting back to California means seeing Hudson sooner, which is a great thing. The whole kiss last night kind of feels like something I dreamed up.

Not to mention, he hasn't texted at all. I don't know why that's surprising me—it's not like he's ever texted even though he gave me his number on the very first day I met him, and I know he has my number. I've only checked my phone a couple dozen times since he left last night, thinking maybe he'd send something to let me know what he's thinking about this...whatever *this* is between us.

"Where'd you go?" Liam asks.

"Ah, nowhere."

I can tell by his smirk that he doesn't believe me.

"Okay, well, now that you've got coffee in you and you know the schedule, I'll leave you to get ready."

"Thanks, Liam."

He gets off the bed and does a fake bow. "Tomorrow you'll be back to waiting on me, so it's the least I could do." He winks and I give him a mock glare.

"I meant thanks for telling Hudson...but thank you for the coffee too. Maybe I won't spit in your food tomorrow."

His eyes widen and he backs his way to the door, hands up. I can't help but laugh. As soon as he shuts the door, I get up and start packing. I'm a little sad that I didn't get to see more of the island, but damn, my moments here have been sweet. I get lost in daydreaming about kissing Hudson. It already seems like a long time ago and it was only last night.

I snap out of it and start hustling. When I leave my room, there are bags by the front door and a few people are already waiting on the couch. Hannah yawns and waves when she sees me. Liam is next to her and he hops up, coming over to give me a hug. I almost forgot we're still pretending in front of everyone else. Winslet walks out while we're still hugging and she rolls her eyes. Ugh. I'd hoped she was leaving on a much later flight than all of us.

Within twenty minutes, we're settling onto our chartered plane. Liam is next to me and Maddie and Hannah are across from us. Winslet is in front of us and has the whole row to herself, the seat next to her and the seats across. Liam pats his shoulder when I rest my head against the seat and I lean over, putting my head on his shoulder.

I wake up to the plane shuddering and sit up, looking around. We dip down, my stomach dropping like I'm on a roller coaster, and someone screams. Our flight attendant walks by and reminds us to keep our seat belts fastened. I grip Liam's hand as the plane takes another drop.

23

GOING DOWN

THE PLANE DIPS AGAIN AND IT FEELS LIKE WE MAKE A SHARP turn. I'm still gripping Liam's hand with one hand and my other is covering my mouth. Hannah and Maddie are crying across the aisle. Winslet is yelling at Joe, the pilot, like it's all his fault.

He gets on the speaker a moment later. "I'm sorry for the turbulence, everyone. I'm turning the plane around and heading back to Oahu."

Winslet shrieks. "We have a schedule to keep. God!" Under her breath, she's muttering about how a professional would've flown out of the storm and gotten us past it.

"Keep it down, Winslet. The man needs to focus. He's as professional as they come," Liam says.

In this small plane, every dip and turn is magnified. I hear someone throwing up and don't try to find out who it is. I'm a sympathetic vomiter—if I see it, it's coming up for me too.

I look at Liam and his eyes are wide.

"You okay?" he whispers.

We take another dip and the plane jolts erratically.

"This is intense," I yelp.

The little oxygen masks fall above us and the flight attendant yells for us to put them on. She reminds us of our seats being flotation devices. It's so different from the movies where there's a team staggering through the aisles helping people. The plane is so small that she's just a few rows over and she's putting the oxygen mask over her face.

"Shit, I can't believe this is happening," Liam says. He gets his mask on and checks mine to make sure it's on right. He glances around and yells for Hannah to make sure she's covered. "Tanner, you good, man?"

"Yeah, you?" he says from behind us.

"We're good," Liam answers.

I lose my stomach with our next drop and Joe gets back on the speaker.

"I'll be landing in Molokai instead of Oahu. We're close, but the plane is mal—" His voice cuts off and we drop again. I scream this time.

We're going down.

My body starts trembling and I shake my head. "I'm not ready to die," I whisper. And then louder, I yell, "I don't want to die."

Liam turns toward me and grips my shoulders, holding me steady. "We're not gonna die. Summer," he says, his hands going to my face. "Listen to me. We're getting out of this, okay? Don't give up on me."

"Oh my god, oh my god," I chant.

Liam leans his forehead on mine, his hands still gripping my cheeks as he whispers my name over and over. I don't know why it soothes me, but it does, and I take one long, deep breath, the tremors in my body tapering off enough to think clearer.

"Okay?" he asks, leaning back to look into my eyes.

I'm about to nod when the plane drops again. And this time it's more like a dive, as we free fall. I'm screaming along with everyone else and tears pour down my face, but I try my best to fight the panic as Liam reminds me of what to do with the seat. I do exactly as he does and then we crash into the water with a vengeance. My head slams back against the seat and I'm stunned silent for a moment.

I feel Liam's hand on my shoulder and blink. I hear him saying my name, but everything feels far away. He gives me a slight shake and I hear him clearly again.

"We have to move, Summer. Come on. Can you hear me?" he pleads and when I finally nod, the relief on his face makes me cry harder. "Get up. Come on, we've got this." He pulls me up.

When the flight attendant moves toward the emergency exit, everything suddenly moves in fast forward. It feels like a dream when she opens the door and the rush of air comes toward us. I have a moment of relief and gratitude that we're all in one piece after that crash, but then I remember we're surrounded by the ocean, who knows how far from shore, and I am *terrified*.

Hannah is the first one out and she makes it look easy.

Then Winslet shoves Maddie out of the way and goes ahead of her. Maddie's next.

Liam moves me in front of him and grips my face. "We're going to be fine, okay? Just hang on and stay calm. You go first and as soon as I'm out, I'll catch up with you and we'll go the rest of the way together."

I nod, and before I know it, I'm dropping out of the plane and landing in the water. My eyes burn from the salt water splashing against me and my teeth chatter, but I'm floating. I can't believe it.

"Summer," Liam calls.

I turn and see him floating behind me, and my eyes blur with tears. He kicks harder to catch up with me.

"We did it," he says. "So fucking badass."

I choke out a laugh that's more of a sob and he grins, but I can tell he's shaken up too.

I look around to make sure everyone is accounted for. The pilot is the last one out and he points toward the shore. It looks so far away, I can't imagine how we'll all make it, but he appears to be calm. I take steadying breaths and focus on surviving. Winslet is struggling and Tanner is closest to her. He latches onto her and helps drag her along. She is weeping and for once I can commiserate with her. This is a nightmare.

I can't believe it's actually happening.

My mind stays hyperfocused on the shore. I blink and it feels like it's even farther away. But we press on. The sun beats down on us, and several times I feel fish near my feet, which makes me shiver, but I try not to think about everything that could be underneath this water with us.

The thought that goes over and over in my mind is: What if we hadn't been as close to one of the islands? What if we'd been in that expanse between that is only water for as far as the eye can see?

Yeah, I have to shut down those thoughts too. We're alive. We're going to make it. We have to, there are no other options.

Every time I feel like I can't go another second, Liam pushes me forward, either physically latching onto my cushion and dragging me, or by distracting me with mindless conversation.

It's hard to tell how much time passes. I feel weak, sunburned, and my skin hurts from the salt water. The shore ahead looks like a mirage and I have no sense of how far it really is. Several of us clump together, helping each other press forward. Liam, Tanner, Hannah, and Maddie surround me. Winslet, Monique, Bella, and the flight attendant—I can't for the life of me remember her name—are staying as close to Joe as they can. They're ahead of us, and Joe keeps yelling out encouragement as we make our way to land.

"I'd kill for a burger right now," Liam says.

"I don't know how you can think about food," I say.

"That's what I'm distracting myself with, thoughts of what I'm gonna eat when we survive."

"You think there's just gonna be a restaurant within walking distance?" Hannah asks.

"In this little daydream I have going, there totally is," he says.

I smile in spite of myself. Joe separates from his group and starts swimming the rest of the way. When he reaches the shore, we all cheer and I start crying again, relieved that we're going to make it.

I kick faster and my foot knocks into something slimy. I yelp and then feel the sting of a bite. Pain shoots through me and I start kicking furiously, thrashing around to make sure nothing else is anywhere near me.

"Something bit me," I say under my breath, even though I am freaking out.

Liam curses next to me and tugs my float closer to his, dragging me the rest of the way. We're almost there. Joe is yelling from the sand, cheering us on. My foot feels like it's swelling and I bite the inside of my cheek to keep from losing it. The pain becomes so severe I feel like I might pass out.

Liam looks at me and curses again, moving through the water faster. When he stands up and starts walking, I can't believe we made it. I try to stand too, but I can't, and he lifts me up, carrying me to shore. Joe runs out to meet us and I see his concern before everything goes dark.

24

DREAMS OR REALITY?

I come to in a bumpy Jeep, bouncing over the sand. Liam is leaning over me, holding my hand.

"Hey, we're going to get you help," he says. "How are you feeling?"

"Hurts," I whisper.

He grips my hand tighter and leans forward. "She's awake and hurting. Are we almost there?"

A voice I don't recognize says, "One minute. This is the best option. Closer than the hospital. We're meeting Modo MD on the beach. They will help you."

"We're not going to the hospital?" Liam's voice lifts at the end in panic.

"What's going on? What bit me?"

"Joe thinks it's a box jellyfish bite, which is more harmful than a normal jellyfish."

The pain is intense. I squeeze my eyes together and try to breathe my way through it.

"Don't leave me. You scared me so bad when you passed out," Liam says, brushing my hair away from my face.

"Sorry."

"Don't be sorry, just stay with me." He smiles and I try to stay focused on him.

We come to an abrupt stop and my vision is getting funky. I also can't get a deep breath, but I'm not sure if that's because I'm panicking or if something more is going on.

A man with long black hair pulls up and apologizes that we had to come to meet him instead of him finding us. "Everyone is backed up with an accident farther down the beach," he says. "Let me take a look. I'm Makani."

He looks at the sting, while pressing a pulse oximeter on my finger.

"We need to act quickly," he says, and he gets a shot ready within seconds. "This is an antivenom. I apologize that we have to do it this way since we're not in a hospital, but from the looks of it, you need this quickly. I will inject it into three different places around your thigh."

The pain is so bad, I just nod and grit my teeth. "Do it," I get out.

I squeeze Liam's hand and the guy takes it all in stride.

"You're doing great," he says. "I would've been yelling my head off and you haven't even whimpered."

"My insides are whimpering," I tell him, and that makes everyone laugh.

"Okay, I'm all done," Makani says. "It will take an hour to feel the full effects of the antivenom, and in the meantime, we need to get you to the hospital. They can administer more there if necessary and monitor you. I can take you."

Joe looks at Liam. "I'll get back to the others. Can you go with her?"

"Of course," Liam says. "I'm not leaving you," he tells me.

An ambulance pulls up then and Makani tells them what's going on while they put me on a stretcher. Liam climbs in beside me and Makani gives me an oxygen mask.

I close my eyes and drift in and out of a weird haze all the way to the hospital. Once we're there, I'm rushed into the ER and it feels like all hands are on me at once. I just want to sleep and they're trying to explain what's happening, what they're giving me next, what they're checking. I'm poked and prodded and tested as I drift in and out. At one point, I hear Liam talking to my dad and Hudson, and he puts his phone in front of me to show them I'm okay.

I think I'm more traumatized over the fact that we escaped our plane crashing than I am about my injury. I keep reliving the plane dropping and that feeling of panic when I thought about us only having water beneath us. My heart rate skitters out of control and they give me something to help me sleep. I drift off, dreaming of blue skies, blue waters, and Hudson's brown eyes.

When I wake up, Hudson is sitting next to my bed and I rub my fists over my eyes, certain I'm dreaming.

"You're not dreaming," he says.

I guess I said that out loud.

"How did you get here so fast?"

"You've been sleeping a long time." His chair is as close

as it can get and he takes my hand. "This wasn't how I wanted our first date to go," he says, eyes twinkling.

"If you're counting this as a date, I think you're setting the bar really low."

He laughs. "Well, I didn't know I'd have to worry that you'd be *alive* when I asked you out." He grips my hand tighter. "Are you okay? God, we were so worried."

"I don't know how you'll get me back on a plane after going down in one. I'm just going to stay right here in this bed for as long as possible to avoid the trip back."

"Take this as chaste or as provocative as you want it, because either way applies: I'd prefer you to be in my bed than a hospital bed." His cheeks lift with how big he's smiling. "I'm so glad you're okay, and I can't wait to get you out of here and hug you until all the stress of the past twenty-four hours is behind us."

My cheeks flush and I glance around to see who else might be in the room since I've only had eyes for him since I woke up.

"It's just us," he whispers. "The story is that I'm sitting with you until Liam gets back. He went to shower at the hotel everyone's staying at, you included, as soon as we can get you out of here."

"Am I good to go? The pain isn't as crazy as it was before. I still feel kind of weird, but nothing too bad."

"Liam said you were so brave through the whole thing. I know they're gonna want to check you out, but the doctor said you should be feeling much better by the time you woke up and even better tomorrow."

I make a face. "Do you think I'll have to stay overnight?"

"If you do, I'm not going anywhere. Okay?"

I settle back into my pillows, feeling weak but happy. Tired but hopeful.

And then I sit straight up. "I need to call my mom!"

"Already done. Your dad let her know what's going on." He leans in and kisses my cheek. I must smell like sweat and salt and medicine, but he doesn't seem to mind. "Rest. Everything's gonna be okay."

25

———

RECOVERY

WHEN I WAKE UP AGAIN, HUDSON IS STILL HERE IN THE CHAIR and sleeping this time. He looks so uncomfortable. I'm tempted to wake him up just to tell him to get in another position, but I feel bad doing that when I know how tired he must be. Jet lag on top of jet lag.

A nurse walks in and smiles, putting a blood pressure cuff on my arm. "You're awake! How are you feeling?"

"Better than the last time I was awake."

"You gave everyone quite a scare," she says. "It's good you

got the medicine when you did." She shakes her head. "Not wise to be swimming where you were."

I don't tell her that my plane crashed and I wasn't just doing a leisure swim for funsies. I'm too tired to say all that, but my eyes must say something because she's quiet while she finishes taking my vitals. Hudson stirs when she undoes the Velcro on the cuff.

"Hey," he sits up straighter, wincing as he tries to stretch his neck.

The doctor comes in and smiles when he sees me awake. "Ah, you're looking so much better."

"I feel better."

"Excellent. The antivenom worked as it should. We had to give you a bit more when you arrived—I'm not sure if you remember that—but it seemed to do the trick. Your vitals look good. I'd like to just assess you a little longer this morning and if everything keeps going this way, I'll let you go this afternoon."

"Great."

He checks a few more things and leaves the room, the nurse going with him. Hudson leans in. "Are you really feeling better or just saying that to get out of here?"

"I really do feel better. The sleep helped. I still felt so groggy the last time I woke up. I didn't think I needed to stay the night, but I'm glad I did. I can't believe you stayed here all night though."

"Liam's been here too, most of the time. He's been so worried about you."

"I don't know what I would've done if he hadn't been there. He was calm and yet acted quickly." My eyes fill with tears when I think about our flight. "It was so scary, Hudson. I don't know if I'll ever want to fly again. I know I have to if I want to get home, but..." I shake my head, wiping my face quickly when the tears spill over.

"We'll ask the doctor to prescribe something for you. I don't think you'll be the only one who needs that going back. Everyone is shaken up," he says.

"Is everyone okay? Do they know what happened to the plane?"

"I haven't heard anything definite yet. Your dad is determined to get to the bottom of it though." He squeezes my hand. "He...he wanted me to let you know that he's been checking in with the doctor frequently and that he's so glad you're okay. He's been working on getting everyone else settled and arrangements for all of us to go back together. I think he feels awful about us not being on the flight with you."

"I wouldn't wish that on anyone. You guys didn't need to turn around and come back either." *Especially my dad who hasn't bothered to show up here once*, I think but keep to myself.

"There's no way we could've stayed put." He stands up and stretches and then sits back down, taking my hand again. "Now, how about you rest a little more and I'll go grab some coffee. I'll be back within ten minutes. Can I get you anything?"

"You don't have to stay, Hudson. I'll be okay. Go get some decent sleep and I'll meet you at the hotel later. Sounds like I'll be getting out."

He pushes my hair back and kisses my forehead. "You're not getting rid of me. Want some coffee?"

"Yes, please."

He moves to the door and looks at me again before he walks out. His hair is messier than usual and his eyes are sleepy, his clothes wrinkled, and he's never looked better to me than he does right now.

I hate that I missed our date and that we're on a tropical island but stuck in a hospital, but I've enjoyed every sweet moment we've had in spite of all the obstacles.

"I'll be back soon. Don't go anywhere," he says.

I laugh and lift my hand, shooing him out. "Pretty sure I'm stuck here for a while."

He's not out the door five seconds before Liam walks in.

"Heyyy, how's the patient?" he asks, looking me over.

Just seeing him makes my eyes well up and I hold my arms out. He leans over and hugs me tight.

"Thank you," I choke out. "I wouldn't have survived any of that without you."

"You would've, but I'm really glad we were together," he says, pulling back and looking into my eyes. "Are you really okay? You're not in pain?"

"I'm good. Not even very stir-crazy yet."

He exhales and leans over to kiss my forehead before taking a step back. He clears his throat and runs his hand through his hair. "Let's keep it that way."

"You look tired. Did you get checked out too?"

He waves me off. "No, I'm fine. If we can get you out of here without any more disasters, I'll be even better. I spoke with your doctor before I came in here and he's going to let you go within the next twenty minutes."

"What? I thought I was here another few hours."

Liam makes a face. "Let's just say your dad got ahold of him and the doctor is confident that you're safe to leave, as long as you make a follow-up appointment when we get back home."

"Oh." I'm not sure how to feel about that. If I'm truly all better or if my dad is just in a hurry to proceed with filming.

I feel bad even thinking that way, but it's difficult not to. "I need something for the flight back."

"I took care of that," he said. "The prescription will be with your discharge papers."

"This is weird—why isn't the doctor telling me all this?"

"Things get weird when showbiz is involved," he says. "But if it helps, I do think everything is checking out. I think you're healing the way you should be, and hopefully it will feel good to get back home."

I don't say anything, the whole thing making me tired and anxious.

When the nurse comes in with my discharge papers a couple of minutes later and I'm free to go, Hudson is still getting us coffee.

26

IT WON'T HAPPEN AGAIN, RIGHT?

HUDSON WALKS IN AS LIAM IS HELPING ME INTO A wheelchair. He hurries to help me from the other side and the nurse looks back and forth from one guy to the other, grinning.

"Someone's a very lucky girl," she says.

My cheeks heat, and even more when Liam says, "We're the lucky ones."

He's sweet. And obnoxious, and the ego on him is the size of New York City, but he's been so good to me. I smile at him and then at Hudson, who rolls his eyes but is smiling too.

"Are you ready to go home?" Hudson asks.

I nod and the nurse pipes up. "She's all set. I've gone over everything with her, and if one of you nice gentlemen wants to pull up to the entrance, I'll see that she gets to the car."

"I'll be right back," Hudson says. He leans over like he wants to kiss me and then thinks better of it, standing up straight again.

It's fun to see him outside his comfort zone. I'm used to being the awkward one. I grin at him and he groans, muttering under his breath. I think I hear, "You're killing me," and it makes my heart well up. I can't wait to get back to exploring where this thing with us is going.

In the meantime, Liam pats my shoulder right before I'm wheeled out of the hospital room. Hudson is already waiting with the car and Liam helps me into the back passenger seat.

"In case you want to stretch out," he says, winking.

After we've picked up my medication, we make the short drive to the hotel. The island is beautiful, and I take in the views as Hudson and Liam talk about the plane crash. I try not to listen too closely because I'm not ready to relive those moments again. That's already happening without discussing it.

Hudson looks at me through the rearview mirror and puts his hand up, stopping Liam from talking. He tilts his head toward me and Liam glances back.

"I'm sorry. We don't have to talk about this right now," he says.

"When are we flying back?" I ask.

"Tonight," Hudson says.

Liam reaches over the seat and squeezes my hand. "We've already lived through a plane crash. It won't happen again."

"That's not really helping me right now." I try for a laugh, but it sounds like a choked-up sob, and I try to focus on the beautiful ocean just past the hotel.

We pull into the parking lot and Liam helps me out of the car, Hudson hurrying around to help too.

"I'm okay. You guys don't have to hover."

"You scared us," Hudson says quietly. "Your dad has been worried too. He'll want to see you when we get inside."

I don't want to see him. I keep it to myself and shuffle inside. I'm a thousand times better than I was, but I'm still weak. My limbs are heavy, especially the leg where I was stung. And it just still kind of hurts, *everywhere.* So weird. I don't recommend it.

We go inside and Hudson leads us to the elevator. We're quiet as we go up. When we step out, Hudson puts his arm around my shoulder and I sink into him. The urge to cry is strong and I'm not even fully sure why. Hudson pulls out the card key and the door opens. It's a beautiful room, but I can't appreciate how beautiful because my father is sitting inside. When he sees us, he stands and rushes toward me.

"Sweetheart, how are you feeling?" His voice and frowny face sound like that of a concerned dad, but I'm not really feeling it at the moment.

"I'm fine. Or I will be." I motion toward the bed. "Is that where I can crash?"

"For a couple of hours, yes," he says. He pulls the covers back for me and I crawl into the bed. "We'll come get you when it's time to go."

"How about you just let me stay here for a few days and recover before I have to get back on a plane?"

My dad laughs like I'm joking, but his smile drops when I just stare at him.

"Oh, that would—that won't be possible. Sorry, sweetie. We need to all get back and I wouldn't feel right about leaving you behind."

"Right. Even though you already left me behind and the plane I had to catch crashed. Okay." I close my eyes so I don't have to look at him, but not before I see him throw a concerned glance at the guys. I don't care if he's embarrassed for me to say that about him in front of them. It's not like it's not evident to everyone else but him, how little he thinks of me. How he's incapable of putting me first.

"I want to sleep now. Wake me when it's time to go."

"Are you sure you wouldn't rather stay awake so you'll sleep on the flight?" Hudson asks.

My eyes open. I sit up in the bed and fluff the pillows around me. "You're right. I wasn't thinking."

"Maybe we can watch a movie or something," he says.

"That sounds good."

My dad slides his hands together back and forth, all smiles. I picture him washing his hands of me, and sure enough, the next thing out of his mouth proves it. "Well, I can see you are in good hands. I'll be making sure everyone is ready to head out." He looks at both guys. "You have the flight details, right? I can trust all of you to get to the airfield in plenty of time?"

"Sure," Liam says.

Neither Hudson nor Liam are making eye contact with my dad. I don't want to cause conflict between him and the people who work with him, but I'm also not going to cover for him anymore. I've spent a lifetime excusing him for not showing up, and I shouldn't have to keep doing that.

He leans over and kisses me on the forehead. "Don't

forget you'll be *Liam's* girlfriend when you get back," he whispers in my ear.

27

BRACE YOURSELF

BOTH GUYS WATCH ME CAREFULLY AFTER MY DAD LEAVES, AND I lean my head against the headboard.

"You know what? I think I'm going to FaceTime my mom and sister. They're going to kill me if I don't show my face soon. We've been texting, but it's not the same."

Liam pats my foot. "Just text me if you need me," he says and walks to the door.

"Will you let me know if you want company?" Hudson asks.

"Yes. Sorry, I'm not the best company right now."

"You don't have to be. You can be a grump, cry, whine, yell, be silent, whatever you need to be, and I'll still be here," he says. He motions over his shoulder. "Or you know, in my room until you want me."

My eyes fill with tears as I look at him and then over his shoulder where Liam is lingering.

"You guys are the best part of my summer." I laugh because that sounds trite, narrowing it down to a season. "Not just summer, but my life right now." I wipe my face and look up at the ceiling. "Go before I get weepy."

"You're stuck with us, Summer," Liam says, and this time he leaves.

"What he said," Hudson says. He presses a sweet kiss on my lips and I close my eyes, soaking it in.

And then the room is quiet.

I have a good cry, my frustration with my dad, the anxiety about the flight home, and the stress of the past however many hours it's been. My internal clock is trashed, somewhere between California and Hawaii and a drugged state. When I have my bearings about half an hour later, I call my mom.

As soon as I see her face and then my sister's over her shoulder, I burst into tears again. They start crying too because that's what we do—when one cries, we all cry.

"We've been so worried," my mom says. "Are you okay? Are you in pain?"

"Yes, but I'm feeling much better. Just shaken up. It was terrifying, the wh-whole thing." I take a gulping breath and feel calmer, just seeing their faces. "Love you guys."

"We love you. So sorry you've been going through this and it feels like you're in another world, you're so far from home." My mom blows her nose and my sister leans her chin on my mom's shoulder.

"We've decided something, if it's okay with you," Autumn says.

"Okay." I wait for her to come out with it.

"I know we talked about me coming later in the summer, but what if I came a little sooner, and Mama too?"

"I could only come for a few days, with work and all, and if it feels like I'm horning in on your time with your dad, I won't do it." Mama stops then, waiting for me to say something.

"Don't be crazy. You're not horning in on anything, trust me. Please come. I miss you both so much!"

"I wouldn't be able to stay long either. I got a job that starts next week, but we could see for ourselves that you're okay," Autumn says.

"I wish you could come and stay," I tell them both.

Autumn makes a face and Jericho barks next to her. She rubs his ears and it makes my eyes fill again. I'm so homesick, it hurts.

"I can't wait to see you, but I don't know if I can handle the stress this summer is causing you," Autumn says. "We'll come, hopefully meet that hot boyfriend, and hug you lots. You're still coming home in August, right?"

The thought of leaving Hudson *or* Liam makes me sad. I'm definitely going home to spend time with Autumn before she goes back to school, but after that...I don't know what I'm doing. Where I'm going to land.

"Yes, absolutely," I say.

"Okay, I'll let you know when I have our flights scheduled. Your dad actually called and insisted on flying us out, which was very generous of him." My mom shakes her head and sighs. "We don't want to be in the way, but I sure will feel better if I can hug you."

"That was...nice of him. You'd never be in the way. I can't wait. I already feel better."

Autumn does a little dance and I wipe my face yet again. But I'm lighter, better, the thought of seeing them soon healing me faster than any medicine or rest. We talk for an hour, and when I get off, I'm still smiling.

There's a knock at the door, and I check the mirror to make sure I look decent before answering. My reflection leaves a lot to be desired, but I've looked worse in the past forty-eight hours.

I look through the peephole and swing the door open wide when I see who it is.

Hannah throws her arms around me and then is apologizing in the next breath. "I'm so sorry. I didn't even see if you were hurting first. Does it hurt to hug?"

"No, come back." I laugh, hugging her harder. "Are you okay?"

"I'm fine. I didn't get stung and nearly die." She puts her arm around my shoulder as we walk to the bed. She sits on the end while I crawl back to my spot with the pillows. I hold one of the pillows out to her and she takes it, stretching out across the end of the bed.

"I think it hasn't fully hit me, everything that happened," I tell her. "How does everyone else seem?"

"You'd think Winslet was the one who'd been in the hospital with the way she's telling everyone about her near-death experience. Your dad has had a talk with all of us, trying to tone down all the talk about the plane crash. It was a malfunction with the plane and I think there's going to be a hefty lawsuit with the guys who checked the plane before we left."

"Joe won't be in trouble, will he?"

"No, someone else is in charge of the maintenance, and

we're supposed to keep our mouths shut until all of it can be resolved."

"Good thing I didn't tell all the reporters knocking my door down," I say.

She gives me a funny look. "Reporters are after you here?"

"No! I was kidding."

She props the pillow up and positions it under her head. "Well, brace yourself, because they will be when we get home."

PANIC

HANNAH ENDS UP WATCHING A MOVIE WITH ME, AND WE HAVE way more fun than I expected to be having today. Hudson and Liam have both texted to check on me, and I've assured them that I'm okay. The girl time with Hannah is exactly what I needed.

My dad sends a group message to all of us, and Hannah and I look at each other after we've read it.

Departure time is in two hours. We will be leaving the hotel in an hour. Everyone, please be on time.

"Are *you* okay getting on a plane so soon?" I ask.

"I've just been trying not to think about it," she admits. "I'm hoping I can sleep through it."

"Yeah, me too."

We switch to an episode of *Love Island* and lose track of time. A knock at the door makes us both jump and Hannah gets up.

"Oh shit, we've got twenty minutes to get to the lobby. I better go grab my bags. I can come back to help you if you can't carry all your stuff." She makes a face after she's said that. "Wasn't thinking that through. You don't really have anything, do you? I only have a couple things I bought last night."

"Makes it easy to get out of here, I guess." I have a moment of sadness about those pretty clothes that are floating in the ocean. "I'll be okay getting down there. I'm going to take something when we get in the car."

"Okay, see you soon. This was fun," she says, hugging me quickly. "I'm so glad you're feeling better."

I shuffle into the shower and even though it's brief, I feel energized when I get out. I still feel sluggish, but all things considered, I'm not in too bad of shape. When Liam and Hudson show up to help me to the car, I'm dressed in the sweats and T-shirt Hannah brought me from the hotel lobby —courtesy of my dad, she said. My hair is up in a wet, messy bun, and I'm as ready as I can be for this.

I ignore my dad, bypassing his little pep talk to everyone by getting in the limo. I take the meds the doctor gave me before everyone gets in, and I still shake all the way to the airport. We're a somber group as we get on the private plane that's only slightly larger than the one we went down in.

Once we're on the plane, I try my best to get comfortable, closing my eyes and feeling the tears roll back into my hair.

"Hey, we're going to get there in one piece, I swear it," Liam says, reaching over to hold my hand. Hudson was sitting next to me at first, but my dad asked him to switch with Liam, which is another reason I'm struggling with my emotions.

I nod and squeeze his hand, willing myself to go to a Zen place.

One time I rode Mission: SPACE at Epcot and had a panic attack. I thought I was going to pass out, claustrophobia taking over and the effects of centrifugal force making me sick. I had to close my eyes and imagine I was in a safe place. Talk myself down from the cold sweat and white dots dancing across my vision, threatening to pull me under. The ride felt as if it lasted forever and I survived, but I was off the rest of the day. And I'll never go on that ride again. No, thank you.

This panic feels like that, only a hundred times worse. But the meds soon take effect and I'm so sleepy that everything feels muted and floaty. Before I know it, we're taking off and I'm drifting into dreamland.

The next time I come to, I'm being picked up and when I open my eyes, Liam is smiling at me.

"Told you we'd get here," he says, smiling.

"You're pretty," I say. "And nicer than you let on."

He laughs. "Thank you, Sleeping Beauty. I think you're pretty special too."

"Special isn't always a compliment," I say, snuggling into his neck.

"The way I mean it is only a compliment."

And that's the last thing I hear him say before I fall back to sleep.

When I wake up again, I'm in my bed at my dad's house. I glance out the windows and am a bit torn with how I feel now, surrounded by so much water. I still appreciate the beauty, but for the first time it feels more ominous than comforting. I take another shower, sweaty from sleeping so hard, and make my way to the kitchen.

Bella is in a deep conversation with my dad and it stops when they notice me. She looks like she's been crying and wipes her face, shooting me an apologetic smile, and my dad looks about as anxious as he's capable of getting.

"How are you feeling?" Bella asks.

"Getting there," I say. I feel like I've been hit with a truck and left outside to let random vehicles take their turn rolling over me. Something tells me now is not the time to share that.

"Great. There's an interview for you and Liam in the morning. It's a big one," my dad says.

"What? I didn't agree to an interview. Dad," I start and he shakes his head, his way of telling me to be quiet.

"Eleven. It'll be after we do our early shoot by the water. Make sure you go to bed early enough tonight to feel your best." He smiles and starts to walk out of the kitchen.

"You're unbelievable," I say to his back.

He pauses and turns to look at me. "You have something to say?" He motions toward Bella. "Feel free to pile on. Everyone else is tonight."

She flushes and leaves the room, her anger palpable.

"You're certainly clearing out the room, Dad. Maybe stop for a second to consider that *you* might be the problem." I scoot past him, my appetite suddenly gone.

29

CAMERA READY

I PULL A NO-SHOW ON SET THE NEXT MORNING. AN ITINERARY slid under my door last night before I went to bed, and I wasn't sure if it was Hudson or my dad or someone else who put it there, but I wadded it up into a ball and threw it in the garbage. And did not have an ounce of guilt about it either.

I sleep until ten and feel good about that too. It's when there's rapid knocking on my door five minutes later and I open it to see my dad's angry face that I think maybe I should've chosen another day to pull this stunt.

"You don't get to just not show up to work, Summer. We're already behind schedule and there is a lot riding on this. I know the crash has been difficult on you, but I need you back to work. I'm counting on you."

"You just can't see anything past work, can you?"

His eyes drill into me and then he sighs. "It's not just about me, Summer. There's a whole crew out there who relies on me. Think about them. I realize you don't like me very much, but I'm trying here. Cut me some slack...please."

"I came out here hoping to spend time with you and am being treated like I'm gum on the bottom of your shoe. Make up your mind about what you're requiring of me because last time I checked, I was your star's girlfriend, your coffee girl, the person who wipes the shit off of everyone's backsides, and your mental punching bag. I didn't sign up for all of those roles, so how about you pick two and I'll see if I'm agreeable."

I slam the door in his face, my insides trembling.

He knocks on the door again and I don't open it.

"Please just do the interview, Summer. I'm sorry for my attitude. It's been a really hard week."

I open the door again. "You're not kidding, it's been a hard week. Not just for me, but for all those who survived the plane crash. The fact that you're acting like a tyrant now of all times shows the kind of person you really are." I shake my head. "I'll do the interview because I agreed to see this through with Liam, and the guy literally saved my life in Hawaii, so this is for him, *not* you. Push me on anything else right now and I'm on the next flight home."

He nods. "Okay, I understand. I really am sorry that I lost my temper. You're right. How I've acted is unacceptable."

My eyes narrow, trying to figure out if he's genuine right now or just saying what I want to hear.

"Do you have everything you need for this interview? I should've asked last night if we needed to replace some of your things."

"Shit. I'll need to borrow something from one of the girls for my hair."

"I'll ask around and make sure it's brought to your room in the next few minutes."

"Thank you."

"Summer?" He puts his hand on the door and his eyes soften. "Part of why I've stayed away from you and your sister is how single-minded I get when I'm working. I'm not trying to make excuses. I know there's no excuse for the way I get. I'll try to do better."

I nod. I want to believe that he means what he's saying, but only time will tell if he does anything about it.

"I shouldn't have to tell you how to be decent."

"You're right," he says. "You're inspiring me to be a better person."

I roll my eyes and he chuckles. "We'll see."

Mae and Anthony from hair and makeup come to my room a few minutes after my dad leaves.

"We're here to make you look magical," Anthony says.

"Oh, okay." I grin, opening the door wide for them. "I apparently only have twenty minutes for that miracle, so you've got your work cut out for you."

"You cannot believe the things we can do in twenty minutes," Mae says.

Liam rushes in about five minutes before eleven. He does a double take when he sees me. "Wow," he says. "You look stunning." He gets closer and I see the nerves bouncing off of him. "I had no idea about this. I tried to get out of it when your dad told me, I swear it. They're already on the way over. We had a long morning of filming, and I—"

"I believe you," I cut him off. "I'll let you do the talking and my job will be to look magical." I smile at Anthony, who's doing the final touches to my lips and he steps back to do a shimmy.

"Check, check, and check," he says. "They're going to want to know when you're hitting the big screen next."

I think about my project, floating in the water with my clothes and phone and everything else I took with me to Hawaii.

"It'll be a long time before that happens," I say. "If it ever does."

Liam looks surprised. "I didn't know you wanted to act."

"I don't. But I hope to write something worthy of being a movie one day."

He grins. "No shit. That's great, Dumpling." He raises a brow and I shake my head. He pretends to be wounded but only for a second, too busy trying not to laugh. "Maybe one day I'll be acting in one of your movies."

"I'd love that."

One of the best surprises out of this fake relationship I've got going here is the friendship I've cultivated with Liam. I didn't see that coming when we first met, but I've gotten attached to him more and more as I've gotten to know him.

A woman knocks on the door and Liam stands up and goes to hug her. "Summer, this is my agent, Catherine. Catherine, my girlfriend, Summer."

Anthony steps back and assesses his work. When he approves, he holds his arms wide and does an air kiss on either side of my face.

"Thank you," I whisper. To Catherine, I smile hesitantly,

unsure of how I should feel about someone who wants me to fake-date her client.

"You're even more beautiful in person," she says. "Liam, don't let this one go. For real," she adds.

30

CAGE ME

"Damn, you look hot," Liam says when we step out of the room. He stares at me for a moment before holding his hand out for me. Our fingers lace together and I take several deep breaths, trying to calm my nerves. "Thank you for doing this," he whispers before we walk down the hall.

When we step into the living room, cameras are set up and the room is clear of everyone but the camera crew and Joann Silvers, the face of the morning news in L.A. It's strange to see her bright, smiley, fully made-up face in our living room, and even stranger when she turns that mega-watt smile on us.

Well, mostly on Liam.

But when her gaze lights on me, I wish she'd stayed focused on Liam. She does a full-body sweep and I can't tell if she's wondering what in the world Liam sees in me or how she can boot me to the curb so she can take my place...it's not clear. Probably both.

Or maybe she sees through our act before we've even said a word.

She stands up and holds out her hand limply for Liam to shake. He does, still gripping my hand tightly with his other hand.

"Joann Silvers, nice to meet you," she says.

"You too," Liam says.

She does the same with me and I have to let go of Liam's hand to shake hers. Her eyes zero in on that and she puts her arm on Liam's shoulder and leads him away from me.

Rude.

Not that I'm jealous, but if I was with Liam for real, that would be super rude, right?

"Let's get you set up over here. The lighting is great in here, but they'll want to do a few test shots first," she says, motioning at one of the cameramen to get ready.

Liam looks over his shoulder to make sure I'm okay and stops, turning toward me and halting Joann from wrangling him away. I have to say, Liam is a pretty dang good boyfriend for someone who's faking it.

He reaches out for me to join them and I can feel Joann's annoyance growing.

She leads us to the couch like it's her place and I suppose for today, it is. We sit down and she perches on the oversized chair across from us. Liam puts his arm around me and we're sitting so close, there's no space between us.

"This is a little soon for a relationship interview, don't you think?" Liam says.

"Exactly why I wanted to be the first to talk to you." She smiles smugly. "And off the record, I also wanted to see for myself if this is a"—she waves her hand between the two of us—"convenient little arrangement to get the press off your back for a while, or if there's something real going on between the two of you."

It's a good thing Liam is an excellent actor because if this were up to me, I would have already messed up. But his arm tightens around my shoulder and he looks at me so adoringly, I'm even convinced for a moment that this is real. He leans his forehead against mine and sighs, his lips curving into a smile that makes girls line up and scream when they see him on the sidewalk.

"We don't have to prove anything," he says, his voice low and intense, "but I'm telling you, this is very real for me."

I gasp a little when he says that, and his smile widens. He leans back and kisses my forehead and looks at Joann.

"We don't have much time, so whenever you'd like to get started, go ahead. I have a full day of filming ahead, and Summer and I are jet-lagged from our trip."

I take note that he doesn't mention the plane crash or my injury and decide to keep my mouth shut as much as possible so I don't say anything I'm not supposed to.

"Okay, let's get started," she says. She glances around at the crew and they give the okay to begin filming.

Someone claps in front of us and we're rolling.

"I'm Joann, and I'm having the best morning, sitting here with the new lovebirds, Liam Taylor and Summer Winters, daughter of Award-winning director Cole Winters. Tell me, Liam, how did Summer manage to tame your bad-boy heart?"

"Well, look at her," he laughs, "first of all, she's gorgeous. Second, she doesn't know it. Third," he looks at me with those heart eyes again and I'm amazed by his skills, "she has a heart of gold. It was easy to hold my heart out and say *here, please take it.*"

Joann looks shocked for a second, but she quickly rallies. "Summer, how does it feel to have captured Liam?" She has a cheesy smile that is so fake, it's just two seconds from cracking.

"He's not an animal," I say, laughing. "I'm not trying to capture or tame anyone—maybe that is what's making it work."

"You can cage me, baby," Liam says, and we both crack up at that.

A muscle in Joann's jaw goes off and her eyes look slightly manic.

"This has all moved relatively fast, hasn't it? There are some who say this is all a little too convenient and that it must be a ploy to win over the bashers after some of your recent scandals, Liam. What do you have to say to them?"

"All it takes is one amazing girl, the *right* girl, to make a man see the light," he says.

I even swoon at that one. Joann almost does except that it's not working with her *expose this fake relationship for all it is* plan.

"Well, you must be quite the person, Summer Winters," she says, teeth bared.

I smile. I don't have a clue how to respond to that. Thank you? Not really? Uh, I'm glad you think so? I settle on saying nothing.

Liam squeezes my shoulder and she moves on to questions about the film. When the interview is done, they take still shots of us and we do everything but kiss in them. By the time it's all over, I need another shower. I'm sweaty and under the Liam/actor influence. That guy is convincing.

31

HOT AND BOTHERED

WHEN I GET BACK TO MY ROOM, HUDSON IS WAITING IN THE hall. He glances around to see if anyone is near us and when I open my door, he lifts his eyebrows as if waiting for permission. I hold my arm out and he rushes in.

When I shut the door, he puts his hands on my waist and pulls me in for a hug. "I've missed you," he whispers. "It's killing me to not be able to do this all the time, everywhere." He pulls back when I don't say anything. "Are you okay?"

"I'm just tired and frustrated by all of this..."

"About Liam?"

"Liam, my dad, how everyone seems to be under his thumb. I just—I need a break and realize I'm not going to get it, not if I stay here. Not that I'm going anywhere either, I'm just...venting. Sorry." I move to the bed and sit down and he looks so forlorn standing where I left him, I feel bad. I pat the bed next to me and he comes and sits down. "My mom and sister will be here late tonight. I can't wait to see them and yet, it will be hard—they're coming here thinking I'm in a hot relationship with Liam."

He takes my hand and sighs. "Yeah, this is pretty fucked up. I'll tell you what, let me handle your dad. I'll make sure someone is around to cover your job while your mom is here. Take time off, enjoy your family, come hang out on the set with them whenever you want. You deserve it, especially after the week you've had."

"Thank you. I appreciate your help. But why is it so hard for me to ask my dad for that? You shouldn't have to be the mediator between us."

"He loses his mind when he's in the middle of filming. I can handle it if he gives me a hard time. But I don't want you to have to deal with him like that."

He puts his arm around my shoulder and I sink into him, nestling my nose into his neck and inhaling.

"You smell good," I whisper.

He lifts my chin and kisses me. It starts out slow and sweet but gets heated within seconds. He pulls me over to straddle him and I whimper into his mouth at the friction between our legs. He rocks me into him and kisses down my neck, and my head falls back, giving him full access.

"Summer," he says into my skin. "I want you so—"

A knock on the door makes me jump, and I get off of Hudson, my chest rising and falling from all the pheromones in the air. His eyes are still hooded with lust and he looks amused as he watches me try to straighten my clothes and smooth down my hair.

I open the door and Winslet stands there.

Full glare. Check.

She peers around me and sees Hudson and her face shifts from vampire pale to cotton candy pink. She puts her hand on her hip and scowls at both of us.

"What is going on in here?" she asks.

"None of your business," I say. "What did you need?"

She walks over to Hudson and softens her tone. "I need you. We're going through that difficult scene in an hour and I need you to walk me through it." Her voice has become a purr the longer she talks and I stare at Hudson incredulously.

I can't believe it when he stands up and smiles at her. "I'll meet you in the living room in three minutes."

She looks back at me and smirks, mission accomplished, and walks toward the door. "I'll leave the door open... wouldn't want people to get the wrong idea about you two. I'd hate to see what the press would do to poor Liam if they thought his new relationship had already—" She mimics an explosion with her hand, and I stand in the doorway and wave my arm for her to hurry up and leave.

She steps into the hall and blows a kiss to Hudson. "Three minutes," she says.

When she walks away, I turn to him, mouth open. "Are you kidding me?"

"What?" he says, chuckling.

"Don't tell me you buy into her innocent act."

"Winslet has never been innocent a day in her life." He moves so he's standing in front of me...and the open door...

and he leans in and whispers in my ear. "To be continued later."

"How?" I fling my arms out. "She just threatened to blow this up for Liam."

"I'll handle Winslet."

My eyes narrow. "That's a lot of handling. First my dad and then Winslet...she's a full-time job. Have you guys ever —?" I pause and I know by how long it takes him to answer that I'm not going to like what he has to say very much.

"We've kissed, but that was a long time ago and I'm the one who stopped it from going any further. You have nothing to worry about."

I fold my arms across my chest. "You'll have to forgive me for not being super convinced. I think she's capable of anything, and I just saw how she was able to work you right out of here."

He folds his arms across his chest, and it feels like we just crossed into hostile territory. "I'm keeping the peace. That's it. You're the one 'dating' someone else, so I don't think you can really get mad at me for a relationship I'm not having, pretend or otherwise."

I don't know what to say to that. All I know is that I'm annoyed. "I told you I was in a mood when you first came to my room. I guess I need to work it out before I try to talk to anyone else."

His expression softens and he leans in. "You're the only one I'm interested in, and the first chance I get, I'm coming back to continue what we started over there." He points to the bed and turns, leaving me hot and bothered in more ways than one.

32

FAMILY TIME

I'm a bit sneaky as I leave the house later that evening, getting an Uber to the airport from down the street. I want this time alone with my mom and sister, without anyone, mainly my father, interrupting us. As with everything when it comes to my dad, I'm torn between feeling like I'm letting him down and being angry at what he's expecting me to do. It's not that I don't mind hard work, or menial work, but I need a little time to recover from the accident, the sting, and well, the Liam thing—that has me all over the map with my emotions. For more reasons than I'm comfortable admitting to myself right now.

Maybe my mom and sister can help me make sense of things. I plan on letting them know what's happening as soon as I can.

Hudson never came back and made good on his promise...not that I expected him to necessarily come back right away, but I know for sure they were done filming for a couple of hours before I left the house.

When I'm dropped off at the airport, I don't bother asking the guy to wait around because I know it could be a while before we get the luggage. My mom texted that they had three bags between the two of them. One is just for things they're going to buy while they're here. Guess we'll be doing a bit of shopping.

I smile in anticipation watching people hugging each other, and I get antsy waiting for my mom and Autumn. When I finally see them walking toward me, I run and collide into them as we have a huge three-way hug.

"You look too thin," Mama says.

"You look awesome," Autumn says. "A little pale, but you have just survived an awful lot."

"Well, you guys look *great*." I smile at them and then burst into tears. They start crying too because of the sympathy-crier gene, but I also think they're just as relieved to see me as I am to see them.

"It feels like it's been forever," Autumn says.

"It has been forever." I wipe my face with the tissue Mama gives me and then blow my nose. She puts her arm around me and we find the baggage claim where their luggage will be.

"How are you doing?" she asks. "I mean, *really* doing."

"I have so much to tell you guys. It's all been so overwhelming, but for tonight, I hoped we could go out to eat and maybe I can just forget everything that's going on at the house for a while."

"About the house..." Mama starts, her eyes suddenly anxious. "Your dad called me this morning and he, uh, he invited us to stay at the house. Insisted, really. And I decided to take him up on the offer. He says it's huge and I'd like to see for myself where you've been staying. And to meet your Liam." She grins when she says Liam and I groan.

"He's not my Liam," I mutter, but they loop their arms through mine and chatter on happily about the pictures they've seen of us together.

"I had to do an interview with him. It's all so over the top, you won't believe it."

"I can't wait to see for myself," Autumn says, sighing. "Oh, there's one of our bags."

My mom stays with me while Autumn gets the bag. "How are you feeling?"

"Still weird from all the meds and kind of weak all over. I'm not sure how long that will last, but it seems like it should start lifting soon. Part of it could be how jet-lagged I am."

"You need to not overdo it. Even without something as traumatizing as a plane crash and a deadly bite," she makes a face, "you've always needed extra rest when you take on too much...or you'll get sick. This has been a lot to deal with, Summer. The good and the bad, you've had so many extremes since the summer began."

I nod. "It does feel like it's catching up with me."

"Well, I'm going to try my best to not let jet lag get the best of me," she says. "Otherwise, I'll be pooping out by 7:30.

But that might be exactly what you need—an early-to-bed kind of night."

Autumn hauls two suitcases to us and then turns to get the last one.

"I should help her."

"She's got it. She's been worried sick about you. It'll be good for her to take care of you a little bit."

I get teary again while I watch Autumn. Her hair is long and has more red in it than mine, and her eyes are brown compared to my blue. She favors our dad and I favor my mom and yet, we still manage to look like sisters.

"I've missed her so much," I say, sniffling.

Autumn bounces up to us with the last bag. "Okay, we're all set."

"It feels so good to hear accents from home." I almost start crying again and when they look at me with concern and a fair share of amusement, I try to rein it in a little.

I get an Uber for us and ask the driver to take us to the City Walk. I haven't been there yet, but I've heard it's got good restaurants and they'll enjoy the shops.

When we pull up and our bags are unloaded, we all look at each other.

"Should've rethought this luggage situation," Mama says.

"We'll be fine. We can each drag one," I say. "Should we eat first or shop?"

"Shop," they say at the same time.

I did not get their love for shopping, but I'm so happy to be with them, I don't care what we do.

We buy matching T-shirts in the first shop we go in and Autumn gets a sweatshirt at the next place. By then, we're all hungry and roll our suitcases into the Italian restaurant.

"So, Dad's called you twice, huh? What's up with that?" I

ask when the bread comes. "How long had it been since you'd talked to him?"

"A long time," my mom says. "I hadn't talked to him in at least five years...since the last time he asked me to come back to him."

33

TAKE ME BACK

AUTUMN AND I STARE AT MY MOM AND THEN AT EACH OTHER. Pretty sure my mouth is hanging open. I know hers is.

"What?" I clench my red cloth napkin in my fist and take a deep breath.

I used to always wish my parents would get back together, as most kids of divorced parents do. But my mom has never mentioned this being a possibility. *Ever.*

I don't really know how to feel about it now. Well, I mostly hate it, so maybe I'm pretty clear on the feelings.

"Is this something that has happened a lot?" I ask. "Dad

wanting you back? I didn't think either of you ever looked back." *And especially not Dad*, but I keep that part to myself. It's no secret that my dad has had many relationships since he was with my mom. I cringe when I think of taking my mom to the house where Bella is living—I'm still not clear on the dynamic she has with my dad, but I've picked up some heavy vibes where the two of them are concerned.

"I never wanted this lifestyle for the two of you," she says.

Autumn is the next one to speak and I'm glad for it because I feel like everything I've always believed has been blown up.

"We always thought you were the one who was heartbroken. That you were too young when you got married, and Dad didn't want to be a dad...he didn't want to be committed to anyone or anything," she says. "So, when you're saying he's wanted to get back together with you...a lot...that doesn't all add up with what you've led us to believe."

Mama's face turns a few shades darker, even in the low ambient lighting of the restaurant.

"All of that is true. He did leave me twice, as you know. He just also wanted to come back, and I never could trust him again. After he left the second time, I'd learned my lesson. There have been low points in my life when I've wondered if that was the right decision—your father can be very convincing."

"Don't I know it," I say through gritted teeth. "So why did he call this morning? Just to ask you to stay at the house?"

"He wanted help with you. Said he thought he'd blown his chances with you and asked for advice. I didn't want to get involved, but I think it would be good to work through some things...together."

Autumn looks at Mama like she's just been dropped off from Mars and has come back a deep shade of purple. Exactly how I'm feeling.

"I don't know what to say." That's my big input for the day.

Mama shrugs. "You don't have to say anything. I wasn't trying to keep anything a secret from you. I haven't let myself really take in anything your father has said about me and him for years. My tie to him is you girls and I'd like to see y'all have a relationship with your father before it's too late."

The waitress comes back around after hovering for a few minutes, seeing that we were in a heavy conversation. We place an order for several family-style dishes and are quiet when she walks away.

"Tell us about Liam and how that's going," Mama says, leaning over and taking my hand.

I wrinkle my nose. "Let's not talk about all that tonight. It's complicated. And Dad and everyone involved have me paranoid that there are ears everywhere."

Autumn's eyes get wide. "Ohhhh," she says. She glances around the room, as if trying to access if we're being eavesdropped on by the paparazzi.

I decide to keep letting her think that just to delay the conversation about Liam. I signed a contract to not breathe a word of this, but it's my mom and sister. Maybe Dad can be there when I tell them the truth and can help solidify the point that they can't tell another soul.

Our food comes and the air clears somewhat as we eat. They fill me in on what's been happening at home, and we order a piece of tiramisu to share. By the time we're done with that, my mom looks worn out.

"That dang three-hour time difference," she says, yawning.

"Let's get you to the house. You can take a little nap on the way." I grab the check before she can and pay for our dinner, which ticks her off.

"Are you raking in the big money now and I just didn't know it?" she snarks.

"Nope. But I can afford to take my mom and sister out to dinner."

"Thank you," Autumn says.

"You're welcome." I grin. "That's more like it."

Mama rolls her eyes but hugs me when we stand up to leave. "Thank you. And you're not paying for another thing for us while we're here."

"I wouldn't dream of it." We each grab a bag and roll them out of the restaurant. "We'll make Dad pay for everything else."

Autumn giggles while my mom shuts down that idea almost as soon as I've gotten the sentence out.

Autumn and I chat all the way to the house, while Mama leans her head back and I think she dozes off. When we pull up to the house though, she opens her eyes and her expression is unreadable. The sun is setting and the house looks especially impressive.

"Wow." Autumn whistles.

"You okay, Mama?" I ask

She shakes herself and pushes her long blonde hair off of her shoulders and sits up straight. "Let's do this."

Something catches my eye outside and I'm surprised to see my dad standing there smiling.

This visit just got a lot more interesting.

34

AWKWARD

MY DAD HOLDS HIS ARMS OUT WIDE AND AUTUMN STEPS INTO his embrace. "So glad you're here," he says.

He stares intently at my mom over my sister's shoulder. My mom's mouth is in a firm line and her cheeks are flushed as she stands stiffly next to me. When Autumn pulls away, Dad comes over to Mama and hugs her too. Her arms stay glued to her sides, and I'd laugh if it weren't my parents and awkward as all hell.

Dad laughs nervously for all of us. "Jenna, good to see you. So good to have all my girls in one place."

"Cole," my mom says and leaves it at that.

"Come in, are you hungry? We have plenty of food still out from dinner."

"We ate," Autumn says.

"Well, how about I take you out to dinner tomorrow night?" he asks. "I have a shorter shoot tomorrow. We could—"

"We have plans," Mama cuts him off. "Thank you, though." She looks at me and smiles. "Let's see your room."

"I've put you and Autumn in a room down the hall from Summer," Dad says.

"We could've just stayed with her. That wasn't necessary." My mom still doesn't look at him.

I think this is the longest I've ever heard them speak to one another that I can remember, and I can tell it's strange for my sister too. Our eyes are ping-ponging back and forth between our parents.

"Nonsense. I want you to feel at home here," Dad says.

I roll my eyes at how over the top he's being. I'm glad he's showing them more of a welcome than he did with me though. If he'd shown this warmth the day I got here, I might have felt differently about this whole arrangement.

We step inside the house and my mom and sister pause to take it all in.

"It's so pretty," Autumn says.

Hudson walks into the living room and smiles when he sees us. "Hey, you made it," he says. He holds out his hand to my mom and introduces himself. "I'm Hudson. Welcome." And when he does the same to Autumn, I think she swoons a little bit. His eyes are all lit up when he looks at me. "Hey, Summer," he says, his voice husky.

"Hey," I whisper back and then clear my throat when my mom and sister look at me. My cheeks flush and I attempt to get my voice to work without sounding like a phone-sex operator.

Pans clatter in the kitchen, causing me to jump, and then something breaks. "That didn't sound good."

Voices raise and my dad mumbles something before walking to the kitchen to see what's going on. The voices get louder. I think it's Monique and maybe Bella too, and it sounds like someone is crying. It gets even louder and then there's the low rumble of my dad saying something. It's too quiet to hear what he says, but the crying gets softer. Monique rushes out of the kitchen, pausing when she sees us standing there, and she nods slightly as she walks past us. Bella comes out a few seconds later, her face red, and she glares at my mom as she walks past us and down the hall.

My dad's face is red when he comes back.

"Lover's spat?" my mom says.

His face flushes even more, if that's possible. I can't say I mind seeing him so uncomfortable.

"Tension is always high when we're at this point in filming," he says.

I snort and he levels me with a look. I lift an eyebrow, daring him to continue his nonsense and he swallows hard. I grin, enjoying his discomfort more than I probably should.

"This is going to be so much fun," I say, putting my arms around my mom and sister's shoulders.

"There they are." Liam walks in from the front door, sweat dripping down his bare chest and looking like pure sin. He pats his face with a towel and leaves the towel around his neck, grinning wide. "I'm sorry I didn't make it back to shower before you got here. I thought you'd be a little later."

My mom and sister both mumble under their breath. *"No worries. That's okay. You're fine."* But I'm not sure he understood a word of it since they're clearly starstruck by Liam Taylor.

He walks over to me and leans in to kiss my cheek. My sister gasps and my mom beams and Hudson glares at me.

And everything suddenly feels more complicated than ever.

How am I going to keep my end of the contract and still have them get to know Hudson too?

"I can take your luggage back," Hudson says, and he manages to roll all three suitcases down the hall. Autumn follows him and my mom and I start to walk back with them too. Dad looks like he doesn't know what to do with himself, but he follows us too.

"I'll take a quick shower," Liam says. He points toward his room like he's questioning if that's a good idea. This is ridiculous. I need to just tell my mom and sister what's going on.

I lean over and whisper in his ear, "I don't think I can do this with them."

"It's okay," he whispers back. "Just in front of everyone else, okay? Especially your dad so he knows we're trying to follow the contract."

"Thank you," I mouth the words and he grins, walking backwards toward his room.

My mom fans herself as he walks away. "How do you get anything done with him around?"

I laugh and walk into their room to see Autumn standing really close to Hudson. She's laughing at something he's said and looking at him with fluttery eyes.

He's laughing too until he sees my face and it's like he suddenly sees how this looks. He runs his hands through his hair and takes a step away from Autumn.

"Will this be okay?" my dad asks.

"It's lovely," my mom says.

Their room is a lot like mine, only there are two beds instead of one.

"You should join us for dinner tomorrow night, Hudson," Dad says, as if my mom didn't tell him we have plans. "Get to know Autumn better. And Jenna," he adds.

The blood boils under my skin. Why is he so insistent on wrecking everything all the time?

He looks at me. "And tell that boyfriend of yours to come too. We'll go to my favorite restaurant."

35

VAMPIRES AND BRICKS

"THAT MAN IS INFURIATING, BUT HE DOES HAVE GOOD TASTE," Mama is still muttering under her breath about my dad when we get to the kitchen the next morning.

There's a bigger spread than normal set out and I don't tell my mom that I think this is my dad's way of showing off for her.

I hear arguing down the hall and frown. My sister and mom pause in piling their plate with eggs and bacon and fruit to listen.

"You can't have it both ways, Cole," Bella snaps. It sounds like she's crying again.

"It's never bothered you for me to have it both ways before," he says. It's more of a whisper-shout for him, and I wonder if he realizes we can still hear him clearly. Somehow I don't think so.

My sister and I share a wide-eyed stare, one that means she doesn't want to be hearing this any more than I do.

"This has gone on too long," Bella says, and my sister's head tilts before she puts her hands over her ears. I bite my bottom lip to keep from laughing.

My mom's face turns red as she shakes her head.

"This was a bad idea," she says. "I never should've agreed to stay here."

"Come on, let's get out of here before they come in," Autumn says.

But it's too late. Bella and my dad come into the kitchen and Bella comes to a complete stop when she sees my mom. My dad pulls a hand down his scruffy chin and then holds his arms out wide.

"There are my girls," he says, his voice bouncing around the walls of the kitchen.

Bella puts her hand on his back and he takes a step forward, making her hand fall.

Oh, ouch. The look on her face is painful to watch and her eyes fill with tears before she leaves the room.

"Harsh, Dad," Autumn says.

He looks at her like he has no idea what she's talking about.

"You're breaking hearts right and left and we haven't even been here twenty-four hours."

"Sounds about right," Mama says.

Pink tinges my dad's cheeks and he clears his throat. "She's known we weren't serious from the get-go."

"Oh, is that why she's living here?" I ask, crossing my arms. "A little casual living arrangement..."

He shakes his head and moves next to my mother. "She knows I only have feelings for one woman." He leans over and kisses her cheek. "And that's this woman right here."

"Lucky me," she says, her voice full of sarcasm.

Autumn and I laugh and my dad's mouth finally lifts into a smirk before he shrugs.

"It's the truth," he says.

"You'll forgive me if I don't believe a word of that nonsense," Mama says. Her shoulders aren't as tight though and she's smiling when she says it.

"This is so weird," I say, finally getting my food.

"Are you guys coming out to the set today? I'm getting ready to leave in about fifteen minutes. We're on a really cool set today, an old Victorian out in the mountains. You could ride with me."

I look at my mom, expecting her to say no right away, but she's in a lockdown stare with my dad. I can't begin to know what this look is conveying, but when she takes a step back and takes a bite of bacon, she nods.

"Sure. Unless Summer had another plan for us today, we're just hanging out together."

"I thought we'd go to the beach today," I pipe up. I don't want to get stuck on a set all day and not be able to leave when we want to, especially if it's far.

"We'll be shooting at Laguna Beach tomorrow. Come with us today. It'll be fun, I promise," Dad says.

Autumn bounces around, excited, and Dad puts his arm around her.

"Sound good, sweetheart?" he asks.

"Yep," she says, smiling.

I sigh and eat standing up. I guess my dad is still calling the shots.

———

It takes an hour and a half to get to the location and it's a dusty, old Victorian house out in the middle of nowhere. Mountains surround it and the rest of the crew has already been out here for hours by the time we arrive. The trip felt like it took forever, with Dad trying to make conversation and Mama shutting him down. I've never been so glad to get out of a car in my life.

I was going to tell my mom and sister the truth about Liam and me last night and I fell asleep before I could. And with Dad around all the time, I haven't had a chance to today. When Liam sees us, he comes over and gives me a hug from behind.

"How did it go?" he asks.

"They still don't know," I tell him.

His eyebrows lift and he laughs. "Am I winning you over, Sum? You've decided you want me, haven't you?"

I laugh. "Sum? That's the lamest one you've come up with yet."

"Don't avoid the question." He puts his hands on my waist and nuzzles into my ear, my back against his chest. "Would you prefer Mer?"

I snort and let my head fall back against him.

"When is your replacement coming?" Winslet says, walking past us. "I'm tired of waiting for you to get 'rested up.'"

"Eat bricks, Winnie," I say, turning away from her.

I hear her sputtering and carrying on and look over my

shoulder. Her face is mottled pink and purple and maybe a little green. I turn and put my hand on her arm.

"Breathe," I tell her.

She does and I can tell it makes her mad to listen to me even in that simple, helpful instruction. But she does and her coloring starts returning back to the blood-sucking paleness we're all used to from her.

"I'm going to make you pay for how you've treated me," she says, stalking off.

"Eat a donut," I yell after her. "You'll feel better."

Hudson walks over then. "What's going on? I've never seen Winslet so angry."

"She was rude to Summer and Summer gave it back," Liam says. "Hottest thing I've ever seen."

Hudson's eyes narrow on Liam and he opens his mouth to say something when Autumn walks up.

She bounces into Hudson with her hip and smiles up at him. "Hey," she says, practically purring.

"Well, this just keeps getting crazier," Liam says under his breath.

36

NO SEX FOR YOU

WE GET THROUGH THE LONG DAY ON SET, THE LONG DRIVE, and my dad still expects us to go out to eat with him after all that. And what is more surprising is that my mom doesn't shut him down. She's full of comebacks and snark and bite, but she's also smiling a lot and looks like she's thoroughly enjoying herself. And Autumn has been in heaven, watching the scenes play out in front of her with Liam, Winslet, Hannah, and all the doubles and extras.

When she's not flirting her ass off with Hudson.

I almost don't even want to tell her about me and

Hudson now because of how much she seems to like him. I should've told her last night. Before she came even.

It's going to be brutal.

And Hudson, he's not making it easy. He isn't flirting back exactly. He's been very sweet and thoughtful with her, but he's also tried to make sure I'm okay every other minute, so I can't even be mad at him. And Liam is just sitting back watching it all when he's not in a scene, laughing and enjoying the show on the sidelines.

I end up steaming an outfit that Winslet has to wear and it's the one time Autumn leaves Hudson's side to come hang out with me. Winslet has ignored Autumn completely and I can tell Autumn is curious about Winslet after all I've said about her.

"You and Liam are so cute together," she whispers as she acts like she's not staring at Winslet.

"About that," I whisper back.

Winslet turns to look at us. "Can you keep it down? I'm running my lines?" she snaps.

"Oh my god," Autumn mouths at me, making a face. "Rude much?"

"Oh, you have no idea."

I finish steaming the outfit and hang it near Winslet, walking away before she thinks of something else she "needs" me to do. I pull Autumn away from the tent we've been working in and try to find a place where no one can overhear us.

"I have to tell you something," I start.

"Okay," she says, but her eyes are back on the crew, probably looking for Hudson.

"Listen, I'm sorry I didn't tell you before now, but I wasn't supposed to. The thing with me and Liam...it's not real."

She turns and looks at me then, her nose scrunching up. "What do you mean?"

"I signed a contract to act like we're dating," I whisper.

"What?" She frowns. "But it seems so—"

"Liam is a big flirt with everyone."

"He hasn't flirted with me. Not once. You think he doesn't like you?" She snorts. "Uh, yeah, you're oblivious."

"I've actually had something going with Hudson." I get the words out and am making a full-on scrunch face—the fear of her really liking Hudson already making me a nervous wreck. *I* liked him right away too—who wouldn't?

She makes a pouty face. "So, what you're saying is that I can't have either one?" She folds her arms over her chest and I'm already feeling better because if she's this playful, she's not hurt. I laugh and she does too.

"You can have Liam, you'd just have to be quiet about it until our little contract thing is over."

She rolls her eyes at me. "You apparently can't see what's right in front of your face."

"What do you mean?"

"The guy has got it so bad for you! Are you kidding me right now?"

I look around, making sure no one is listening to us. And then I lean in to whisper. "He's one of the best actors out there right now. He is *playing a part*."

So maybe I've done some Liam Taylor homework when I should've been sleeping and now know his work very well. Can't believe I've been missing out all this time. He's good. *Really* good.

"Then why is he looking like he wants to back you into that wall and have his way with you right now?" Autumn whisper-hisses.

I turn to find Liam staring at me, his eyes roaming my

body like he's imagining it naked, and I flush. Autumn sighs next to me.

"What have you done to these guys? Now that I know, I see it with Hudson too. Damn you." She laughs to soften her words, and I groan.

"Liam knows about Hudson and me. He's tried to help that happen. I don't think he would if he seriously liked me."

"If you love 'em, let 'em go," she quotes and I pinch her arm, making her yelp. "What? Maybe he's using that old philosophy."

"Well, Dad is determined I make it look real with Liam. He's really pushed the whole thing. I think Liam is just trying to make his agent and Dad happy. Period."

"Go ahead and delude yourself. I've always been the smarter one." She jabs me in the side with her elbow and I roll my eyes.

"Are we sure we're glad you're here, Auto?" I tease and she acts wounded again.

"Oh my, look at this." She tilts her head toward the right and we watch as our mom walks toward us. The look on our dad's face is both priceless and gross.

"Why have I never noticed how into her he is?" I ask.

"Maybe he's finally realized he can't live without her."

"I can't believe he's dating Bella and still hitting on Mom."

"Looks like the apple didn't fall far from the tree," she says, laughing when I glare at her.

"Enough. I am not dating two guys at once. Well, not fully." I shake my head at her and then see that she's distracted. I turn to see what she's looking at and Clyde, the barista from Starbucks, waves from where he's set up coffee.

"Is there no shortage of cute guys here?" Autumn asks, grinning.

She walks over to get a cup of coffee and by the way he's smiling at her, I can only hope she'll have a good distraction from my love life.

My love life that has the least amount of sex in the history of any single girl in Hollywood ever.

37

HOT MAMA

THE THREE OF US ARE GETTING READY FOR DINNER IN MY room. My dad has insisted we eat with him again. It's the most I've seen him outside of work since I got here. We're going to a place about half an hour away, and Liam, Hudson, Winslet, and Hannah will be there too. I'm not sure why my dad is trying to torture me this way, but I've agreed to it because my mom has never been as smiley as she's been the past couple of days. She's not just pouring it all on my dad— although I've seen her smile at him more than I expected to

—but she seems calmer. It could simply be that she was long overdue for a vacation.

We went to the beach earlier today and drove around celebrities' homes. It's something Autumn has always wanted to do and I was surprised by how much I enjoyed it too. I'm not one hundred percent certain the celebrities listed on the Celebrity Homes Tour Map *actually* live in the homes or if it's a scam, but it was still fun.

And now I'm putting on makeup next to Autumn in the bedroom because our mom has taken over the bathroom.

"I think she's even wearing eyeliner," I whisper. Our mom is a mascara, lip gloss kind of girl, nothing more, ever.

"What? Are you sure? What's happening? What if they get back together?" She hisses the last words and I flinch like I've been hit.

"We've gotta do something." I stop abruptly when Mama comes out, smiling at us, and she looks beautiful. "You look so pretty, Mama."

"Is it too much?" She turns to the side and smooths down her fitted grey dress. Her hair is in long waves, she's wearing a full smokey-eye, and her lips are a matte dark plum. It's news to me that she even knew how to do all of this. She's always been gorgeous, but this is next level.

"Not at all. I'm...stunned." I walk over to her and put my hand on her arm which feels like satin. "You're so soft and so beautiful. Why haven't you taught us any of these tricks?" I burst out laughing and so does she.

"No shit, Mama. How did you learn to do a smokey eye like that and can you do mine?" Autumn shimmies over to her and pets her other arm.

"Had I known I'd get so much attention from the two of you, I would've pulled this out long ago." She shrugs. "I don't know. Once I got serious about making a living for us and not relying on anyone else...it just felt like it took all my energy to work and be your mom." She holds up a hand. "Please don't think I am complaining. Not even a little bit. But making this much of an effort when I didn't really want the attention anyway...it was an easy thing to stop."

"Dad's gonna blow his load when he gets a look at you," Autumn says.

"Ew." I smack her arm. "Please don't make me imagine Dad blowing any loads."

"Well, one of us is getting lucky tonight and it's not gonna be either of us at this rate. Miss I've Got All the Choices...I don't see you sealing any deals." She smirks and I scowl at her.

"When did you start talking like a college boy?" Mama asks, laughing.

"Are you gonna tell Mama or should I?" Autumn says, hand on her hip.

Mama looks at me and I exhale, putting my head on her shoulder. "I need to finish getting ready, but my sister is being so annoying."

"Someone's gotta tell the truth around here." Autumn lifts an eyebrow and sticks her lips out when I try to spear her with daggers from my eyeballs alone.

"What is she talking about?" Mama asks.

"I signed a contract to 'date' Liam. We're not really dating, so it's not real. We're pretending to date. But I like Hudson and he likes me, and this thing with Liam is Dad and Liam's agent's doing."

Her lips form into a pout, much like Autumn's did when I told her. "So, you and Liam aren't—? But he seems so—? And Hudson? I mean, I like him, he's a doll...but Liam just acts *so* into you."

"Exactly. He's acting. And Hudson is trying to act like he's not into me, so there's that." I wish he wasn't doing such a good job at it, to be honest.

"I did catch Hudson eye-fucking her earlier today," Autumn says, nodding.

Mama and I both smack her arm this time and she jumps out of the way, eyes wide. "What? It's true. He was. Hurt my pride, but once I talked to Clyde, I felt a lot better."

"Who is Clyde?"

"That hot coffee guy who was on set."

"I didn't notice him," Mama said. "So, why did you agree to this contract and why is Dad forcing you to do it?"

"I'm getting a lot of money. A LOT." I waved my hand across the room. "Which I feel weird about, but it will take care of so much. I wanted to tell you guys so bad, but Dad made me promise I'd stick to the contract...and that means you can't tell a soul."

"But Hudson knows?" Autumn asks.

"Liam told him because he knows how much I like Hudson."

"Are you *sure* you don't like Liam too?" Mama asks. "The way he looks at you..."

"Liam and I survived a plane crash together and he's really been there for me, so I have had moments of...confusion," I admit. When I say it out loud, I'm surprised by how long it's taken me to admit that much.

"Well, take your time and enjoy the attention," Mama says, smiling. "Hudson is really, really—" She fans herself and we laugh.

"I'm so glad y'all know everything now. I hated keeping it from you." I pull them to me and we hug it out, before Autumn squeaks and ruins the moment.

"We've gotta be fabulous in three minutes. Let me go," she says.

I roll my eyes, but we break up the fun and hustle to get gorgeous. Well, Autumn and I do...Mama's already got it covered.

38

THE BEST KIND OF TORTURE

WE'VE ONLY BEEN TO THE TRENDY RESTAURANT NEAR THE Venice Boardwalk for a few minutes and I'm already anxious. Seated in an oversized booth, everyone and everything feels too close for comfort. I'm squeezed between Hudson and Liam. Autumn is on the other side of Hudson and next to our mom. Mama sits next to Dad and oh yeah, there's also Hannah, Winslet, and *Bella*. It's great to have Hannah—I would love for her to get to know my mom and Autumn better, but Winslet and Bella are a dark cloud hanging over the group. I don't know why Bella would come except to cause trouble, and I feel bad for thinking that, but I also wish she'd had the good sense to stay as far away from this awkwardness as possible.

My dad seems oblivious to any drama and he keeps leaning in close to my mom's ear to whisper things, which is making Bella see red. I'm afraid she's going to blow at any second. And my mom keeps scooting as far away from him as she can and trying to include Bella in the conversation.

Liam, I think in an attempt to make me laugh, starts upping his flirting game. It works for about two seconds when he says, "I wish I was your dress..."

"Why?"

"So I'd have a reason to be up against you."

I burst out laughing at how ridiculous he is and visibly feel Hudson bristle next to me. I turn to look at him apologetically.

"He doesn't mean it," I try to subtly whisper.

Hudson stares straight ahead and Winslet thinks he's looking at her. She leans against the table, trying to create cleavage she doesn't have. I mean, she still looks like a freaking movie star, so she's clearly not suffering.

"I guarantee he means every word," Hudson says through gritted teeth.

When I turn to look at him, he takes a long drink of iced water and won't make eye contact with me.

I ask Liam to let me out of the booth and since I'm in the middle, there's a small line of people that have to get out to let me through.

"Sorry," I say as I head to the bathroom. There are four unisex bathrooms in the darkened hallway and there's no line, so when I close the door behind me, I sag against the door and take deep breaths, willing myself to relax. The peace is momentary, a loud knock making me jump out of my skin.

"Summer? It's me. Hudson," he adds. "Can I come in?"

I open the door a crack. "What if I'd been using the bathroom?" I look down the hall and it's still quiet. I open the door wider and he comes in, closing the door behind him and locking it. His hands find my waist.

"I was hoping I'd catch you just in time. Did you need to?"

I smile despite being a tiny bit annoyed with him for being annoyed with *me*. "No. I just needed some air."

"And you found it here?" His head lowers to mine and I close my eyes.

It feels good to be near him.

"I've missed you. I'm sorry I've been so foul tonight. It's just...I want to get to know your family and they have no idea who I even am to you."

"I told them tonight before we came."

"You did?" He pulls back and the smile on his face is enough to make me weak in the knees.

His lips hover over mine, his hands squeezing my waist and venturing lower and lower. I tilt my head back and he kisses along my neck.

"Hudson," I whisper.

He slides his hand through my hair and gives it a tug as he gets my mouth right where he wants it. When his lips land on mine, I want to crawl out of my body and into his. It's consuming, this kiss. I forget about everything and everyone else and let his kiss rip apart every expectation I had for tonight. Because this is much, much better than anything I could have imagined.

He hitches my leg around his waist and presses against me, showing me how this kiss is affecting him. I groan into his mouth and he reaches up my dress and between my legs, his fingers finding that spot that is begging for him.

"You're driving me crazy," he says, his voice gravelly. "I don't know how long I can keep doing this, living with you every day and pretending I don't want you. Being close to you and not ripping your clothes off." He moves my lacy scrap of material aside and I lose all sense when I feel his skin against mine.

"You can rip my clothes off any...time." I groan as his fingers pick up their tempo and his tongue teases the edge of my mouth. I kiss him hard, pulling his hair and unable to be still with the torture he's inflicting on me.

The best kind of torture.

"Come for me," he says. "I want to go back to that table and know that I'm wearing you on my skin."

His words, along with the next level he takes his fingers —it sends me over the edge. He inhales my gasps, his kiss searing into me and setting my body on fire. I hold on for dear life as the shocks rush through my body and when I open my eyes, he's watching me, the lust nearly knocking me over.

"I'm committing every second of this to memory. In case it's too long before I get to do this again. God, I hope I can do this again soon." He grins and withdraws his fingers, putting them in his mouth and sucking them clean.

"Oh, please do that again soon." I smooth my dress and jump when there's a knock on the door.

I glance down sadly at his situation and give him an apologetic look.

He leans in and kisses me one more time before yelling, "Occupied."

"You know it would probably be safer to sneak into my bedroom than this was..."

"Noted." He smirks. "You better get back out there. I'll be in here until this isn't quite so obvious." He points at the bulge in his pants.

I laugh and turn to the door. "It is so sad to leave that behind," I tell him. I peek out the door and am relieved when it's just Autumn out there. "Go to the next one," I whisper.

Her eyes widen and she pumps her fist. "You are so bad," she whispers. "I am so impressed right now."

WHEN I GO BACK TO THE TABLE, THE TENSION HAS ESCALATED. My mom looks uncomfortable and Bella is leaning forward, her hands slamming into the table, as she whisper-shouts at my dad.

"What have we been doing all these months?" she asks.

My dad just stares at her.

She pounds on the table and he looks around. The restaurant isn't full—I don't know if he's paid to have the restaurant empty for our dinner tonight or if it's just quiet—

but the waitstaff is paying close attention. We're giving them a show whether we want to or not.

"Answer me. Tell me. I sold my house and moved in with you because *you said we were good together*."

I have to admit I'm surprised it's only been months and she's selling her house and cohabitating? But whatever. I guess when you know, you know. It's just my *dad* doesn't seem to know.

"Please keep it down, Bella." My dad leans in and speaks in a low voice, which makes Bella throw her head back and cackle.

I've always liked Bella and I feel bad that there's any kind of sadness for her where my dad is concerned, but I also don't want to be here for this conversation.

"Bella, could this wait?" I ask.

She glances at me apologetically and nods before standing up. She wobbles slightly before leaning down on the table with both hands. "You're right, Summer. This can wait. He'll be coming to my bed later tonight and we can resume this conversation then." She laughs again like she's on the verge of losing it and I feel sorry for her.

My dad gets up and takes her by the arm, and she trails next to him, sputtering something in his ear the whole time.

"I think Bella missed her calling as an actress," Winslet says.

The rest of us sit there, willing the dinner to be over soon. Liam attempts conversation a few times and my mom jumps to answer, happy for the distraction, but the topics dwindle down to nothing while we wait for my dad to come back.

When he finally does, he's alone. "I apologize for that. Bella had a lot to drink, even before we came tonight, and she would normally not indulge in such petty confrontations."

"It seemed to me she had reasonable concerns," Mama says.

My dad leans over and starts whispering in her ear, and I just want to get out of here. I look at Autumn and give her wide eyes.

"Can we get an Uber out of here?" I ask quietly.

Liam and Hudson both hear me.

"We'll go with you," Liam says. "We've got drivers lined up, remember?"

"Oh yeah, I forget that you have someone to do your bidding at all times," Autumn says. "That must be nice."

He makes a face. "There are some perks and some drawbacks."

"Mom, we're gonna go. Do you want to ride back with us?" I ask.

My dad says something else to her and she looks a bit torn. "I'll stay a little longer. Go ahead."

Hannah and Winslet slide out of the booth and the rest of us follow. Hannah has her phone out for an Uber.

"Just come with us," I tell her.

"It's okay. I think Tanner is meeting me for a drink soon." She winks and I grin.

"*Oh.*"

"Mmhmm." She does a little shimmy and then we hug.

"I'm happy for you," I tell her.

"I can't tell who I'm rooting for," she whispers. "Liam or...Hudson?"

My eyes get huge and she winks, putting her fingers up to her lips like she's locking them.

We wait for a few moments and Liam gets a text saying our driver has pulled up. We step outside and it's as if every flash goes off at once. Photographers are yelling and snapping pictures on either side of us. Liam puts his arm around me and hustles to the car.

A photographer yells, "Give us something to work with. Kiss the girl!"

We rush to the car and before Liam opens the door, he dips me back and gives me a long, scorching kiss. Cheers erupt as his hand slides up to my hip and he squeezes my waist. His tongue dips into my mouth and I'm so stunned that I put my hand on his cheek to have something to hold onto. The next second, he swoops me upright and I pull away in a daze.

I look back and Hudson is staring at me with the saddest eyes I've ever seen. Autumn is standing next to him and he turns to her and motions for them to get in the next car. I feel terrible as I get in our car and Liam follows behind me.

When we're inside, I turn to him and give him a shove. He laughs and laces his fingers through mine.

"What?"

"You know what. Why do you keep doing that?" I turn and face the front, pulling my hand away, arms folded over my chest. I'm so mad I can't even look at him right now.

"Do what? I gave them something to get them off of our backs for a while. It should give us a little freedom for the next few weeks."

"I didn't think that was how it worked. Pretty sure it's not."

"Is kissing me so bad?"

"No, it was a great kiss. But you didn't really keep your word about the kissing. And you make me feel terrible because I kissed Hudson not even fifteen minutes before. I'm not this person." My voice breaks and he puts his hand on my knee, pulling it away abruptly and back to his own leg.

"Hey, you're right," he says softly. "I'm sorry. I wasn't thinking, but you're totally right. I'll do better. Hudson knows it's just for show though."

"Is it? Because even I'm confused at this point."

"Do you...want it to be real?"

I sigh and stare out the window as we put more miles between Hudson and me.

"Liam, I like Hudson. I'd like to see what we have—give it a chance. Or I don't know...I'm not sure he'll keep hanging in there to give me a chance since you keep making it so difficult."

He laughs and when I look at him, he rolls his eyes. "If he can't handle a little conflict, he's not worth it. *You* are worth fighting for."

40

IT'S ON

WE DON'T DO MUCH TALKING ON THE WAY BACK TO THE HOUSE. For some reason, I get the impression that Liam is mad at *me*. Therefore, my anger with him stews and swirls and boils and by the time we pull into the driveway, I hop out before he can stop me.

"Summer, wait," he says.

"What, Liam?" I say, turning back around to face him, the annoyance in my voice very clear.

"I just want to know...are you *sure*? You're sure he's who you want?"

"You seemed clear on this before. Why are you so intent on clouding the issue now?"

"I enjoy being with you. You're fun and beautiful and it's so easy when we're together. I care about you. I think...we could be great together."

"I'm comfortable for you because I'm your friend," I remind him, my heart softening slightly toward him. "Do you have any friends?"

He laughs, but it falls off quickly. "I don't think I do. Not real ones anyway."

"I'll be your friend. But let's not complicate it, okay? I like hanging out with you and think you're great and fun too..."

"Easy on the eyes?"

"Very," I say, grinning.

"Okay, I guess I'll put up with friendship. It's just hard because I really want to kiss you."

"Well, rein it in. Next time you pull a stunt like you did outside that restaurant, I'm kneeing you in a place where the sun don't shine." I motion toward his crotch and he cringes.

"Okay, okay. Message received. No need to get hostile."

Another car pulls in behind us and I'm relieved to see my sister and Hudson in there. They get out and Autumn presses her lips together as she gives me a loaded look. Hudson walks past us, not looking at Liam or me.

"Someone's not happy," Autumn whispers. "Why don't you go see about Hudson? I'll chat with Liam."

"Are you sure?" I whisper back.

"It is no hardship for me, I promise you that."

I roll my eyes and she tries not to laugh out loud as Liam turns and walks toward the door.

"Well, problem solved, I guess. I'll see if he needs soothing inside." She winks and catches up with him.

"Good night," I call out.

Liam lifts a hand and waves without turning around and Autumn looks back at me and grins.

"Night, Season," she says.

"Night, Auto." I think about waiting up for my mom, but when I get inside, I go to my room to change first. I check my phone and there's a text from her.

I'm fine. I know you're worrying about me and you shouldn't. I'll be smart, I promise. :)

I text back. **Well, that sounds like trouble waiting to happen. But if you say so.**

I do. Love you.

Love you, Mama.

I'm down to my underwear and heading to the bathroom to wash off my makeup when there's a soft knock on the door. At first I think I've imagined it. But then it happens again.

I open the door, hiding carefully behind it.

Hudson. His eyes dark and unfathomable, and his mouth in a tight line.

"Can I come in?" he whispers, looking down the hall.

"Oh, yeah." I open the door without thinking about the fact that I'm in my bra and panties until he steps inside, closes the door behind him, and stares at me.

I glance down and then look around for my robe, but before I get to it, one hand clutches my waist and the other tugs my hair and he kisses me like a man possessed. I melt into him, hands going everywhere at once, and his hands land on my backside. He moans as he kneads my cheeks and then picks me up, wrapping my legs around his waist. I pull my head back, looking at him, breathing hard.

"You're not mad?" I ask.

"Oh, I'm mad, but I'm not mad at you," he whispers.

"Well, maybe a little." He chuckles and grips me tighter around him. "Do you want this—me?"

I nod, my hands on either side of his face. "Yes."

"I don't want to waste any more time acting like I don't care about you."

"Then let's not."

He turns out the light and walks over to the bed, the moon shining through the windows like a spotlight.

"It's beautiful out there," I whisper.

"Not as beautiful as in here."

I hope it's dark enough that he can't see me flush. But he lays me back on the bed and stands over me looking like a highlighted god. I sit up and unbutton his shirt, splaying my hands across his skin. He undoes his pants and I help him out of them, not letting myself get too intimidated by the bulge at eye level. He gives me a slight shove back onto the bed and leans over me.

"Just so you know, I'd be happy just holding you all night," he says, kissing up my neck. "I just don't want to be lying in my room imagining you lying in yours for another second."

"I'd be happy with whatever we do as long as we're together, but I'd rather..." I reach down and let my hands roam on the parts of his body that I've been dreaming about for what feels like forever now. He kisses me, soft at first, and then when I start stroking him up and down, the barrier of his boxer briefs still between us, our kiss intensifies. He thrusts into my hand and I gasp into his mouth. He breaks away from me and kisses down my skin, his hands warm against my body.

"I'd much rather do this too," he says against my stomach. He tugs my panties down and I unclasp my bra. He takes off his briefs and I motion toward him.

"Do you have a condom?" I whisper.

He reaches for his pants pocket and grabs one out of there. "I can't wait to be inside you..."

41

BASHFUL AND A VIXEN

"Is this really happening?" I whisper as he kisses his way down my body.

He gives each breast his undivided attention and murmurs, "Yes, it's absolutely happening," against my skin.

And then he goes lower and lower and I'M DYING. It's like I'm bashful and a vixen all at the same time. I cover my face with a pillow, but I arch into his mouth, and when his tongue and mouth and fingers start going crazy on me, I lose my mind. I'm so glad I have the pillow; otherwise, the whole house would be able to hear me right now. Who knew

Hudson Callihan would be a freaking force of nature in bed?

I knew. I did. It's part of why he's always had me under his spell, and it's why it's a good thing we haven't done this before now.

He takes it to another level, sucking that most sensitive part of me and dipping his fingers inside. He takes his time, murmuring his approval when he comes up for air every now and then.

"You're the taste I will be craving from now on. So sweet," he whispers before unleashing his tongue with a new determination. I don't even know what he's doing right now. He might be sucking out my brain cells—I can't think straight—but I don't even care because it sends me cresting over the edge again. I whimper into the pillow. He pulls it away and I look at him, whimpering again when I see him between my legs.

"You are...too much," I say, trying to catch my breath. "I don't know how I'm going to get anything done around you."

He grins and leans over me, sliding the condom on and settling between my legs. My eyes close when I feel him nudge my entrance.

"Look at me," he says, his voice raspy. "I don't *want* you to get anything done when I'm around. I want you to be in a lust-filled haze every time I come into the room. Then you'll know at least half of the agony you've put me through since the day we met." He grins and then it's wiped off his face when he thrusts inside of me, going as deep as he can go. He groans and it's the most erotic sound.

"Don't ever stop," I say.

His head falls back and I put my hands on his face, bringing his eyes back to mine.

"I'm the one who's at your mercy," he says. "God, you feel good."

I do. I feel *so* good. Better than I've ever felt in my life.

We start moving slowly. This pulse, this living, breathing fire that is palpable, it feels bigger than us. It doesn't matter what we haven't said, what hasn't been promised, what may have happened before...the way our bodies communicate with each other—there is no going back.

Our bodies are glistening with sweat, the moonlight casting shadows over us as we lose ourselves in each other. My legs are wrapped around him, my hands roaming through his hair, down his back, and landing on his perfect ass. I feel close to losing it again and he flips us over so I'm on top. I sit up and lean my hands back against his thighs as his hands cup around my breasts, giving my nipples a tug. I rise and fall on him and his fingers move between us, making my insides squeeze him like a vise. My head falls back and his fingers move faster as I feel him get even harder inside of me.

"I want this to last forever, but you are the best thing I've ever felt," he says, slamming up into me.

Harder, faster.

I ride him until I am crying out his name and he leans up to kiss me. When I start to slow down, he sits up until our chests are flush with each other and drives into me again and again and again. I see stars, my hands holding onto his shoulders for dear life. It feels so impossibly good. I clench around him as he swells inside and he moans my name as he pulses with his release. I feel every twitch, every shudder, and when we sag against each other, spent, I'm completely sated.

He pulls me against him as he lies back, my head on his chest, still connected.

"Wow," he says.

"Yeah."

Definitely robbed my brain cells. I think I might've taken some of his too.

"I can't wait to do that again." His fingers trace down my back and I shiver against him. He sighs and says, "I'm sorry to do this, but I'll be right back." He pulls out of me and I sigh. "I know," he says.

He goes to the bathroom to take care of the condom and when he's done and back in bed, I kiss his shoulder and go to the bathroom myself. I hardly recognize myself in the mirror.

"Sex goddess," I whisper to the mirror and giggle. I take care of my business and clean up a little before going back into the bedroom. I get a hitch in my chest when I see him lying in my bed, his hands under his head.

"Come here." He holds his arm out and I nestle into his shoulder. "Are you okay?" he asks.

"I'm better than okay."

"Yeah?"

"Yeah." I laugh. "I feel thoroughly sexed up. Wrung out. Like you put me through the spin cycle."

He laughs and traces his fingers down my chest. "You definitely spun me out. My heart is still going nuts." He puts my hand on his chest and I feel it pounding.

"Do you think anyone heard us?" I ask.

"No. Hear those waves out there? That and your pillow did their job." He kisses my forehead and I tickle his chest. "Keep doing that with your fingers and I can't be responsible for the sounds *I* make."

My body is wrapped around his. Leg over his thigh, my head on his chest, skin to skin. My energy is zapped from how thoroughly he has ravaged my body. I grin against his chest and shiver, and his arms tighten around me. As tired as I am, I don't want to sleep. I don't want this to end.

"How's your writing going?" Hudson asks.

"I still haven't replaced my laptop since the crash."

"What?" He looks down at me and lifts up my chin. "Why is that?"

"Well, it's been a little busy, for one thing. I need to get a new computer and I will. I guess I'm just mourning the loss of that work. I didn't do a good job of backing it all up, and I'm kicking myself over that now. I'll have to start over and that just feels really daunting right now. I've barely had time this summer to do anything but work and swim to safety and try not to die from getting stung." I laugh, but it sounds weak. His fingertips tickle down my back and I lean my chin on his chest, looking up at him. "I don't know that I had anything important to say anyway. You know? All the time I've committed to my writing and wishing I could move toward more screenplays...I'm just not sure I'm cut out for it."

"Has being on set turned you off of it that much?" he asks.

"No. If anything, I want to be part of this business more than ever. Not being an errand girl necessarily," I laugh, "but I'm not complaining. I do want this. But being around my dad...it has kind of clouded everything."

His arms tighten around me and he kisses my hair. "I'm sorry it's been that way. I hope things can change before— well, I don't even like to say the words *before you leave*."

I make a face because I don't like to hear those words either. But as far as direction goes, this summer hasn't really helped nail down my future plans the way I'd been hoping it might. I can put money toward rent somewhere, which is huge, but the cost of living is astronomical in California, and for this Charlotte girl, I'm just not sure I have what it takes to stand out here anyway.

"I don't want to ride my dad's coattails, and yet, I'm not sure I know how to do it without his help either. It's just...it's hard to even be around him full-time. I thought I was fairly well-balanced for having a dysfunctional upbringing, but it turns out being around him is reminding me of all of my hang-ups."

"What's the biggest hang-up you have?"

I sigh and pull in my bottom lip with my teeth. "Trust," I whisper.

"Do you trust me?"

"I think so. I want to."

I want to trust that this is real. But this night has already been too surreal. I don't want to say too much or jinx anything or scare him off. What I've come to realize this summer is that my abandonment issues are very much a part of how I approach relationships. I'd rather be a *good-time right now* kind of girl than make him feel like he owes me anything after tonight.

"Hey, are you okay?" he asks.

"I might've been getting inside my head a little too much," I admit.

"I'm not going anywhere. And I hope to God you're not either. Please don't break my heart," he whispers.

I pull back, until his eyes are meeting mine. "I'm afraid you're going to break mine."

His lips turn up. "I think you haven't fully grasped how into you I am, Summer Winters. I'm all in." His arms tighten around me and I let my eyes close. And before I fall asleep, I think that maybe I will make an exception for Hudson. Maybe I will truly let him in.

I want to give my heart and trust to someone who deserves it and I think he just might be the one.

42

STAY

THE NEXT DAY AFTER I WORK A FEW HOURS AND MEET MY
mom and sister for a late lunch, I buy a new laptop. The
little nudges Hudson gave me last night put a voice to what
had been looping around in my mind for a while. I've
pushed aside my dreams to the back burner and even
while I've been busy working and keeping my commit-
ments—who knew I'd be committed to a fake relationship
with an actor, among so many other things?—it is time to
remember what I set out to become. I love to write. With
more work, I could shop the novels and screenplays I've

already written. Or work on something new. I don't need to let my dad's agenda get in the way of any of this for another second.

Even if nothing changes with my schedule the rest of the summer, I need to keep up with my writing to stay sane. And now that I've made the decision to not let anything stop me, I'm feeling the itch to get back to the house and write.

"Do we have to go back there?" my mom asks. "It's just a lot, being in that constant...drama."

I guess we won't be going back to the house any time soon.

"What happened with you and Dad last night?" Autumn asks. "He's not getting to you, is he?"

A nervous laugh bursts out of Mama, and Autumn and I glance at each other before looking at her. Twin expressions from her daughters, I'm sure: pure concern with a side of grossed out. She sees it all because her face crumples and she covers it with her hands. Her shoulders shake and I put my arm around her shoulder and find a bench outside the store we just hurried out of and help her sit down.

I don't know what to say, so at first I just keep my arm around her, but the longer she cries, the angrier at my father I get. I know I need to keep my mouth shut, but I just can't.

"Who does he think he is?" I ask. "Hasn't he learned anything by now? He's the ultimate player and wonders why he doesn't have anyone stick around...or does he even wonder that? I don't know. It's just—gah, I am so—"

My mom puts her hand on my arm and I stop and look at her. Tears are running down her face and she looks like she didn't sleep all night.

"He wants me to give him another chance," she says.

Autumn and I both start talking at once. Neither of us saying anything particularly nice or helpful.

Mama holds up her hand and we stop. Autumn plops down on the other side of her, dejected.

"Is he even out of a relationship with Bella?" Autumn asks.

"He says Bella and her cousin will be moving out of the house today. He wants me to stay—not in his room," she hurries to add, "but at the house, or at least in California, and give this a real chance. I've never wanted to leave Charlotte, never wanted this life. Although that house isn't bad." She snorts and then winces and more tears fall down her cheeks. "I've tried to teach you girls to be stronger than I was when it came to men, and you are. Both of you are so much stronger than I've ever been."

"You've always shut him down before, right? I mean, I never knew he'd pursued you really until seeing him with you this time. Now that I'm older, I remember him being like this with you and you just always being aloof yet kind. Were you dying inside?" The thought of her wanting to be with him and not giving in to that all these years is crushing.

"Yes," she whispers. "I have always loved him beyond reason. The two of you were my safety rafts that I so desperately needed. I haven't wanted this life for you. And yet, here we all are. Summer, you seem invested here, and Autumn, I know you're chomping at the bit to be here more too. Have I done the wrong thing for you all this time?"

I scoot in closer and lean my head on her shoulder. "I've loved our life. Dad made his choice—it was his career over us, Mom. No matter how you look at it. I don't doubt that he loves you. But he has never chosen you or us."

She takes a shaky breath. "I know you're right. I just sometimes wonder what it would've been like if I'd tried harder to fit into this lifestyle. I made him choose and that wasn't really fair of me either."

"Well, the important thing is, what do you want now? Because you don't have to worry about raising us anymore," Autumn says. "We've turned out pretty good, thanks to you. And it's time to think about what *you* want."

"She's right. And we won't stand in the way of that. Even if you choose Dad." Yes, it hurts to say that because I want to tell her to run far, far away from my father, but more than anything, I want her to have the life she wants after all the sacrifices she's made for us.

My phone has been vibrating like crazy and I've been ignoring it.

"You should check that," Mom says. "I'm okay, I promise."

"I'll look at it on our way back. But first, I think we should talk about the possibility of you staying." I bump her shoulder with mine. "Is that something you'd really consider?"

She bites her bottom lip and shrugs. "It would be really nice to not work so hard anymore. And to have less humid summers. And to look at this ocean all the time." We all stare out at the water and are quiet for a few moments, enjoying the beauty.

"What would Jericho think of all this sand?" Autumn asks and we laugh. Our dog would lose his mind in the sand. He'd be rolling around in it all the way up to the water.

"Maybe I'll know better how I really feel once I get back to Charlotte," Mom says.

I sag back against the bench. "So, you *are* going back tomorrow?"

43

MAGIC

When we leave the restaurant, someone calls my name. I turn and a handful of photographers snap away on their cameras. I'm caught off guard and try to rush past them.

"How does it feel to be the one to settle Liam Taylor down?"

"Is it serious?"

"Will there be a wedding anytime soon?"

"Can you turn to the right? No? That's okay, I got a good shot."

"What's your story, Summer Winters?"

My face is red and I'm shaky as I try to get to the car that's waiting for us. They never stop taking pictures as they conduct a one-way conversation, trying to get something, anything, out of me. I try to smile but know I probably look more like a wild animal in a trap.

When we finally get inside the car, my mom and Autumn are wide-eyed.

"That was intense," Mama says. "Please be careful going anywhere—I don't think you should be alone. They're relentless!"

"I'm sure it will die down quickly. Especially if Liam isn't with me when I'm out."

"Just be careful."

"Yeah, I will."

I text Liam about what happened and tell him his plan is working. They definitely believe we're together.

I'm sorry. I didn't think about what it could mean for you when I'm not around. It's best to just smile for a few pictures and say very little. I really am sorry, Summer. That's too much.

I don't say anything back because I am a little freaked out over the fact that they followed me or that someone at the restaurant maybe tipped them off. It's bizarre that anyone would be interested in me.

When we get back to the house, Liam is waiting for us. "Are you okay?" he asks, hugging me.

"It shook me up a little bit, but they weren't too bad. I was just surprised to see them out there."

"Be careful, okay? Let me know if you need to go somewhere and I can come to ward them off." He shrugs and still looks apologetic. "Or you know, just take someone with you, doesn't have to be me. My driver can take you anywhere you need to go."

"I tried to tell her that too—to make sure someone is with her. Thanks for the backup, Liam." My mom smiles at him. "It was so nice to meet you. I probably won't see you before we fly out, so I'll say my goodbyes now," she says.

Liam reaches out and hugs her and then Autumn. "You guys should stay. You fit right in around here."

"I've been saying the same thing," I say.

"We have a puppy who would be so sad if we didn't at least come get him," Mama says. "And more than a few loose ends to tie up." She sighs. "What am I thinking? I don't think I could leave Charlotte."

Autumn hugs me and whispers in my ear. "If you end up staying out here, I'll come once I'm done with school."

"Perfect."

I hug my mom and she and Autumn make their way down the hall to their room. I turn back and Liam is still standing there.

"You must be tired. It's after midnight," I whisper.

"Are we okay?" he asks. He steps closer but stops just short of touching me. "I feel bad about the way we left things last night."

That feels like such a long time ago now. So much has happened with Hudson since then. I don't know why I feel slightly guilty about that in front of Liam. There's no reason I should. Except that he looks so sad right now.

"Things are okay on my end," I tell him. "I'm not mad at you and...things are good with Hudson." It's obvious my face gives me away because Liam's expression changes from sad to slightly gutted. How is that possible? He's Liam freaking Taylor. "I'm sorry, Liam," I whisper.

"Don't be. I'm happy for you. Sad for myself," he says.

I reach out and take his hand, squeezing it for a second

before pulling away. He ducks his head, his eyes still on me, and then turns and walks to his room.

I'm exhausted, and yet I still wish I could knock on Hudson's door. It was strange going the whole day without seeing him after our night together. I haven't stopped thinking about him for a second, that's for sure, and I still feel the reminder of where he's been. It's the best kind of ache, and certainly not painful enough to not revisit the whole scenario again tonight. I open the door to my room, deciding to set my things down and think about it a little more before going to Hudson's room.

He's sitting on my bed and stands up when he sees me there, looking as sleepy as I feel. "I'm sorry. I should've texted you that I was in here. I tried to sneak a note under your door and heard someone coming, so I just came in before I got caught."

I step into his arms and laugh. "I'm glad you're here. I wanted to sneak over to your room, and now I don't have to." He leans down and kisses me and I let my body sink into his.

"I haven't been able to stop thinking about you all day," he whispers.

"Same.

"How was your day?"

"It was an adventure."

When I don't say anything else, he kisses me again, and in seconds it's so heated, he almost makes me forget all about the photographers, Liam's sad eyes, and the fact that my mom and sister are leaving tomorrow.

44

HARD WORK PAYS OFF

When I come out of my room the next morning, Dad is in the living room talking to my mom in hushed tones. Mom's luggage is next to her and my dad is leaning close, saying something that has her on the verge of tears.

"What's going on?" I ask.

Her head shakes slightly and I'm not sure if it's directed at me or my dad. Autumn walks down the hall toward us, rolling her suitcase, and comes to a stop next to me.

"Everything okay?" she asks.

"Just wish you guys could stay longer," Dad says.

"Don't start." My mom takes a step back and gives me a huge hug.

"I'm taking you to the airport," I say in her ear, unsure why she's hugging me so hard now.

"I've got a car coming." She pulls back and smooths my hair away from my face. "I hope you don't mind—I didn't want you to have to make that trip and then drive all the way back here alone. And it's hard to prolong our goodbyes." Her eyes fill with tears as she puts her hands on my cheeks. "You get what you need out of this time here, Summer. I hope you're going to get inspiration for your story now that you've got a new laptop and are seeing the filming process firsthand." She glances at my dad and doesn't bother lowering her voice when she says her next sentence. "Don't forget to follow your dream of being a screenwriter and don't let your dad or anyone else get in your way of that."

"What's that supposed to mean?" If he weren't trying to get her to stay, I'm sure he'd sound angrier than he does right now.

"Did you even know she writes screenplays?" Autumn asks.

We all turn to look at my dad and he stands here with his mouth slightly open.

"Exactly," Mom ends up answering for him. She looks at me again and repeats it. "*Exactly*. Don't let his plans for your time this summer get in the way of your dreams for your future." And then she sets her eyes on my dad with an expression that has my heart pounding hard. It's full of steel and colder than I've ever seen her be.

"I've always wanted y'all to have a strong relationship with your father—and you know how I feel about a strong work ethic and want you girls to know the meaning of hard work—but the day you put work before your family is the day I'll know I've failed as your mother." Her face lightens as she tries to smile at Autumn and me. "But hard work pays off, no matter who it serves, and I believe it will pay off in spades with both of you. You both have what it takes. Just remember what's most important." She grips our hands between hers.

Damn. My dad's face is red and he looks like he's a mixture of livid, confused, and hurt. Whatever happened between the two of them during the night has my mom unloading all of her bullets.

Autumn and I look at each other and she gives me a big hug. "I'll call you later," she whispers.

"Please do. I need to be filled in on whatever this is that's happening," I whisper back.

"Hell yeah. I'll get to the bottom of it."

She pulls away and Hudson walks up then, looking rushed. He grins at me and then directs his attention to my dad. "The last scene went well, but Winslet isn't nailing this one. I told her and Liam to take a break and we'll start again in twenty."

"I'll be out there for that," Dad says. He takes a step back and then it's like he changes his mind again and kisses my mom on the cheek. When he pulls away, he looks at all of us. "I've made a lot of mistakes. With all of you...but your mother most of all. I know I just keep doing the wrong thing and I'd like a chance to make it up to all of you."

My mom makes a face. "Work on making things right with your daughters and do me a favor—leave me out of it."

My mouth drops. She grips my arm. "I love you, baby. Don't forget what I've said, and don't get taken advantage of for another second of this summer, do you hear me?"

I nod dumbly, too shocked to say anything. She walks toward the front door and Autumn hurriedly catches up with her, opening the door for her and looking back to wave at me before they walk out. Part of me wishes I was going with them, but Hudson moves into place next to me and puts his arm around my shoulder.

"I like her," he says. "Both of them...*all of you*." He looks at me and winks, and then we both look at my dad, who's watching the door like he's willing my mom and sister to walk back through it.

Liam rushes in the door then, distracting all of us. When I see the look on his face, I feel a sense of dread.

"What's wrong?" I ask.

"It's not good," he says.

"What's going on, Liam?" Dad asks.

"I think we need to break up," Liam says, still looking at me.

"About time," Hudson says.

"Not so fast." My dad holds up his hand. "What's going on?"

Liam looks at me apologetically and holds out his device. When I look at the screen, all the blood rushes from my face.

45

FALLING

THERE ARE A HANDFUL OF PICTURES OF ME—TWO ARE WITH Liam, one is me by myself, and the other two are with my mom and Autumn. The problem is, with the exception of the one with Liam, I look awful in the rest of the pictures. It's like they purposely took the worst possible pictures of me and made sure to use a good one with Liam.

Why is Liam Taylor's new love so sad?

Summer Winters was seen on Liam's arm earlier this week and then out shopping solo with her mom and sister. Take a look at the expression on her face when she's with Liam, compared to how she looks when he's not around. Looks like there's trouble in paradise already.

"Don't pay any attention to what they're saying," Liam says as I'm reading it. "I just don't like how they're already turning on you."

"You warned me it could be like this, but...that sure was fast," I say, handing Liam his phone.

"I don't like it at all," he adds. "I don't feel right about dragging you into this."

"I'm fine. It feels weird to know they were watching me when I didn't even know it for some of these, but I'll just be more careful. If I ever leave this house again," I add, laughing.

Both Hudson and Liam don't crack a smile and my dad puts his hand on my shoulder.

"It'd be a good idea for you to have someone with you at all times, preferably Liam or myself," he says.

"I'd be happy to contribute to the *watch out for Summer* plan too," Hudson says, smiling at me.

My dad looks between me and Hudson but doesn't say anything. I want to tell him then that Hudson is the one I like and that I think we have a chance at something *great* if I wasn't...say..."dating" someone else right now. But Hudson seems to read my expression and he gets a panicked look on his face.

It stings.

Maybe I'm misreading everything since we're not talking about it outright, but I decide to have the conversation with Hudson before saying anything to my dad. Who knows? This could all just be a fling with him. He might not be in it for more than the summer...and that would be really embarrassing if I acted like we were more than we are.

"Say the word and I'll end this today," Liam says.

"That would make your agent so upset. She got that interview for us and everything. Let's just take a breath and wait it out." I didn't know I'd be the one to calm everyone else down about this when it's me they're talking about, but there really are more important things to care about right now.

The main one being if the guy I slept with last night is really into me or not.

"Maybe don't go online for the unforeseeable future," Liam says grimly.

"I won't. And just let me know if it's something I *need* to know; otherwise, it's probably best if I just stay in the dark about what they're saying about me."

"Okay. Thank you, Summer," Liam says, kissing my cheek. He steps back and my face flushes with all the attention focused on me. My dad and Hudson are both studying me closer than I'd like and Liam is being extra sweet.

"Well, this is feeling weird, so I'm gonna go. I think I'll write for a while. My mom encouraged me not to give up on what I'm passionate about, so I'm going to listen to her advice." I turn and start walking to my room.

"Will you be up for returning to work tomorrow?" Dad asks.

I stay facing the hall to my room and don't turn around. "Sure. And we can talk about my schedule for the remainder of the film. Once summer is up, I need to get a job and start looking for a place...figure out where I want to be..."

When my dad speaks again, he's right behind me and he puts his hand on my shoulder again, turning me around. "I hope you'll stay here. I'm not ready to see you go. You're comfortable here, right?"

I shrug. "It's fine, but I'm not sure how I'll feel when the next film begins and there's a whole new crew."

"I heard what your mom said and I took it to heart," he says. "I want you to be happy here. Are you not happy with the job I've provided you?"

It takes everything in me not to roll my eyes. "I'm meant to do more than be an errand girl, Dad. Not that I'm putting down the job, it's just that I have my BA in creative writing, and I'd like to get a job that pays me while I pursue my dream. I'd think you, of all people, would understand that."

"It's like you insist on believing the worst in me," he says darkly.

I sigh. "If you keep choosing to not understand, then I'll really have no choice but to go."

"No, I'm trying. I'm really trying. I just don't know what more you want from me. I mean, look at this place. You're living on beachfront property. You've gotten money from Liam," he says under his breath, "and you're working on a blockbuster film. I don't know what more you could want."

"I guess we're just not going to see eye to eye on this," I tell him. "It's great for right now. I know I have to start somewhere. But wiping Winslet's nose and tweezing a stray eyebrow is not furthering my writing career, and hiding away in this house isn't either."

He exhales loudly but seems resigned to what I'm telling him. I'm not trying to be difficult, but the man seems to have a block about some subjects when it's something that doesn't fit his agenda.

Hudson comes up to us and puts his arm around my shoulder. "You should also know that I'm falling for your daughter."

46

SUCKY TIMING

My dad's eyes narrow just as I turn to face Hudson, my mouth dropping as I try to form words.

"What?" Is what finally comes out of my mouth.

Hudson grins. "You heard me. I'm falling for you." He takes my hand and brings it to his lips, kissing my palm. He looks at my dad. "With all due respect, Cole, I have not wanted to rock the boat with you over dating your daughter, and I tried to fight it, but..." He shakes his head.

My dad puts his fingers over his eyes and squeezes, saying a few choice words under his breath.

"They're good together," Liam says, grinning.

"You knew about this too?" Dad asks.

"Yeah," Liam says, snorting. "When smoke blew out of his ears every time I came near Summer, it was a pretty good indicator. I let him know our arrangement was just that—an arrangement."

"Well, I'm glad you guys have it all figured out." Dad's voice is full of sarcasm and his expression is granite. "I would've hoped you'd respect our working relationship and keep things professional between the two of you," he says to Hudson. "I don't even know what to think."

"It doesn't affect his job, so it shouldn't affect your working relationship," I say.

My dad snorts. "How's it going to be when the two of you break up? Because you will, you know. Nothing lasts forever in Hollywood."

"Is that why you were pushing so hard for Mom to stay? So you could break her heart again when you got tired of her in a few months?" I narrow my eyes at him, my heart racing in disgust. "Sometimes I really dislike who you are."

My dad takes a step back, his face turning red. His eyes are sad, but he doesn't say anything to soften what he's already said.

"What happened between the two of you anyway? Why was she so angry with you when you left?" I ask.

"I don't want to talk about this right now." He takes another step back and starts to turn and walk away. I reach out and grab his arm.

"Why not? Nothing seems to be sacred in this house, so why can't we all just speak freely now? You've had a girl-friend while hitting on Mom." My hand falls off of his arm. "You've expected me to fake-date Liam, yet you have the audacity to get angry that I'm actually dating Hudson.

What's with all the double standards? It's a moral whiplash, trying to figure out where your integrity lies."

There's a deep intake of air all around. I'm not sure who gasped the loudest, but when I look at Hudson and Liam and my father, they're all stunned speechless. I can't tell if they're afraid for me or proud or something not so easily defined. The layers of manipulation seem to run deep where my father is concerned.

"Unless we can figure out how to communicate, I won't be staying as long as I thought." I turn toward my bedroom and start to walk away.

"Wait for me," Hudson says, falling into step next to me.

"Where would you go?" my dad calls. "I thought you wanted to work in Hollywood."

"I can go be someone else's right-hand person. Liam will give me a good recommendation, won't you?" I smile at Liam, who is already nodding.

"You know I will."

My dad glares at Liam and he shrugs, still smiling.

"It's not easy to find an affordable place to live," my dad starts.

"We can go to my apartment," Hudson says. "There's plenty of room."

My heart starts to pound at the thought of living with Hudson. It's too soon, but the thought that he'd stand up to my dad for me and offer his place warms my heart.

"This is getting out of hand," Dad says. "No one needs to go anywhere."

"Okay, then talk. What's going on with you and Mom? And Bella?"

"This is ridiculous," he snaps.

"I agree. You're ridiculous." My cheeks heat when I say it because as angry as I am with my father and as fed up as I am with this roller coaster that I just want off of, I'm not used to being so mouthy with him.

"Well, first of all, I don't owe you an explanation. And second, I'd rather not do this here. Can we go somewhere more private?"

Liam and Hudson look at me, waiting for me to say what I want. I've never been more grateful for these guys than I am right now.

"We're all living here together. That's what happens when you invite a bunch of people to live under one roof." I'm about to give in though. It's not like I want to hash everything out in front of the whole house, but he's infuriating me with his sudden desire for privacy. He's the one who forced the close proximity.

"She's pregnant, okay? Are you happy now?" he says. He shoves his hands in his pockets and stares down at the ground, while I stare at him with my mouth hanging open.

"Who's pregnant?"

"Bella."

I swallow hard, unsure of which emotion to tackle first. "And you thought that would be a good time to bring Mom back into your life because...why exactly?"

"I don't expect you to understand," he says. "I just-I love her and I hoped she'd give me another chance."

"I'd say your timing is the worst."

47

COCKY MUCH?

I SLAM THE DOOR HARD—WELL, AS SOON AS HUDSON IS safely inside my room too. I pace the floor, back and forth.

"Can you believe him?"

"No, I can't," he admits.

"I wonder how many other babies he has floating around out there." I put my hands on my hips and keep walking. He puts his hands on my waist and I pause, my head falling back on his chest. "My poor mom. I wonder if she was hopeful this time. She seemed to actually be—I don't know—entertaining the thought of him while she was here. I can't imagine what she's thinking now. Well, I guess I can because I've never seen her as angry as she was this morning."

I hear myself blabbing away, but I can't seem to stop myself, and Hudson's hands rub the sides of my arms, calming me down a little more with each pass.

"I know you need to be at work," I tell him. "Don't worry about me. I'll be okay. I need to think. I don't know what I'm going to do, but I need to think."

"Will you let me know if you need me? I don't mind getting out of work today. In fact, it'd probably be a good idea."

"I'll let you know if I need you." I turn around and put my arms around his neck. "I'm so glad you told him. About us." He lowers his head until it's touching mine. "You're falling for me?" I whisper.

He kisses me and for those few moments, I forget about everything else.

My phone rings and I jump back, startled. I hold onto Hudson's shoulder. "Sorry. Don't know why I'm so jumpy."

I check my phone and don't recognize the number, so I decline the call. But it starts ringing immediately again. And again.

"Guess I should see who that is..." I answer the phone and a woman with a raspy voice says hello.

"I'm with *The Hollywood Enquiry* and I wondered if you have any comment on your relationship with Liam Taylor."

"No, no comment." I hang up the phone and toss it on the bed. "How did they get my cell number?"

"Probably got it from a friend of yours. They have their ways of getting that out of people."

"Ugh."

There's a knock on the door and then Liam says quietly, "It's me."

Hudson checks to make sure I'm okay with him opening the door. When I nod, he walks over and lets Liam in.

"Hey. You okay? Quite the bomb to drop on you," he says.

"Yeah, I'm okay." I wave it off like it's no big deal even though the news that my dad is having a baby with another woman after trying to get back together with my mom is doing a number on me.

"Well, listen. I meant what I said earlier. We can let everyone know we've broken up and that would be one less thing for you to worry about."

"Catherine won't like that."

"I just got off the phone with her." He shrugs and grins. "She'll just have to get okay. She asked that we wait until our big spread comes out and then break the news."

"When will that be?"

"Another week."

"That's not bad," I say. I glance at Hudson, who doesn't seem happy about this, but he doesn't look mad either. They both just look concerned about how I'm taking everything. "I can hang out here for another week."

"You're leaving?" Liam asks, his forehead creasing in the middle. "No, don't do that."

"I haven't decided what I'm doing yet. I don't know how I can keep staying in this house though."

Hudson takes a deep breath and goes to stand by the window.

"We'll keep your dad occupied and you just do whatever you need to do until the movie is over. We're almost done. It won't be the same if you leave before we're done filming."

"I don't want to miss out on that," I admit.

"Let me handle your dad. Just don't leave," Liam says.

"I'll think about it." I smile at him and he walks to the door.

"So we can make a statement the day after the spread comes out—sound good?" he asks.

"That just feels like such a waste. I won't be taking your money when I'm not even doing all we committed to, just so we're clear."

"You're not giving that money back. You could use that to get a place here," he says.

"Or stay at my place," Hudson reminds me.

"You have options," Liam says.

I sigh. "Thanks. You both have been amazing to me. It hasn't even been that long since I met you, and yet you've both changed my life."

"It's not every day you survive a plane crash together," Liam moves back by me, putting his arm around my shoulder. He drops it when he sees Hudson's face and grins. "Or you meet Hudson Callihan and pick him over the hottest actor Hollywood has ever known."

Hudson snorts. "Cocky much?"

Liam rolls his eyes, but he's still wearing that grin that rarely leaves his face.

I put my hands on both of their backs and push them toward the door. "Go. I need to think or write or plot my dad's demise. I can't tell which yet."

"No demises except in fiction," Hudson says. He bends to give me one more kiss and they both reach the door. He opens it and looks back. "How about I take you to my apartment when I'm done for the day? You can see what you think. And you can have it to yourself if you're not ready for me ... well, you can see what you think about all of it later."

I smile. His nerves are endearing. "Sounds good."

I shut the door behind them and pull out my new laptop.

Once I start typing, I can't stop.

48
───────

THE HIGH

SINCE THE STORY I'D BEEN WORKING ON IS SOMEWHERE ON THE ocean floor right about now and I sucked at keeping back-ups, I scrap the story idea I'd been working on. It wasn't flowing as quickly as I would've liked anyway.

What comes out is different than what I was expecting...

Death didn't flatter him in the slightest.

What? Didn't see that line coming, but I go with it anyway and keep typing.

After a life of privilege, Carl didn't expect his end to come in such a nondescript way. He'd had the finest money could offer— not just houses, clothes, cars, but also women, opportunities, experiences. His was a life well-lived, so it was a surprise to him when he woke up on the last day of his life...alone.

He knew it was the end, you see.

Well, he'd been told his end was imminent. He just hadn't believed it could be true. Until now.

He knew his sins had caught up with him. Because along with his life of luxury and all he could ever want, he'd been operating under the mistaken theory that nothing would ever catch up with him. He'd learned only the week before that he'd been so wrong.

"An eye for an eye," the woman had said.

He'd been at a Broadway show in his usual box, and as always, he enjoyed a glass of whiskey at his seat during intermission. It was brought to him by the attendant who served him each time he visited, and that night the guy didn't linger. Also as it had always been. What was different this time was the woman who came in afterward. Carl was looking across the theatre and didn't hear when someone entered his box.

She'd put her hands over his eyes and whispered in his ear, "Your time is almost up. What will you do to atone for your sins?"

"I don't live a life of regrets," Carl said, chuckling.

He'd tried to pry the fingers off of his eyes, but the woman had a surprisingly strong grip. He squirmed a little bit, uncomfortable for the first time since he'd heard her voice. She smelled like tobacco and vanilla, his favorite combination.

I type away for hours, getting in five thousand words before the day is over. A record for me. Especially after not writing in so long. I feel energized and a plan is brewing. My first drafts are written in novel form, even though I see the story playing out in my mind as a film right away. I'll go back and change the format on the second or third draft as more scenes begin to take root.

When Hudson knocks and sticks his head in my room later, I wave him in excitedly.

"Feeling better?" he asks.

"Definitely. I needed a day like this. Writing, not being around everybody—not you," I add.

"It's okay if you need a break from me too. It's a lot, everyone living in each other's space all the time."

"Yeah, I didn't realize how intense all of this would be. I feel better though. I always do after writing."

"Do you still want to go see my place or do you want to keep writing?"

"How about we wait? Let the article of Liam and me come out, and then maybe a few weeks after that, we can 'break up' and I won't be so nervous about whatever comes out online when we're seen together..."

He smiles and tugs me toward him. "You're a good person. I guess I can stay another month in this love triangle."

I roll my eyes. "You know it's no love triangle."

He lifts an eyebrow. "I'm not always sure Liam doesn't think so, but I believe you."

I laugh and am relieved that we're talking this out. It feels good to have everything out in the open.

"I have this idea," I tell him. My hands are on his chest and it's hard to think straight when he's looking at me like he wants to strip my clothes off and throw me onto that bed, but I forge ahead. "An idea for a movie. I'm writing it as a novel now, but I envision it as a movie..."

"Tell me everything," he says.

We talk for hours about the story idea. A man who gets his comeuppance. We talk right through dinner and don't even think about eating until around midnight. We're both charged and the ideas have been flowing for hours. I really think we're onto something.

"We should pitch this to your dad," he says before we sneak to the kitchen. The house is quieter than it usually is, even at this time of night, and he peeks down the hall to see if anyone is around.

I frown. "I don't want my dad involved with this."

"*Oh.* I know you're wanting to do it on your own, but... you should really consider..." He sees the look on my face and stops. "Or I know someone else we could pitch it to."

"Why are you just now telling me that?" I whisper, getting the giggles with the way we're sneaking down the hall.

"I don't like to jinx things, so I won't say too much, but —" He wriggles his eyebrows and I clamp my hand across my mouth to keep the cackle in.

If you've never had a day of almost manic creativity flowing through you, I'll explain it like this: it's like every nerve and every thought and every cell is electrified with *purpose*. The impossible seems possible. The dormant crackles to life. Hope infuses with promise and there is only what is right in front of you, and that thing, that creation, is incredible.

Now the next day or month or year, whatever the case may be, when you come crashing down and see your work as crap and everything is just mediocre, blah, and meaningless—that will come and that will be as devastating as the flip side was brilliant.

But when the flow is happening, you embrace it and ride that wave for as long as possible.

To have that connection with Hudson is almost too good to be true, and if I were not in the middle of such an amazing high, it would scare me.

49

SLOW BURN

I CALL MY MOM BEFORE WORK THE NEXT MORNING, GRATEFUL for the time difference for once.

"Hey, you okay?" she asks.

"Checking to see if you are. You texted to let me know you made it home, but you didn't answer my call...which was fine, but I just needed to hear you to make sure you're okay."

"I'm good," she says, bright and cheery and fake.

"I know about the baby."

"Oh." I hear the crack in her voice and she's quiet for a

moment. "I can't believe I believed him for even a second. He really almost had me convinced that I should give him another chance." She laughs and then it turns into a sob. "I thought I knew better by now! And he has a girlfriend! I feel like the worst person."

"I've just assumed he was with Bella—he's downplayed everything about her with me too and I'm living with them. I'm so sorry, Mama."

"No, I'm sorry. I'm embarrassed about what a bad example I've been to you girls, to even consider putting all of us in that position again. I've learned my lesson. Never again."

The sadness in her voice is more than I can take. Tears drip down my cheeks and I try to get it together before I speak again. "Can I do anything to help?"

"I'll be okay," she says. "I've survived him before and I'll do it again."

"I can come home. Today even," I tell her.

"Don't you dare change your plans for me. Just like I was saying about your dad getting in the way of your dreams for the future, I'm not going to get in your way either."

"I know, but this is different. I want to be there for you and you're not Dad. I'd do anything for you."

Her voice breaks again as she says, "I know you would, baby girl, and that means everything. The best thing you can do for me is to do what you love. Chase your happiness. And don't let any man derail that."

"Okay. I hear you." I wipe my face and take a deep breath. "I love you. Please talk to me whenever you need."

"Thank you. I will. Please don't worry about me," she says.

I laugh. "Yeah. Impossible, but okay."

We hang up and I finish getting ready. I'm on my way to

the kitchen when Bella comes around the corner. She comes to an abrupt halt when she sees me.

"Summer—can I talk to you?"

I nod and we head back to my room. I shut the door and she leans against it, her eyes filling with tears.

This morning is starting out great.

"I'm really sorry for how I acted while your mom was here. I panicked. My hormones have been all over the place and I just...I didn't know what to do." She looks so forlorn, her arms wrapped around herself like she's shielding herself from everyone and everything.

"Are you going to be okay?" I ask. I put my hand on her arm and she looks up, surprised.

She wipes her face and I hand her a tissue.

"I don't really know." Her face flushes. "Your dad told me you know about the baby."

I nod and her face breaks as she cries again.

"I know I'm crazy for hoping he'll be here for this baby, but I feel like I have to at least try."

"Well, I won't pretend to understand your dynamic with my dad, but I'd like to be in my brother or sister's life whether my dad ends up being involved or not."

"He says he will be," she whispers.

"I know, but he doesn't have a great track record. Just promise me you'll take care of *you* in all of this."

She throws her arms around me and hugs me. "I can't tell you what this means to me. I thought you'd hate me."

"I don't hate you. I'm angry with my dad right now, but I don't hate you."

Her smile is wobbly, her eyes still glassy as she nods and opens the door. "Thank you."

I smile and walk out with her. Not much time for breakfast in the house, so I walk outside and get my coffee there, arriving on set at the time I usually do. Everyone seems surprised to see me there, but I do my job, ignore my dad, and when we're done for the day, Hudson and I hole up in my room again, writing and plotting. I might not have my life figured out as well as I need to yet, but I could coast this way for a while and be okay.

Later, I'm on top of Hudson, his hands on my breasts as he thrusts into me. We've been doing this for a while now and every time we get close, we slow down, enjoying the buildup.

"I think I've finally found what I enjoy more than movies," he says, grinning up at me. His hands find my backside and he clenches me tighter.

"Speak for yourself," I whisper, cackling when he jabs my side.

I drop my chest to his and kiss him and he flips me onto my back. This time we're unable to savor the slow burn and we race each other over the edge.

50

INTEGRITY

THE MAGAZINE IS OPEN TO MY SPREAD WITH LIAM ON THE dining room table a few days later. I look at all the pictures first, glad that I at least look my best if I'm going to be playing the part of *Hollywood's Hottest Actor's Girlfriend.* That's what it says in bold letters...

HOLLYWOOD'S HOTTEST ACTOR HAS A GIRLFRIEND!

It appears Liam Taylor has finally found the girl of his dreams. The daughter of director Cole Winters, with whom

Taylor has worked on several films, Summer Winters claims she didn't know much about Taylor's work before she met him. Hard to believe, since her dad and boyfriend have worked together on other projects.

"From what I've seen since meeting him, I'm definitely a fan," she insists.

You and the rest of the world, Summer Winters!

When asked if the chemistry between them was instant, Liam jumps in and says, "Hell, yeah. I mean, look at her. I haven't been able to keep my hands off of her since the day she gave me permission to kiss her."

I roll my eyes but have to laugh at that. When has Liam ever asked permission for anything?

The true superfans of the longtime bachelor will be sad to note that Liam seems completely smitten with Summer.

"She makes me want to be a better man."

If that doesn't make the hardest heart swoon, what will?

This couple survived a harrowing plane crash and another brush with death when Summer was stung in the ocean by a box jellyfish. If this sounds like a movie to you, we agree—we'd love to see these two heat up the big screen!

When asked if they have any plans to act together, Summer is the first to say that she is not an actress. She will, however, be pursuing a career as a screenwriter and possibly director, in the steps of her father. Let it be said that we will be the first in line should Ms. Winters ever make a film based on her relationship with Liam Taylor.

. . .

I flip to the last picture and it shows the two of us looking at each other and laughing. My head is thrown back and he's leaning in, looking at me with adoration. The guy is good, I'll give him that, and for all my talk about not being an actress, I sure am hanging in there. It makes me cringe that this is what's out there now about me. I'll be known as Liam's girlfriend, the one who made him settle down and then the one who either breaks his heart or gets her heart broken, depending on how it's spun.

I toss the magazine back on the table. It happens all the time in Hollywood, and as quickly as it got all amped up in the press, it'll die down even quicker when the next hot story comes out.

At least that's how I hope all of this goes down.

————

After working all day on a set an hour from the house, we shuffle back inside after an annoying day of stops and starts. There were scenes that took far longer than planned. Winslet was in a foul mood and didn't know her lines. There were camera glitches and the lighting wasn't working well. My dad lost it on the crew, and all I want to do is take a bath and work on my story.

I've been staying off of social media because the article is everywhere I look. I hope this helps Liam in the way his agent is counting on.

I'm stripping to get into the steaming tub when someone knocks on my door. I grab my robe and crack the door open.

Hudson stands there with a bottle of wine. I grin and open the door wider, letting him in.

"I thought we should celebrate my girlfriend's beautiful photo shoot," he says, holding up two glasses.

I grin and lean up to kiss him. "That's quite a healthy attitude to have."

He sets the bottle and glasses down and wraps his arms around my waist, kissing me hard. My robe ends up on the floor and I'm on the bed before I know it.

"Since I'm the one who gets to do this, I'm feeling great about the whole thing," he says, kissing down my neck.

It's much later when I remember the bath I'd planned on taking. I have to add hot water to the bath as we both climb in it.

"Never thought I'd be taking a bath in Cole Winters' house," he says, shuddering as he tugs my back against his chest.

"Please don't bring my dad up when we're both naked."

"I know. It's not working for me either." He laughs.

I flip over and face him. "How much longer do you think it will realistically take to be done filming?"

"Another four weeks at most, why?"

"I've decided that's how long I'm giving my dad—I'll work for him another four weeks and then I'll pursue what I want. I can't stop thinking about the story we're working on. I have a good feeling about it."

He pulls me flush against him, his hands on my backside.

"I do too. It'll be another six months or more before we're done with post-production, which gives us a lot of time to be working on the story in the meantime."

"What will you tell my dad when you're working with me?"

He's quiet for a minute. "I guess we'll deal with that when the time comes," he says finally.

The look on his face makes me nervous and he seems to realize it because he jumps in to add, "Seeing how all of this has gone with you—it's important to me to surround myself with people of integrity. This summer has brought a lot of things to light and I'm ready to make some changes...but...I do know your dad means well."

I don't say anything.

"Just think about showing him this story when we're done," he says. "I won't keep pushing it, but just promise you'll think about it."

51

THAT GOOD

THE NEXT MORNING, I LEAVE A FEW MINUTES EARLIER THAN usual to go to the shoot. It's the last of our scenes on the beach near the house, and in about a week and a half, if all goes as planned, the rest will be finished up in a studio about half an hour from here. As I walk out on the patio, my phone starts buzzing. I ignore it, hoping to check it before I start work but wanting to get to the set on time.

I'm about to round the corner, out of our gate, when I run into a man with a hat and sunglasses on, his camera already poised to take my picture. I stumble back, nearly losing my footing, and there's another photographer there who steadies me while also snapping a photo.

"Step away from her." Liam's voice is low and as intimidating as when he's played an assassin in his films. I'd be scared if I were these guys, but they just smirk at me and then look back at him as if we're all buds. "You're on private property," Liam says. "I'll give you ten seconds to get out of here and forget how you found the place."

"Come on, man, we just need a good shot of you and your girl. Smile for the camera?" The guy closest to me snaps at least five pictures in the time it takes Liam to reach my side.

"You're not getting the message. You need to get out of here now, before I call security. You won't like their approach," Liam says. He puts his arm around me and scowls at them and they snap, snap, snap more pictures.

The quieter one nods and turns to go. "Thank you. We'll see our way out."

We watch as they walk away from us, down the beach in the opposite direction from the house.

I sag against Liam. "I'm surprised they haven't been here sooner."

"I'm not sure why our security didn't catch them this morning. I'll look into that, and we'll need to tell your dad they were here." He turns to face me. "The only problem is, I'm not so sure he isn't the one who told them where to find us."

"You think my dad was behind that? Why?"

"I'd be more surprised if it wasn't him," he admits.

"Ugh, he just doesn't make it easy to like him, does he?"

"It's an old trick," Liam says. "Don't take it personally if it was him. He's just trying to get exposure for this movie."

"And using me to do it."

Liam makes a face and tugs me into his side. "I'm sorry about all this. Are things at least good behind the scenes?" he whispers. "You and Hudson disappear at night, so I'm assuming things are going well?"

I nod, trying to hide the grin that wants to take over my face. "Really well."

We're about a hundred yards from the tent where we're set up for the day, and so far, it's only the film crew and a few of the actors getting their makeup done. I don't see my dad anywhere.

"Good," Liam says finally. "Don't let anyone ruin it, not even me."

I turn to look at him and see what he means by that, but he takes off toward the water and starts doing warm-ups with his double. I look around for Hudson and he isn't here yet. He left before I woke up this morning.

I've thought about what Hudson said about my dad way too much. It's leaving an unsettled feeling in my gut that I'm trying to override.

The two of them show up a few minutes later and we get to work.

Later that afternoon, Liam shows me his phone and there are photos of us on several online sites. All of them show us scowling at the cameras.

"Don't you love how the camera adds twenty pounds, Summer?" Winslet chirps over our shoulders. She reaches out and swipes up to see the next photo and laughs. "More like thirty in this one."

"Shut up, Winslet," Liam says. "Summer is beautiful, and you know it. Otherwise, you wouldn't take every opportunity to try to tear her down. It just makes you look pathetic."

She shrugs and smirks when I look at her over my shoulder. "The camera doesn't lie. Just like it doesn't lie every time you and I kiss, Liam. I haven't seen the chemistry between the two of you that you and I have when we're acting out this *trash* movie. I think that says a lot right there." She starts to walk away, and he puts his hand on her elbow and turns her to face us again.

"This 'trash' movie is going to make your career, so I wouldn't let anyone else hear you saying that. And what our chemistry says is that I'm a better actor than you realize. Because every time I have to kiss you, it actually physically turns my stomach." Liam makes a disgusted face and I feel hot with how uncomfortable this conversation is, but I can't lie and say it isn't a little bit entertaining to hear him give it to Winslet as hard as she dishes it out. "Kissing you is like kissing a fish who is trying to be a mermaid. It just never adds up. But I make it *look* good for the camera because *I am that good*."

She's gone even paler than usual by the time he's done, and I feel a little bad for her when she presses her lips together and takes a step back.

But in true Winslet fashion, she rallies. "If you guys are so tight, why do I keep seeing Hudson sneaking into her room every night?"

52

GET OUT

Winslet puts her hand on her hip, her eyes gleaming in uncontained delight.

Liam laces his fingers through mine and leans in close to her. "We're working on a project after hours. You think I'm not in there with them?" He shakes his head, grinning when she can't hide her disappointment. "Aw, you thought you were telling me something I didn't know..." He kisses the side of my head and I look at him like he hung the moon because he *is* pretty great. "Quit messing with my girlfriend, Winslet. It won't end well for you."

She gives us both a withering look and walks off.

I start laughing and cover my mouth when it's too loud. Liam looks proud of himself, and I don't blame him. He handled that like a pro.

"I need you around to slay all the rude people who come my way," I say as we walk toward the house.

"I would be happy to slay all the dragons for you, Summer Winters."

My arm is around his waist, and I squeeze him hard. "You are a most excellent boyfriend, Liam Taylor," I tell him.

He grins down at me and then frowns when a huge crash comes from the pool area. Yelling follows and we rush to see what's going on. There's a pile of Oscars on the patio and Bella is tossing my dad's clothes out next.

Monique is trying to stop Bella and my dad is fuming while Bella yells her head off.

"I will not be treated no better than a maid when I'm carrying your baby. Get out of here. Get everyone out."

"This is my house," my dad roars. "If anyone should get out, it's you. You're acting like a child."

"I have cooked and cleaned and done your laundry for so long it's not even funny. I've fed your dinner parties; I've replaced things that were broken from your careless guests...I've stitched clothes for you that you never even acknowledged me fixing. I have lived for you, and yes, I've gotten to live in this pretty house, surrounded by pretty things...and that is the *least* of what I deserve. I have not been in this for money—you wanted me to give up my job to stay with you and I did...a good job." She shakes her head and sobs. "God, I was so stupid. I just need a little time without goddamn Winslet snarking at me every second. I need time to figure out how I'm going to have a child with a jackass father. Get everyone *out of here* or I will make a real scene," she yells.

"You don't think that's what you're doing?" My dad is incredulous, and I cringe because he seems oblivious to the fact that he's only stirring her up more.

"Dad," I say, putting my hand on his back, "why don't we give Bella space and find an Airbnb somewhere, a hotel even? Hudson and I can stay at his place and I'm sure everyone else will be fine going somewhere else for a few nights."

"This is crazy. This is *my house*," he yells.

"No one is disputing that, but if you want to keep the peace, you should give her a little space right now. She's distraught, Dad, look at her. Give her a break."

He looks at Monique helplessly and she nods. "Please," she says.

He points at Bella, stabbing the air with his words. "Take a few nights and get yourself under control. I don't owe you this house. I don't owe you anything. You tricked me with this baby and I'll provide for it, but you need to stop with the theatrics. I only have time for that on set—it has no place in our relationship."

He stalks into the house, leaving Bella sobbing. Monique holds her arms out and Bella falls into them.

"You're exhausted," Monique says quietly. "You have to sleep. Are you sure you wouldn't rather get away? Go somewhere just the two of us?"

"I'm too tired to go anywhere," she sobs. "I just need the quiet."

Monique leads her inside, and Liam and I look at each other as we go into the house.

"This is why it's probably not a great idea to all live in the same house while shooting," he says. "I'm going to suggest we all figure out our own lodging...most of the cast lives within an hour of here anyway." He leans in and whispers in my ear, "And this will give you and Hudson the privacy you need."

"You really think we can get away with staying at his place right now with the paparazzi on us? Seems risky now that I think about it."

Hudson comes into the kitchen while we're looking for a snack and lifts his eyebrows. "I missed the fallout. Were you around?"

"We were. It was brutal."

"I just got a text from your dad saying to let everyone know we're moving to an Airbnb tonight...and that I need to find the Airbnb," he says, making a face.

"About that. How about everyone just goes home—I think Hannah and Maddie are the only ones who don't live as close, and I'm ready to go home, man. Aren't you?"

"Well, I don't live in as cushy a house as you, but yes," Hudson says, grinning.

"Hannah and Maddie can stay with me," Liam says.

"Won't that look strange when you have a girlfriend?" Hudson asks.

"You guys are welcome to come too. There's plenty of room. I thought you might want the privacy."

"Oh, we do." Hudson looks at me.

"You're right though," I tell him. "We shouldn't go to your apartment. And Liam, you shouldn't be in your house with two girls who aren't your girlfriend. This is so crazy. Why are we still doing this?"

"You don't have to keep doing it. I'll come up with a good story of why we're over, trust me." Liam grins and grabs a beer out of the fridge, popping the top.

"No, we'll come stay too," Hudson says, sighing. "Not much longer though, okay?"

"It can end today if you want." Liam shrugs.

"No, after all of this, we need to do it right. You're not getting rid of me that easily." I smile at Liam and squeeze Hudson's hand.

I'll have to make it up to him later.

53

RELOCATE

I PACK A WEEK'S WORTH OF CLOTHES AND GO FIND HANNAH
and Maddie. They've heard about the drama with my dad
and Bella, but they don't know that everyone is following
Bella's wishes and leaving.

"Is this movie going to happen?" Hannah asks. "I'm
starting to worry."

"I think everything will go on as planned, at least I hope
so. This is just a small hitch." I don't know why I'm trying to
smooth things out for my dad, but it's not just his career at
stake—his choices affect every single person working on

this film, from the actors to the cameramen and makeup artists. "Liam offered his house for those of us who don't live close, so we can continue without too much of a stall. Hudson and my dad are talking right now, and hopefully, they'll work out all the logistics. I'm obviously the wrong one to ask since my dad doesn't keep me in the loop with all of this," I roll my eyes, but I keep my tone light, "but Liam and Hudson seem hopeful."

"Good enough for me," Hannah says, smiling back. "Well, this will be fun. Have you ever seen Liam's place? I've heard it's amazing."

I pause before answering, knowing it's strange that I wouldn't have been to my boyfriend's place yet. Despite our spacious living arrangement, most new couples would want time alone, especially if there is a house not too far away where we can escape.

"No. It's been too busy with filming and then recovering from the crash and all that craziness. I'm excited to see his house." I laugh weakly and decide to get out of there before I say too much. It will definitely be harder to hide what Liam and I are *not* with a smaller group around. Especially when Hannah already suspects something.

About an hour later, I roll my suitcase down the hall, my computer bag over my shoulder, and see Liam first. Hannah and Maddie come in a few minutes later.

"You ready?" Liam asks me.

I nod, looking around. "Where's Hudson?"

"He's still talking with your dad. He texted that he'll meet up with us later."

It's weird that he didn't text me, but I'm sure he has a good reason.

Tanner comes into the room with his suitcase, grinning

sheepishly. "Got room for one more?" he asks. He winks at Hannah and Maddie. "We can share a room."

They both flush and my eyebrows lift to the ceiling. How did I miss *this*?

Liam grins at them. "Sure." His eyes are laughing when he looks at me. "This should be fun."

I don't know why my nerves just kicked up. It's not like I'm a prude. Okay, maybe I am a little bit. I'm not *judging* them for having their fun, all three *together*, but talking about it openly still makes me feel like I'm the inexperienced newbie to the Hollywood lifestyle. Is this just what most people in their twenties do no matter where they are? I was too busy studying in college to know.

I try my best to act unfazed and smile back at Liam and the others. Hannah is avoiding my eyes, so I think it's safe to say that she's embarrassed too.

"Can we all fit in one vehicle, you think?" Tanner asks.

"Summer and I will go ahead," Liam says, putting his arm around my shoulder.

We walk out and as I stop in front of the car door, I look back at the house one more time. "Are you sure we should go ahead without Hudson?"

He holds up his phone for me to see the text. It clearly says that he'll meet us there later.

"Okay." I shrug. "Let's do this."

Liam gets behind the wheel, and he looks good in this sleek sportscar.

"Is this your car?"

He nods. "I went and picked it up earlier. What do you think?"

"She's pretty."

He grins. "I think so too." And then he laughs. "You

should've seen your face earlier. You gonna be okay with sexy times happening underneath your roof?"

I make a face and laugh. "I was that obvious, huh? Well, I'm assuming it's been happening under the roof we've been under for a while, so what's another roof?"

"Good point."

"They won't be having sex in the living room for everyone to see or anything like that, will they?" I shudder and he laughs harder.

"I almost wish they were, just to see your reaction." His eyes drop to my lips and his teeth tug on his bottom lip before he turns back to the road.

I don't even want to know what he's thinking.

I tap nervously on the armrest as we drive, and eventually, Liam reaches over and puts his hand over mine.

"Relax. I won't let anything bad happen to you, I promise, Petunia," he teases.

"*Petunia?* Where do you come up with these?"

We laugh and I lean back into the seat and enjoy the ride, his words calming me even though I'm being ridiculous. These are my friends. I can be as progressive as the next person...right?

Liam points out various celebrities' houses as we get closer to his place.

"Did you know you were surrounded by all these people when you bought your house?" I ask.

"My real estate agent made a point of letting me know when I was wondering if I should buy." He laughs. "Some people buy into all that hype about who you surround yourself with and real estate agents around here take that literally. I just liked the house." He pulls up to a gate and punches in a code. When it swings open and we drive toward the house, I gasp.

"I can see why. Liam, it's beautiful."

He beams proudly. "First house I've ever owned."

"It's something else."

"Wait till you see the pool."

There's a circular drive with a fountain in the front and lush flowers everywhere I turn. The house is more traditional than I would have expected from Liam and yet, when we walk inside, the place is a nice mixture of homey and modern.

"I love it, Liam."

"Thank you. I'll give you the grand tour in a minute, but first, let me show you our room."

"Our room?" I laugh, thinking he's joking.

He turns and looks at me, and it's one of the few times he hasn't been grinning. He's completely serious. "Hudson didn't tell you? He thought you and I should stay in a room together until we come out with the truth."

54

FINDING ME

"He was ready for us to be done with this dating sham when we all spoke earlier. Why is he saying this now?"

Liam shrugs, eyes wide. "I thought the two of you must have decided on this together."

I shake my head, too mad to say anything else. I check my cell phone again and there's still nothing from him. He hasn't gone this long without texting or calling since we started sleeping together. And this with Liam is a big deal... something he should've talked over with me first.

Maybe I'm making a bigger deal out of it than I should, but something isn't sitting right with me.

"Are you okay?" Liam asks.

"Not really." I put my shoulders back and draw in a long breath. "Let's see your room." I smile at him, determined to not let this blow up in my mind until I've had a chance to talk to Hudson.

Liam takes my hand and pulls me down the hall. "The rest of the rooms are upstairs, but ours is down here." He winks and I roll my eyes.

"You don't have to look so excited about this," I tease.

"Having a beautiful houseguest staying with me for an indefinite period? Can't say the thought has ever excited me before, but..." He lifts a shoulder and grins at me, his eyes bright.

I give him a little shove and when he opens the door to his room, I gasp. It is not what I expected at all. I thought he'd be the typical male with blacks or browns or dark greys, but it's much lighter. The walls are a pale grey and his massive bed with the tall cream tufted headboard is covered with a plush cream comforter and tons of pillows. There are floor-to-ceiling windows that look out into the pool area that is more exotic jungle than Southern California. And behind the comfortable grey couch is a plant wall. I've only seen pictures of something like this at the Amazon head-quarters in Seattle, never one in real life.

"How do you take care of that?"

"There's a timed watering system built in there. And the plants in there are ones that thrive with a comfortable temperature, not too humid. If I'm on location too long, I have someone come check things out to make sure it's all working as it should, but if I'm in town, I make sure to swing by and check it myself."

"I had no idea you were capable of something so—"

He laughs and motions for me to keep going. "So what?"

"So spectacular." I laugh too when I realize how that sounds, but it's just true. I've gradually seen for myself that there's more to Liam than meets the eye, but this far exceeds all expectations. "I am in awe. Truly. This is a work of art. And the fact that you're keeping it all alive—I am so impressed."

"Well, I do have help, remember, but yeah, I feel like I need things that ground me when I'm not shooting a movie. Otherwise, all of this just feels like too much. I don't deserve all of this, I really don't. And I suppose having a plant wall could prove that I'm as bougie as the next bastard, but I like being curious about things I know nothing about. Next project will be growing vegetables." He smiles, embarrassed suddenly. He rubs a hand over his face. "Enough about that. Let me show you the closet and the drawers that will be yours."

"I'm good with living out of a suitcase. This will be short-lived, don't you think?"

"You already looking for reasons to leave, roomie?"

"No. I just don't want you to go to a lot of trouble for me."

He puts his hand on my waist and gives me a side hug. "You are no trouble."

We walk to the closet and it's the size of a bedroom, as is the bathroom. The shower could fit ten people and the tub is not far behind.

"See? Plenty of room. If you get sick of me, I can always sleep in the closet." He takes my suitcase and puts it on the luggage carrier to the side of the closet built-ins. He points to several drawers in the closet and the bathroom. "Take all of those."

"Where are Hudson's things gonna go?" I ask, my voice light.

He doesn't say anything, and I look at him. He walks back toward the bedroom, and I follow.

"Is something going on?" I ask.

"I don't know," he says. "Now that I know you and Hudson weren't communicating, I'm not sure. But we won't worry about that now, okay?"

"Okay." I nod.

The doorbell rings and I jump. Liam moves toward the bedroom door and turns back before leaving.

"I'll get everyone settled and you can make yourself at home. I hope you'll be comfortable here, Summer."

He turns and I hear the girls and Tanner going on about the house. As they go upstairs, the sound is muted, and then I don't hear them. *Guess I won't be hearing their threesome.* I giggle to myself and decide to take Liam up on using the drawers. I unpack and then look at the plant wall for a long time, only stopping to open the glass doors and walk outside to explore this gorgeous yard.

I lose track of time, walking through the trees and flowers and stopping at the pool. It stretches out across the yard and has elaborate stonework around it with fountains and a slide built into the stone. The flowers and trees surrounding it are so inviting, I get a sudden urge to get in it and so, I do. I strip down to my underwear and dive in.

I do laps across the pool, feeling more like myself than I have since the plane crash and my stint in the hospital. More myself since coming to California...

55

LEFT FIELD

When I come up for air, Liam is standing at the edge of the pool.

"I couldn't resist," I say, laughing. "Come in! It feels great."

He doesn't smile right away, which should have been my first indicator that something is wrong, but then he turns and grabs a towel from the lounge chair.

"Summer, you might want to come inside. Your phone has been ringing like crazy and...Hudson is trying to reach you."

I hustle out of the pool as fast as I can, his expression throwing me off so much that I feel a lick of fear in my belly.

"What's wrong?" I ask.

His eyes are hard to read and that's so unlike him, I clutch his arm, wrapping the towel around me.

"Liam, you're scaring me."

"There are some ridiculous accusations that have come up...I don't believe them, but you should talk to Hudson, give him a chance to explain."

Now I'm really scared.

I move past him, snatching my clothes in my arms and finding my way back through the jungle maze. The beauty of Liam's room hits me again, despite my stomach being in knots this time and the worry that's causing me to shake.

He comes up behind me and rubs his hands over my shoulders.

"Do you need a quick shower to warm up?"

"No, I'll be okay."

He motions toward my phone on the bed. "I'll give you some privacy."

I nod, my eyes blurring as I try not to cry. I don't have a good feeling about this.

I press Hudson's name without reading the texts or listening to his voicemails.

He answers on the first ring. "Summer," he breathes out.

"What's going on?"

"I'm so sorry, Summer. I wanted you to hear about this from me, and I—I wish I could be there in person."

"You're scaring me, Hudson. Just tell me."

"I have agreed to be Winslet's boyfriend for the next several months."

"What?" My towel falls to the ground, and I can't breathe.

"An arrangement like what you have with Liam. I'm sure you've noticed she could use a little help in the PR department. I'll also be paid a good amount of money. This will give your dad time to adjust to the thought of you and me, give him a chance to warm up to the idea before we tell him about our movie. And my relationship with Winslet will get my name out more too, which will only be a positive for us in the long run."

"My dad shouldn't factor into our relationship, Hudson, or our movie...and your name is already out there because of your *work*. I thought you wanted me to get out of this with Liam. We were almost done. When did you agree to this? Or was this your idea?"

"Today. And it was her idea."

"You agreed to all this without talking to me?"

"You didn't exactly talk to me when you agreed to date Liam."

"Have you been holding this against me the whole time? We weren't sleeping together then—we weren't even together." My voice raises and I try to rein it back in. "We hadn't even kissed. I'd say things are a lot different now than they were when I agreed to this." The tears spill over my cheeks, and I bat them away. "How could you do this? And with *her*?"

"She's not as bad as she seems, and it won't be long. I hoped you'd understand since you're in a similar situation."

"I don't understand. I should've never agreed to this with Liam, but you and Winslet...no. I can't do this, Hudson."

"Summer, think about it. This can be really great for us... if you just think it all the way through."

"Everyone knows already?" I ask, my voice cold. I pick up my towel and walk toward the bathroom, sitting on the edge of the tub.

"Winslet shared a selfie of us that alluded to the fact that we were together, yes."

"Were you telling me the truth when you said you hadn't slept with her before?"

He's quiet for a long time and my heart thunders in my chest. "Yes," he finally says. "I told you we kissed and... things have gotten heated in the past. Before you."

"I hope you'll be happy together."

He says my name, but I hang up on him before I hear another word.

I run a bath and get it as hot as I can stand it. When I sink into it and dunk my head under, I wish I could be weightless and float away into nothingness. The hurt and the betrayal...I didn't see that coming. Not now. Not from Hudson.

He seemed like the real deal in a world of fake and scammy and make-believe. I thought he was the truth. The honesty that I crave and hotter and sexier than the guy-next-door, but every bit as dependable.

How the hell have I been so wrong?

I wrestle with myself too. He's right—I am in a similar situation. One I never imagined I'd get myself into. But does he not see that we're in such a different place than we were when I promised my dad and Liam I'd put up the pretense of dating Liam?

And it's Winslet Barry of all people. Someone he has a history with. He says he hasn't had sex with her, but Winslet will do everything she can to change that. Liam might not have been Hudson's favorite person when all this began, but they've come to understand one another.

I will never understand Winslet. There's nothing redeeming about that girl. And the fact that Hudson is convinced there is...it does not bode well for us.

I stay in the water until I'm a prune and when I get out, I sit on the edge again, a towel in my hair and around my body.

There's a soft knock on the door. "Summer? Are you okay?"

"No," I say quietly.

I get up and open the door and he holds his arms wide. I fall into them and have a good, long cry.

56

PLAYER

I STAY TO MYSELF FOR A FEW DAYS, TRYING TO KEEP MY BROKEN heart from ruining the mood of everyone else in the house. Liam tells them that I'm not feeling well, and he checks on me frequently. He seems to have a sixth sense for when I need company and when I need time to myself. And I haven't had much of an appetite, but he's kept a steady stream of snacks and meals and drinks flowing since I got here. He comes in after I've fallen asleep and slides into bed next to me, careful to stay on his side. I couldn't have asked for a more understanding friend and the perfect place to hide while I nurse this heartache.

But when Monday rolls around and I'm due back at work with the rest of them, I can't hide any longer. I allow extra time to get ready, applying more makeup than I normally do to hide the circles under my eyes. I wear the softest cardigan I own, tugging it closer to my body to ward off the early morning chill. I'll probably be shucking it off in an hour, but for now, it's comforting me.

Liam brings me coffee while I'm putting on my shoes, and I look up at him in surprise after I take a sip.

"Did you make this?"

He nods, his constant smile softening some of my blues.

"How were you hiding all these skills?"

"It's just a fancy coffeepot that does all the work. And I've seen what you put in your coffee enough times."

"I've been getting *your* coffee this whole time."

He sobers and bends down until we're almost at eye level. "As long as you're in my home, I will take care of *you*," he says.

I reach out and hug him. "Thank you."

He stares at me for a long moment. "Anytime. I won't complain if you get coffee for me when we're on set, though," he adds, laughing as he stands up. "I have a reputation to uphold."

I roll my eyes, acting like I'm offended, but we both know I'm not and that he doesn't mean it anyway. Mr. Hollywood keeps surprising me.

"You know Hudson is making a huge mistake and I have a feeling it's going to bite him in the ass sooner than he expects. I'll be telling him that when I see him today." He puts his hands on my shoulders when I stand up.

"Don't bother."

He shrugs. "It's the truth."

"No, really. I don't want him to think I'm as hurt by this as I am. He acted like it wasn't a big deal, and I'm afraid if he tries to talk about it today, I'll cry. I don't want to make a fool of myself with Winslet gloating nearby."

"You're sure she knows about the two of you?"

"Don't you remember her asking why Hudson was sneaking into my room every night?"

"But we covered that. She believed me," Liam says, narrowing his eyes. "Don't you think?"

"I think she knows you're not really into me and that I have something going on with Hudson...and that's why she came up with this plan for them to date."

"To let you know she knows?" He makes a face. "Is she that petty?" He covers his face with his hand. "Forget I asked that."

"I do think she's that petty, but more than that, she wants Hudson."

We walk toward the door, and he stops before opening it. "There's just one thing that you don't seem to be understanding..."

"What?"

"I *am* really into you."

I flush and shake my head and he turns toward the door.

"I know you don't want to hear it, but it's true. I'm not going to push you to be with me, Summer. Especially not with you forced to live with me and forced to pretend."

"You've tried to get out of this several times—you're not forcing me to be here."

"I hope that's really how you feel. But make no mistake —I know the amazing person you are, and I know how I feel about you."

"Liam—"

He turns back to look at me, his smile back in place. "You don't have to say anything. I know I'm making it awkward as fuck. I'm only saying it because that dickwad has given your self-confidence a dive, and you've had the impression that I couldn't possibly have real feelings for you being the player that I am...and I'm just saying, I'm not going anywhere. Not now. Not as long as there's a minute chance for me in your life." He takes a step toward me and my heart stutters in my chest. "Because there's one thing about players you may not realize..."

"What?" I whisper.

"We know better than anyone when we fall."

He allows his words to sink in, and I want to ask exactly what he means by that.

He leans in like he knows what I'm thinking and whispers in my ear, "And I haven't even put my best efforts in yet." He takes a step back and his eyes are light. It's impossible to look away. "Now that you're free, maybe I'll start... when you're ready, that is."

"What makes you think I will be?"

He puts his fingers on the pulse of my neck. "The way this is quickening right here. And the way we keep being faced with adversity and riding it out...*together*. I thought for sure the plane crash would make you see the light, but I'm willing to keep proving myself." His eyes crinkle with his grin and his dimples are on full display.

And then, like he's not wreaking havoc on my emotions, he nonchalantly taps the door. "Shall we go?"

I nod, too afraid my voice will be wobbly if I speak, and we walk out of the house and into the sunshiny California day.

57

UNCOMFORTABLE POSITIONS

I SEE HUDSON BEFORE HE SEES ME, AND I WALK TO THE opposite side of the building. Today we're in a studio in Hollywood, and it feels strange to be inside after doing most of the filming outside. Hannah and Maddie rush over to see if I'm feeling better.

"So much better," I lie.

A throat clears, and I turn to see Hudson standing there. Liam is by my side in seconds.

"I need to speak with you about something—" he starts.

Hannah and Maddie move away, and Liam doesn't budge.

"Alone," Hudson finishes.

"No, thank you," I say, turning to walk away.

His hand catches my arm and I look back.

"Please," he says.

"No."

"You heard her, man," Liam says quietly.

"This doesn't involve you, Taylor," Hudson says between his teeth.

"Maybe not, but you don't need to upset her at work. You've had all weekend to make things right."

"I've been blowing up your phone all weekend," Hudson says to me. "You're just ignoring me now?"

"I turned it off to take a much-needed break from social media," I say in the most saccharine voice.

"We need to talk." He folds his arms across his chest, and I face him and do the same.

"Have you broken up with Winslet?"

He looks surprised, and then we both are, when Winslet walks up and puts her head on his shoulder. "Did I snore too much? You left before I woke up this morning." She pouts and then looks at me and smirks. "It's been just like old times..." She leans in and whispers, "Except the sex is even *better*."

My mouth drops open and Hudson pales as he turns toward me. I turn around and walk off, fighting back the tears but not winning. Liam keeps up with me, his arm finding my shoulder and squeezing.

"It doesn't mean anything. We slept in the same bed last night too," he says. "She's probably just saying that to upset you."

"Summer?" Hudson calls and I try to keep walking, but

his hand stops me. He moves in front of me and looks conflicted when he sees my face.

"Did you lie to me?" I ask softly. "Did you have sex with her?"

"We didn't have sex last night, I don't know why she—"

"But you have before, right? And you lied about it...twice."

His chest rises and falls as he stares at me, and I jump when my dad calls Hudson's name.

"It was before I ever met you. I don't know why it matters," Hudson whispers. He looks over my shoulder toward my dad.

"It matters that you lied about it." My voice breaks and I can't bear to look at him another second.

I move around him and when he tries to stop me again, I shove his hand off of me. Liam opens the door for me and we step into the hall as I pace and try to catch my breath.

"I know you have to get in there," I tell Liam. "I feel crazy right now. Am I overreacting?" I feel a pain in my stomach and I lean over, hands on my knees.

"You have every right to feel what you feel," he says. He puts his hand on my back and I take a deep breath. "I can get you out of here right now, just say the word."

I stand up and try to wipe my face. "Thank you for trying to make me feel better. I'm not going to let them—" I put my fist over my mouth and roll my eyes when my voice cracks again. "I'll be okay. I just need to keep my distance from both of them today."

"If you're sure. You don't have to prove anything to them, Summer." He waits and when I nod, he does too. "I'll do my best to keep you away from them."

And he tries, he really does. He tries to be demanding enough to keep me busy, but Winslet sees through that and ups her demands. She sends me out to get different food than craft services and when it's not to her liking, she sends me to two different places to get the salad she likes from one place and the salmon she likes from another.

When she's not in a scene or sending me for food or having me steam her skirt while she's wearing it...she's leaning into Hudson's side, her hands on his chest, her hands in his hair, her hands *all over him.*

I go into self-preservation mode and become numb all over. So, when Hudson comes up to me at the end of the day and says, "I'm sorry, Summer," it barely registers.

It's not until later, when I'm back at the house and taking a long bath, that I think about his apology.

Sorry for what?

Sorry for breaking my heart?

Sorry for ruining our plans?

Sorry for being in Winslet's bed this weekend?

Sorry for being a fucking *liar*?

I decide to do what I should have done my first week here. I call my dad when I'm out of the bath. There's a plush violet robe that magically appeared while we were gone today, and I have a feeling Liam got it for me. It's even more comforting than my softest cardigan.

"Hey," Dad says. "You okay?"

"I've been better."

He sighs. "I was afraid you were on your way to heartbreak. Hudson has a—"

When he doesn't say anything else for a moment, I try to push. "Has a what, Dad?"

"You probably don't want to hear this coming from me."

My heart turns over and I clutch my stomach, afraid I'm going to be sick. "Just say it, Dad. What about Hudson?"

"Well, he has a lot of similarities to me."

I sit on the ottoman in the bathroom, staring at the tile and trying to make sense of what he's saying.

"Why do you think I never pushed the two of you together?"

"I thought you didn't want your right-hand man and your daughter getting involved in case things went south... like you'd said. That would be an uncomfortable position for you."

"True, but I can handle uncomfortable positions. Like an idiot, I had your mother stay in the same house as me and my girlfriend," he says quietly.

I would laugh if my stomach wasn't in knots. "Yeah, I suppose you're right. You're not one to back down from a mess."

"He has a lot of drive. You think I don't know he wants my job one day?"

"That's not a bad thing."

"No, but there's a difference in what he's willing to do to get there. Who he's willing to use to get there. He will follow what serves him best, sweetie."

"Don't call me that."

"I'm sorry...Summer. And I'm sorry for the hurt you're going through. I'd hoped he meant it about his feelings for you."

"You don't believe him, do you?" My insides shake and the knot in my stomach tightens. "He claims he's doing the same thing I'm doing with Liam—that it's all for show...and money."

"Well, for your sake, I hope that's the truth." He sounds skeptical though.

"He lied to me, so I have no idea what the truth is right now. I need you to let me out of this job, Dad. I'm sorry if I'm letting you down, but I don't want to face the two of them every day."

"I understand."

"Thank you. Do you know any other jobs open right now? You know what, don't answer that. I'd rather find something on my own."

He laughs. "So independent. But...you're staying in town?"

"For now. I still want to give my career here a shot. This hasn't changed that."

"I'll help you in any way I can," he says.

"I appreciate that."

"I'm really glad you're staying."

"Is, uh...is Bella okay?"

"She's talking to me again, so that's a good sign."

"Good."

"Please stay in touch, okay?" His voice is gruff, and for some reason, it makes a tear drop down my cheek.

"Okay, Dad."

"I love you, kiddo."

I slam my hand across my mouth, as tears fall rapidly now. "Love you too," I whisper.

And I hang up, feeling more confused than ever.

58

PDA AND TATTOOS

IT FEELS STRANGE TO NOT GO TO WORK THE NEXT MORNING. I get up at the same time as Liam, and when I see Hannah and Maddie, I'm sad that I won't be spending as much time with them anymore.

"I wanted you to hear it from me that I'm not working on the set anymore," I say as we're grabbing coffee in the kitchen.

"Oh no. What happened? Is it about all this with your dad?" Hannah asks.

"Well, kind of. I've been trying to ease my way out of

working with him for a couple of weeks now and was willing to wait it out, but he was good with me leaving now, so I'm jumping on it."

"Makes sense." Hannah nods. She puts her arm around me. "I'll miss you though. And now Winslet will really be unbearable."

"Hudson will keep her in line," I say, forcing a smile. "Did you hear they're dating now?"

"I know. I hate it." Her head falls back. "Ugh. Anyone but her. I didn't want to believe it. I was hoping it wasn't true."

"Hudson told me." I focus on the half and half in front of me, and I think my voice sounds steady. I'm not as good of an actor as everyone around me, but she seems to buy it.

"Well, that sucks royally. I'm not sure I can ever hang out with him again if he's interested in someone like her," she says.

"I know the feeling," I say.

Liam walks in and comes up behind me, kissing my neck. The few times we've all been together since moving in here, he amps up the PDA for their benefit. Sometimes it's hard not to laugh because I feel certain they're going to see through it, but so far, no one seems to suspect that Liam and I are anything but a happy couple. Hannah seems to fully believe I'm with Liam now, and I'm sure Winslet seals the deal.

"I'm gonna miss you today," Liam says. I turn around and he puts his hands on my waist.

"You'll miss having someone wait on you all day, I'm sure," I tease.

He tugs me closer and wraps his arms around me. "You know I'll miss more than that," he whispers.

Hannah sighs and so does Maddie. "God, they are so cute, aren't they?" Maddie says.

Tanner walks in and slaps both of them on the backside. "Nice ass times two."

Maddie snorts and rolls her eyes.

"You need to take note of Liam," Hannah says. "Learn from the master on how to treat a woman." She flicks Tanner on the arm and he rubs it, scowling.

"You guys weren't complaining last night," he says, a slow grin forming as he tries to grab Maddie when she walks past him.

Maddie shrugs. "Meh." She looks at Hannah and giggles. "We'd probably be just fine without you actually."

Tanner's mouth drops open and so does mine.

Hannah and Maddie laugh hysterically and Tanner dives between the two of them, tickling both.

I make a face at Liam and start laughing too, still unsure if they're being serious or not. "I guess it's working for them," I tell Liam.

He lifts a shoulder. "Seems like it."

He kisses my cheek and leans back, studying me. "Are you sure you're okay? Do you need anything before I leave?"

I shake my head. "No, I'll be good. I'll make a few calls, see if I can find a job doing something somewhat enjoyable."

"Or you could always write. You've got the time now."

"I can't just take advantage of you forever, Liam. I need a job so I can move out."

He wrinkles his nose. "Do you though?" His hand goes back to my cheek and his forehead leans against mine. "I want you to stay as long as you want, I mean it. Please stay."

"You're really hard to resist."

His eyes are bright when he steps back. "Really?" He looks hopeful and that damn dimple, goodness.

I shove him away, laughing. "Get to work."

"Yes, ma'am. I'll call you when I know what our schedule will be like."

I nod and take my coffee to the yard outside our bedroom. There's a side yard that's gorgeous too, but the area outside our room is my favorite. I drink my coffee and scan a site that my dad texted me about this morning. He also sent a few names but promised that he wouldn't butt his nose into it.

I fill out a few online applications and then Google the names of the people he mentioned. The first one is Joanna DeGenali and while she sounds somewhat intimidating, she seems like a total badass woman who's killing it in film right now. When I see a couple of the movies she's done, I'm surprised that I didn't know her name before now.

The second is Sean Scott and he's a hard pass. I've heard too much about him and his proclivity toward young actresses. I don't need that kind of trouble in my life and don't want to support the career of a man like that.

And the third is a woman I've met before, Sophia Lakelyn. She's a friend of Dad's and has always been nice when I've seen her. She's more of an indie filmmaker than the big box office type and I'm a fan of her work. I decide to call the one I think I want to work with first and dial Sophia's number.

A guy answers and I'm caught off guard for a moment. Then I realize it's probably one of her assistants.

"Hi, my name is Summer Winters and I was hoping—"

"How did you get this number?" he interrupts.

"Uh..." I really don't want to use my dad's name, but I don't want to miss this chance either. "Cole Winters gave it to me."

"You said you're Summer Winters...oh my god, are you

the one dating Liam Taylor right now?" His voice goes up at least ten decibels, and I pull the phone away.

"Yes?" I say and laugh when he squeals. "You're a fan, I take it?"

"Uh, yeah, I'd say so. I have a tattoo of him on my back. I know I'll probably get it removed when I'm like, forty or something, but right now it is *sick*."

I laugh. "I can't wait to tell Liam about this conversation."

"Oh my god," he says again. "My name is Sven, S-V-E-N, Gardner, G-A-R-D-N-E-R."

I lose it at that but try to do it away from the phone so he won't hear.

"So I'm Sophia's assistant. What did you need?"

"Well, I wondered if she might have any openings for a job. I've worked on my dad's set all summer, and I have an interest in making movies too, so I'm wanting all the experience I can get. I have a BA in—"

"Sophia's picky as hell about who works with her, but I'll see what I can do," he jumps in. "Do you know her films?"

"Yes. And I've met her before. I'm not sure if she'd remember me or not, but—"

"If I tell her you're dating Liam Taylor, you stand a great chance of getting *in*."

59

CARBS AND CANDLES

WHEN LIAM GETS HOME THAT NIGHT, I'VE MADE DINNER FOR everyone. I have the table set just because it's fun. Liam has such pretty things and he said to make myself at home, so I did.

Liam's eyes light up when he sees me. "Wow, you look incredible." And then he sees the table and grins. "Are we having a party?"

"I mean, we could call it that, but no, I just made lasagna. Everyone can eat it as they come in, if they're not all here at once."

"Aw yeah, I do think they might be going to a screening of something tonight. I didn't hear where or when they'd be back, but I *love* lasagna." He looks shy all of a sudden. "I could open a bottle of wine..."

"That would be great," I say, smiling.

My talk with Sven put me in a great mood, and even better, he called back to say Sophia would meet with me tomorrow morning in Malibu.

Liam follows me into the kitchen and washes his hands. "I could use another shower. I took one on set, but that feels like a while ago. It was hot out there today."

"There's time if you want to."

"Yeah?"

"Sure. It's just heating in the oven now, ready for whenever."

"I'll be no more than eight minutes."

"I'm timing you," I tease.

He lifts an eyebrow and grins. "I'm glad to see you... happier tonight," he says over his shoulder, walking toward his room.

I put the salad together and check the loaf of bread. Everything is ready. I'm even wearing one of my favorite summery dresses, a light blue cotton dress with intricate lacework at the waist and not much of a back. It feels casual and special all at once, and deep down, I'm glad it's just Liam and me tonight. We can be ourselves and I want to thank him for *everything*.

I have big band music playing. It's what my mom always plays while cooking and it makes me feel closer to her to have it going now. She's been immersing herself in work lately, I think to try to get past this latest thing with my dad. If my mom can work through everything she has with my dad, I can handle this hurt about Hudson. I take a deep

breath and then dance around while I check the mini straw-
berry cheesecakes in the fridge. They're almost chilled
enough.

When Liam walks in, I jump and turn around, hands at
my throat.

"Sorry, I didn't mean to startle you. I might've been
staring a little too long at your back in that dress." He's
looking at me with an expression I can't read, his eyes
shining and that sweet smile playing at his lips. Sometimes I
still can't believe that I'm so comfortable around this guy
that is so incredibly talented and well...HOT.

I wave him off. "I'm fine. I was in my own little world."

"Do you really not know how beautiful you are,
Summer?"

"Uh. No?" I make a face and shake my head. "I mean,
look at you. You are the epitome of beauty, the perfect speci-
men." I laugh and he groans, wiping his hand down his face.

"So, you think I'm just making it up when I tell you
you're stunning or that I'm into you."

"Uh, yeah. No. I think you just *think* you're into someone
like me. I get that I'm a novelty because I'm not, you know,
falling all over you all the time..." I pull the lasagna out of
the oven and he picks up the salad.

"I can get the bread out of the oven too," he says.

We go to the table and set it down and then he goes back
for the bread and then disappears again, coming out with a
couple of candlesticks that are usually on the fireplace
mantel. He lights the candles and sits next to me.

"I hope this is good." My nerves kick in then as I realize
how long it's been since I've actually cooked.

He reaches over and lays his hand on top of mine. "I've
never eaten at my table, never had anyone make a meal for

me...never had anyone sleep in my bed with me. You're all kinds of firsts for me, Summer."

The moment pauses as we stare at each other.

"Thank you, Liam. I'm glad it's just us tonight because I wanted to somehow show you how grateful I am for the friend you've been to me. I don't know how I would've survived the past few days without you, much less the past few months. I'm just so glad we met."

He pours wine into both of our glasses and lifts his, his smile gone but the kindness still in there. "Friends forever," he says.

I beam, relieved that he seems to understand what I need from him. We take a sip of wine and then pile the food on our plates.

He moans for at least thirty seconds when he takes the first bite of lasagna. "I can't believe you can cook too," he groans. He attacks his plate like he's starving and talks while he chews. It doesn't even look gross on him. "This is going to up my workout time, but I don't even care. This is worth every bite. My beach scenes are almost done anyway."

"Oh no! I'm sorry, I didn't really think to ask what you might not be eating right now."

"I am eating whatever you throw down."

I laugh and tuck into my food, startled when the doorbell rings.

He looks surprised and stands up, walking toward the door. "Maybe someone forgot their key..."

He opens the door and Hudson stands there. He looks past Liam and sees me at the candlelit table for two and his face goes stormy.

"Well, this is cozy," he says.

60

CARBON COPY

"No, you don't get to do that." I set my napkin down and watch as he stalks into Liam's house.

Hudson runs his hand through his hair, looking at me with sad eyes and then giving Liam a pointed look. "A little privacy?"

"You don't have to go anywhere," I tell Liam. "This is your house." I realize it's stating the obvious, but with the way Hudson's storming in here throwing out demands, it needs to be said.

He nods at Hudson and his expression softens when he

turns to me. "I'll be in the kitchen if you need me." He starts walking toward the kitchen and then comes back, picking up his plate and piling it with more lasagna. He winks at me and carries it back.

Hudson moves toward the table and stands there awkwardly, waiting for me to say something. I don't.

I pick at my food and finally set the fork down and wait for him to say whatever he came to say.

He glances at the lasagna. "This looks good." He seems to notice the rest of the place settings now.

I don't say anything.

"God, Summer. Look at me. Say something."

I look up at him but don't know where to even begin.

"Can I sit?" he asks.

I hold out my hand for him to take the chair across from me. He does and then it's quiet for unbearable seconds.

He clears his throat and leans his elbows on the table, his hands stretching out to reach mine. I don't meet him the rest of the way.

He pulls back, frustrated. "I can't believe you're being this way."

"What part of this confuses you?" My brows frown so hard, Mama would be fussing at me about the wrinkles I'm surely adding to the later years.

He shakes his head. "Do we really have to go over all of this again? You're literally doing the same thing right now with Liam and you're angry because I want to jumpstart our life together with a cushion."

"There's so much more to it than that, and you know it. I'm sorry you don't want to *go over all of it again*, but I think it's really telling that you didn't talk to me about any of it first. You and I are in a far different place now than we were when I made this arrangement with Liam. And even if that weren't the case, Winslet is a different human than Liam. If you're not already, I give it three weeks until you're sleeping with her. And last but definitely not least, you lied to me. That, in itself, is enough for me to—" I leave it hanging and shake my head.

He makes an exasperated sound and leans his forehead on his hands, staring down at the table. When he looks up again, he sighs and moves to the chair closer to me, scooting it until our legs touch. He takes my hand and weaves our hands together.

"I'm sorry I lied. I didn't want you to worry about her. You have *nothing* to worry about, Summer. Nothing. And I'm not sleeping with her now either," he says. "I wouldn't do that to you."

"You can. We're not together anymore."

"Summer!" he says, his head going back as he glares at the ceiling. "Stop. You don't mean that."

"I do," I whisper. My lips tremble and I have to look away because I don't want him to suck me back in with his puppy-dog eyes and perfect hair.

He leans closer, his thumb rubbing the outside of mine and it feels nice. I pull my hand away and he sits up straight, clearly at a loss of what to do with me. I don't blame him. I feel numb and cracked—I will not allow myself to think I'm broken even if I am. What is there to do with that?

"What about our story?" he asks.

"You mean my story idea that I mostly wrote?"

He shoves away from the table, getting up and moving to the other side. He puts both hands on the table. "We worked on it together. You wanted me to be part of it. I *am* part of it. It's just as much mine now as it is yours."

I stare at him, and tears blur my vision of him until he

looks like what happens when a movie shifts into a dream sequence. I blink, the tears fall, and he's crystal clear again.

"My dad was right about you."

He pulls his hands from the table and crosses them over his chest. "What do you mean?"

"He said you're like him, and I cannot believe that I didn't see it sooner." I push my chair away and stand up. "How was I able to see who he was all this time and not spot his carbon copy from the very beginning?" I shake my head incredulously, the tears falling again now. I swipe them away as fast as they're falling.

He looks alarmed and walks toward me, his hands reaching for my arms. I back away so he can't touch me.

"You liked that I'm driven like him. You know I'm not like him in the ways that matter," he argues. "I meant what I told him though, Summer—I-I *am* falling for you. We can chase our dreams together. You have qualities of him in you too, and together, especially the *three* of us, we can make this movie more successful than anything he's ever done before."

Panic flashes across his face when I start laughing. "I remember when I heard you tell him that—that you were falling for me. I was so excited. I thought we were on our way to something amazing. But if you're still *falling* for me and haven't landed yet, I doubt you're going to." I laugh again. "You can have the story idea. I don't want it anymore. That's the real reason you're here, right? You got worried that my screenplay was out of your hands now? You want me as long as I can finish that story, keep the peace between you and my father, and have Winslet's name backing you... that'll give your career the exact push it needs...right? Is that how this was all playing out in your mind?"

His mouth opens and closes, and he truly looks bewildered. And I believe he is. I also believe I'm right and he might not even realize it yet.

I wipe my face and take as big of an inhale as I can, feeling the air finally reach my lungs.

I thought this summer might bring me closer to my dad and it seems it just did. Because even if I don't necessarily have the relationship with him that I want, his insight about Hudson just saved me years of heartbreak.

61

IT ALL BOILS DOWN TO THIS

"You're wrong about this." Hudson's jaw is clenched and he's withdrawing into himself right before my eyes. "You're so off it's not even funny."

With a lot more nonchalance than I'm really feeling, I shrug. "Maybe so. I guess only time will tell."

"*I'm* telling you. And that should be enough. You know me, Summer. I've never lied about my ambition. I've worked my ass off for years in this industry. I've been nothing but loyal. I've done every single thing your dad has ever asked me to do for such a long time and have nothing to show for it but experience and a shitty apartment, while you're shacking up with the biggest player of all time in *this*." He waves both hands around the luxury that is Liam's house. "I'd say if one of us is like your father, it would be you. You have the perfect setup here, don't you." He laughs and wipes a hand over his face. "This is so fucked up. I don't even know what to say to you right now."

"You're doing a pretty good job of saying plenty."

His eyes flash with anger. "It's like I don't even know you right now."

"Kettle, black," I say, my hands going to my hips. "And I might have similarities to my dad, but I got out."

"What do you mean?"

"I'm no longer working for him. I'm out. I'm interviewing elsewhere."

He snorts. "If you think your name doesn't get you places, you don't know how it works around here. Along with the fact that you're dating Liam. See? We're the same, Summer."

My face flushes with anger. "I've had enough of this conversation. We're going in circles and it's not getting us anywhere."

"Our story has *hit* written all over it."

"I love how you keep circling back to that. It's not our relationship you're fighting for, it's the rights to my story. Take it. I'm starting to believe you were only ever with me because of my dad. And then my story was just a bonus. I hope when it wins an Oscar, you'll thank me for being the brains behind it."

He looks angrier than I've ever seen him. He starts to say something and then shakes his head and turns, walking toward the door. I want to say something petty about

Winslet but refuse to let any more venom shoot out of this mouth. I've said all I need to say.

He turns back and his expression is cold. "Enjoy your fantasy world with Liam. I'm sure he'll take you everywhere you need to go in this career."

He slams the door behind him.

Is he right? Are we just alike?

Liam comes out of the kitchen tentatively, studying me. I turn and put my arms around him and he pulls me close, engulfing me in a hug. Neither of us say anything for a long time and when I finally pull back, he looks angry. I wipe my face of the damn tears that won't stop leaking out.

"Do you want to talk about it?" he asks.

"I'll tell you what happened and then I don't want to talk about him anymore."

"Okay."

We clear the table and take everything to the kitchen. I start washing the dishes and he takes my hand. "That will get taken care of later. Let's go sit down." He points to the bottle of wine we barely drank. "Wine?"

I nod and we take it back through his bedroom and to the couch outside his bedroom windows. I already feel better being outside.

I tell him everything and watch as his face shifts from anger to murderous to compassion and everything in between. When I've said all I can say and am spent, he takes my hand in his and looks at me earnestly.

"You know how I can tell the difference between the two of you?"

"How?"

"You're in this arrangement with me to help *me*. He's in the arrangement with Winslet to help himself. It's as simple as that."

I press my lips together to keep from crying again. But it's such a consolation to hear that.

"He made me feel like my motives for doing this with you were to get ahead and I'm sure he's right—it *will* help. It helped me get in with Sophia tomorrow."

"But you didn't go into this for that and you stayed with me even when you were at risk of losing your relationship with Hudson."

I think about that and wonder if that should've told me something about Hudson and me...

"Maybe he felt I had one foot out the door the whole time."

"Did you?" he asks.

"I didn't think so, but now I'm wondering. I'm rethinking everything. I think I need to be a lot more honest with myself than I've been." I take a sip of the wine and watch the way the breeze flutters the greenery around us.

"I admire the way you question yourself. Most would just get defensive about it and think there's no way it could be true if it's something they don't want to hear. But you think about it and try to examine the ways it could be true first."

"Learning I could be so wrong about someone is going to make me question everything for a long time." And he lied to me. That fact keeps hitting me like a hammer to the heart. I lean my head back and turn to Liam. He's looking at me, a soft smile playing on his lips, his white linen shirt unbuttoned to show just a sliver of his tan skin. "Thanks for listening," I whisper. "I'm done. I don't need to dissect the daylights out of it."

"You can. I'm here for it," he says, his smile growing. "My sister Lara and my mom monopolize the dissection technique—your processing is a millisecond of theirs." He laughs, but his expression gets that far-off look it does on the rare occasions he talks about his family.

"Is Lara in a relationship with anyone? I don't think you've said."

"She's been in a relationship with one of my friends from high school for the past year—Barrett. But before they got together," he shakes his head, "it was a lot of agonizing, *so* much discussion." He laughs and holds a hand up. "Not that there's anything wrong with that."

I laugh too. "No, I get it. That's how my sister is, and she and my mom wish I was more like that."

"Don't let anyone change you, Summer Winters. I don't know if anyone's told you today, but you're spectacular as is."

62

EXTRA GRILLING

A BREEZE BLOWS THROUGH THE TREES, AND I SHIVER.

"Should we head inside?" Liam asks. "It's getting cooler out here."

"Yeah, I should get to bed. I have that meeting in the morning. How early do you have to be out of here?"

"Six." He makes a face. "I guess I should get to bed too. Hey, Troy can take you if you'd like. He's on the schedule this week and Ben is working next week. When I'm not with you, I'd feel better about you navigating the paparazzi with one of them around. They can drive you wherever you need to go—you've seen both working as security on set, right?"

"Are you sure you don't need Troy tomorrow?"

"He can probably take both of us. What time do you have to meet Sophia?"

"Ten."

"Plenty of time for him to do both. He'll be happy to do something other than just wait around on set."

"Okay, great. That will save me arranging an Uber."

He grins and we stand up, stretching after sitting on the patio furniture. He opens the door into his bedroom and there's an awkward moment as we figure out which direction we're going. He ends up flopping back on the bed, crossing his ankles, and I point toward the bathroom.

"Do you need to get in there before I wash my face?"

"No, it's all yours."

When I come back out, he goes into the bathroom and takes a shower. Not that I'm counting, but that's his third or fourth shower today. I try to focus on my book as he walks back in with a tank top and shorts and gets in bed with me. But the need to keep talking to him is too strong.

"You know, our roommates are here so little, we could probably get away with spending the night in separate bedrooms," I say, turning to face him.

He turns on his side and faces me too. "What would be the fun in that? We wouldn't get to have these slumber parties."

I grin and he smiles back, reaching out to caress his thumb across my cheek. He pauses, listening.

"I think they just got home. See? Best we keep it up," he teases. "Sleep tight, roomie." He bops the end of my nose and moves his hand under his face.

"Night. Thanks for being such good company."

"It's easy when I'm with my favorite person," he whispers.

His eyes close and I stare at him for a moment, my heart warmed by the sweet things he says.

I picture Hudson in Winslet's bed, but I can't imagine them having heart-to-hearts or anything beyond a shallow physical attraction. Maybe I'm wrong about that too though. If he did have feelings for me at all and is hurting right now, I could almost feel bad for him. Winslet can't possibly be the best friend Liam has turned out to be.

I close my eyes, willing sleep to shut out all thoughts of Hudson. It's best I don't think about him, which is still impossible, but I'll get there. *God, I hope I get there.*

In the morning, there's a note by the coffeepot, which has hot coffee waiting for me. I taste it to be sure it's fresh and wonder how Liam pulled that off, leaving so early this morning.

The note says:

Go rock their world.

XO, Liam

I smile and take my time getting ready, excited to meet Sophia. Troy knocks on the door a few minutes before I'm scheduled to leave.

"Whenever you're ready," he says, smiling politely.

"I'm good to go right now."

When we pull up to the address, I'm surprised to see a beautiful house on the beach in Malibu, rather than an office building.

"I'll be waiting," Troy says.

"I can text you, if that would be better, so you're not just stuck sitting here."

"It's a beautiful day," he says. "I don't mind sitting outside in this."

"Thank you."

"Anything for Liam's girl," he says.

I'm smiling as I walk up the brick-lined path and ring the doorbell. The door swings open and a tall, thin, gorgeous guy clasps both my hands and tugs me inside.

"Sven," he says. "You are even prettier than your pictures."

"Oh, thank you," I say, surprised.

"I admit, I wasn't sure anyone could keep up with Liam in the looks department, but—yes." He takes in my whole look and nods approvingly.

I laugh. "Well, I take that as high praise coming from someone who looks like you. Your outfit is awe-inspiring, and knowing what a huge appreciation you have for Liam, well, it's very kind of you."

He motions for me to follow him. "I don't just appreciate Liam Taylor. I know every movie, TV role, lead or bit part he's ever done. As I said, I have a tattoo...that you may or may not one day see, should we bond." He pauses for effect and I can't help but laugh. "He also did a deodorant commercial. Did he tell you that?"

"No, I did not know that." It's both endearing and a little terrifying that Sven knows so much about Liam. I hope that if I get this job, Sven won't drop me like a hot potato when Liam and I break up.

"Sophia will be meeting with you in just a few minutes. One of her phone calls was running long and she asked if I'd put your basic info in the system."

"Oh, okay. What would you like to know?"

He leans in. "After our little chat on the phone, I told her she had to hire you, so you're in, darling. But go ahead and act surprised when she tells you," he whispers. "If you could fill out this form, and this one." He pushes the forms across the table, and it has a nondisclosure agreement, saying the things that I learn at Lakelyn Film will not leave my lips. I sign my name and hover over the slot for my address, moving on to my social security, and then fill out my banking info, so they can direct deposit me for payment. I hover over the space for my social media links, knowing I'm in Hollywood if they care about that here.

"I'm not really very active on social media," I tell him.

"Fair enough. Just fill in where you have accounts, and that'll be enough.

I pause over the address, still unsure about what to put there.

Sven glances over. "All set?"

"For the address, is it okay if I just give a general location?"

"Absolutely. Los Angeles is fine."

I breathe out a sigh of relief, not wanting Liam's superfan to show up on his doorstep until after I get a sense of whether he's trustworthy or not. I'm not getting any weird or stalkery vibes about him, despite his ability to quote the names and years of the roles Liam has had, which he does, while we're waiting for Sophia to come out.

He makes me laugh and I'm thoroughly relaxed by the time Sophia comes into the room.

The first thing she asks once greetings are behind us is, "So tell me, is this a real relationship between you and Liam Taylor, or are you doing what every actor in Hollywood does at some point and just pretending to be the love of his life?"

63

CUSSING, JESUS, AND FILMS

MY MOUTH DROPS AND I STARE AT HER, SPEECHLESS.

She laughs and waves her hand at me, pulling me into her office. "I'm kidding, I'm kidding. It's none of my fucking business who you or Liam Taylor dates, and don't you forget it." She leans closer. "There are fucking sharks in this town and if you're on my team, I want you to know I am a safe place. I cuss a lot, love Jesus, love making fucking films that matter, and I don't tolerate shitty people."

I nod, tucking that description of herself in my vault for

later examination because I feel like she just gave me a lot right there.

She laughs again and says, "You are so cute. Cole okay with you being here?"

I take a deep breath and smile, the shock of her opening receding quickly. I try to subtly glance around her office. It's gorgeous. A ton of white and black with a huge vase of pink peonies on her glass desk. There's a beach right outside her windows, prime location.

"My dad knows I'm applying for jobs, and you were one of the few people he recommended I try."

"Well, that is so fucking nice of him," she says and the warm smile on her face suggests there is no irony in that statement. "I think a lot of your dad. He's got a genius mind."

"He thinks a lot of you too."

"Tell me where your skills lie," she says.

"I've spent the summer doing everything on my dad's set. Coffee, whatever the actors want or need...I've learned to find things at incredible speed..." I laugh. "Things I never thought I'd have to do, but it's been a learning experience."

"But you must want to do more than that," she says.

"I do."

"That's what I want to hear about."

"I'm a writer," I tell her. "I received a bachelor's in creative writing and my goal is to be a screenwriter.

She leans forward. "Now it's getting interesting. And what do you like to write about?"

I think about the things I've written, my heart caving a bit when I think about the story I worked on with Hudson. I sit up straighter. I'm not letting him hold me back. I'll write something better.

"I like to write about the truth. Raw, gritty, quirky reality...usually with a love story in there somewhere, but more emphasis on capturing real life than anything. I don't have to wrap things in a tidy bow. I prefer if it's not, if that's what the story needs."

"I like you," she says, pointing her pen at me. "I'd love to read something you've written." She pats the pile of paper next to her. "These are screenplays that I'm supposed to be reading through...with a few manuscripts that have the potential to be turned into a screenplay. I wasn't sure what I'd have you do, honestly. I wanted to meet you first. But after hearing what you like to write about, that tells me all I need to know. If you're willing, I'd like you to go through these and find the ones worth fighting for. I'd like to see your writing because something tells me Cole Winters' daughter has something special, especially if he's sending you my way." She winks. "If your writing is what you just described to me, he knows you'd be a better fit with me." She nods, grinning wide. "I like that about him."

I smile at her. "I like you," I tell her.

"We are going to get along just fine," she says. "How long was the drive for you?"

"About twenty-five minutes. I was surprised. So far everything has taken forty minutes to an hour."

"We can do this however you'd like. You can read these at home and come in a day a week to discuss. Or there's room for us to set up an office here if you'd like to come in full-time. Some prefer working outside of the home—they get more work done—but I don't know where you land on that, and I'm easy."

"I graduated from college and came straight here, where I've been on the set every day, so I've never really worked at home before. I'm willing to try that if it's the simplest."

"Why don't you follow me? I'll show you where your office would be, and you can get a feel for it. There are five other employees who work in and out of here regularly. Ten who are happier working from home. When we're shooting a film, you might decide you want another role, and we can discuss it when the time comes, but for now, I desperately need help with those scripts."

I follow her out of her office, and she introduces me to Otis, who waves and shouts, "Hey!"

Next is Randall, and he smiles shyly from his office. Blair is in the next office and she's the chattiest, warming up the more Sophia gushes about how I'm going to be a great addition to the team. And in the last office is a woman with stern features and slicked-back white hair.

"And this is the woman who is responsible for it all," Sophia says. "My beautiful mother, Ana Claire."

When Ana Claire smiles, her entire face comes alive, and I can't believe I thought anything about her was stern. She beams and stands up, her hands landing on my shoulders. "Welcome to the team," she says. "We are so happy to have you."

"I love that the two of you work together," I say, smiling wide at both of them. "I'm close to my mother and...I love it when I see other mother-daughter relationships that are close like this."

Sophia puts her arm around her mother. "I think we have a keeper with this one."

"I have a good feeling," her mother agrees.

"So, your office would be the one across from Mother Dearest here," she says, chuckling. She leads me to a smaller office across the hall. It's got a thick wood table for a desk and the walls are lined with white bookshelves. "It's in need of a little TLC. It hasn't been updated since Lauren went on maternity leave. She's decided she wants to work from home, so this is all yours, if you want. If there's anything you'd like us to provide in here, we can; otherwise, we have a full office up front by Sven that has the printers, copiers, etc."

"I will be set here," I say, liking the feel of the room a lot. It's cozy and won't take much to make it comfortable. "I'd probably divide my time here and at home, if you're really okay with that."

"Absolutely."

"So, I have the job?" I ask, laughing.

"You're hired," she says.

She reaches out to shake my hand.

64

BABY ARM

IT'S FRIDAY NIGHT, LATE, AND WE CAME TO HIDE IN LIAM'S room after we had dinner with Hannah, Maddie, and Tanner. We all enjoyed a few bottles of wine, and they got a little looser with each other the longer we hung out. When they started having a make-out session on the couch in front of us, Liam and I exchanged a look and snuck out, barely making it around the corner before we were giggling and shushing each other to be quiet.

We've been facing each other in bed for about an hour now, talking about the past few days at my new job and how much I love it, about a new role he's considering, and about his day on the set.

"I have a question to ask you," he says. "You can say no, of course."

"Ask away."

"Quinton Rivers has invited us to a party on his yacht on Sunday," he pauses, his lips twitching as he tries not to laugh.

"Do you ever have momentary freak-outs that this is your life?" I ask, laughing.

"All the time," he says, his eyes crinkling at the sides with his smile.

"You're such a big deal," I tease. He reaches out and tickles my side and I yelp, wriggling around until he stops. And then I reach out and tickle him, cackling when I realize he absolutely cannot handle being tickled. He jumps out of bed, and I do too, and we chase each other around the room. I throw a pillow at him, but he gets me anyway, tickling me until I'm wheezing. "Truce. Truce!" I yell.

He holds his hands up and backs slowly away, still not trusting that I won't attack.

My side hurts from laughing and I crawl back into bed, looking up at him as he stands on his side of the bed, staring at me.

"What?" I whisper.

He shakes his head slightly and seems to come out of his daze. He gets back in bed and turns on his side again to face me.

"I'd be happy to go with you to the schmancy yacht party. He really wants you to take this role, doesn't he?"

"Seems to." He shrugs slightly, still quiet.

"Are you okay?" I ask. His mood seems to have shifted in the last few moments.

"I am," he says softly. "Just thinking about how our time is almost up. Do you think we can still hang out sometimes?"

I reach out and put my hand on his cheek. "I would be devastated if we didn't."

"You mean it?" he asks.

"If you don't *know* that I mean it, then I have not done a good job of conveying how important you've become to me. I can hardly believe how much we've been through together." My voice gets a little shaky and I swallow hard, taking a deep breath. "I'll be here for you, no matter what, Liam. Wherever you go—you're already at the top, so I can't say, *when you get to the top*—" We laugh, and he reaches out and brushes the hair that falls into my eye. "But I promise I'll be in your life as much as you want me to be."

"You better not say that if you don't mean it." His eyes burn into mine. "Because I want you with me all the time."

My heart tumbles over itself and I try to catch my breath.

He leans over and kisses my cheek, lingering there for a few moments as my heart thunders inside.

"Night, Honey Bunches."

I groan. "Nope. Not it. Night, Hotshot."

"Sweet dreams."

I fall asleep thinking of all the fun we've had together. When we're not working, we're together, and when we're not together, we're texting or sending each other funny pictures or videos. Long dinners together, walks along the nearby beach, his patience when showing me how to take care of the plant wall, and how we'd like to try growing avocados next since we both love them so much. And never, ever running out of things to talk about.

It isn't that I haven't been sad about Hudson, I have been. Mostly sad that I let him in as much as I did. That I was intimate with him at all. Although realizing I probably never knew the real Hudson has replaced some of the hurt with anger. But Liam has kept me so busy I've hardly had time to dwell on Hudson.

Just one more reason to be grateful Liam's in my life.

———

On Sunday morning, I wake up with Liam's arms around me, his chest to my back, and his...*holy hell of a hard cock* resting between my cheeks. I squeeze my eyes tight as my core clenches, and I barely breathe for fear of waking him up or amping up this situation.

Now it makes sense why I woke up all hot and bothered from the most erotic dream of my life.

My skin breaks out into a cold sweat when I think of the details of my dream. Liam was leaning over me, thrusting into me so hard, I can almost feel it right now. My body shifts of its own accord and a small gasp escapes from my mouth.

"Well, this is a new development," Liam says, his husky voice sending another jolt between my legs. "I was so proud of myself for keeping my dick on my side of the bed." When he laughs, said dick surges and he curses. "I'm going to slowly back away. My apologies on behalf of the wood. It is my sincere hope that no creatures were harmed during the filming of this scene."

I snort before dissolving into a loud burst of nervous laughter. "It could have just as easily been me who mauled you in my sleep. The dreams sometimes—"

He tightens his hand around my waist, his nose and lips

burrowing in my neck. "Oh? Tell me more about these dreams..."

I giggle, my eyes closing as I feel him swell against me again. We're playing with fire, and I know it, but neither of us move. Every part of my body wants to stretch out and collide with his. My mind tells me that would not be smart. My heart is in no shape for that kind of confusion right now.

It's as if he can read my thoughts because he sighs and pulls away, getting out of bed. I know I should keep my eyes to myself, but they have a mind of their own and are drawn to the enormous...*e-nor-mous*...bulge in his boxer briefs. Damn. How has he been hiding that thing?

My respect for him somehow grows even more, knowing how hard he's worked to maintain the boundaries between us while dealing with something the size of a baby arm between his legs.

I put my head in my pillow and laugh until I cry, my nerves and hormones fried. When he comes out of the shower, his hair wet and messy, in his effortless, laid-back attire of a blue linen shirt and light linen pants, I can't even look him in the eye.

65

CALM ADORATION

I WEAR A SHORT AND FLIRTY WHITE SUMMER DRESS, MY LEGS and arms a warm golden brown in contrast.

Liam grins appreciatively when I step into the living room, standing up from the couch where he's been waiting. I flush when his eyes roam down my legs and squeeze my hands into a fist. I don't know where all this nervous energy is coming from, but it needs to stop. This is Liam, my friend, and a sex dream about him does not mean *anything*. And neither does the size of his schlong.

Not helpful, Summer. Not helpful.

I fan myself and murmur that I'm ready if he is.

Troy drives us to a private marina in Newport Beach, where the yacht is waiting in the water. Even from here, I can tell it's full of beautiful people and my nerves kick up.

"You've been awfully quiet," Liam says, taking my hand as we walk toward the boat. "You sure you're okay with this? You're not...you're not upset with me about this morning, are you?"

My face feels like it's on fire, and I swear, if I could and it would work, I'd tell it off right about now for throwing me under the bus. I'd guess it's either dark red by now or maybe a purplish hue.

"Not at all," I tell him, looking at my feet.

He chuckles and with his thumb and index finger, he turns my chin to face him. "Are you sure? Because you haven't looked me in the eye since last night."

I turn to face him all the way, needing to say this before we get on a boat with strangers. "Nothing you do upsets me, Liam." I fan my face, hoping my coloring is returning to normal. "I am constantly surprised by you. I have the best time with you. You have been unbelievably kind and funny and entertaining and sweet and-and hot. Um, I mean, well, yes, hot, but that wasn't what I meant to say—"

He's looking at me, smiling that crinkly-eyed, smirky, dimpled smile that I've thought was just his signature movie star smile, but there's something different I've noticed lately, when we're this close. It's the way he looks at me. It used to be flirtatious and that's all still there, but it's more than that. There's a calmness to him that wasn't there before, and I wish I knew what he's thinking when he stares at me with what I can only interpret as adoration. He doesn't even try to hide it.

"I think this is the quietest you've ever been," I say awkwardly.

Someone yells his name, and he lifts a hand, waving behind him, but he doesn't move away from me.

"Just listening to what you're saying about me," he says, his smile growing.

"Do you have anything to say?" I ask.

"About the things you're saying about me?"

"Or...anything else?"

"I'm sorry if I made you uncomfortable this morning," he says. His voice is low and hypnotic, curling around my skin like billows of smoke. "I can sleep on the floor tonight if you'd prefer. But either way, I can't wait to get done with this party and get you back home where I can have you to myself."

My skin heats again and I put my hand on my neck, wishing I could cool down.

He leans in, his mouth to my ear. "Getting to know you more every day only solidifies it for me, Summer." He backs away slightly, looking in my eyes to make sure I'm hearing him before he leans in again. "I'm in love with you, you know."

I gasp and he pulls away, lifting my knuckles up to his lips and kissing them.

"Shall we get this party over with?" he asks.

I nod dumbly and we walk onto the yacht. People rush toward us—well, Liam, of course, they have no need to rush toward me—and he introduces me to everyone, even the girls who have no interest whatsoever in acknowledging me.

We make our way through the people, heading to the other side of the yacht, as the boat starts moving. Quinton Rivers is on the couch and he waves us over, standing up as we approach.

He takes my hand in his and holds onto it obnoxiously long. "Who is this beautiful woman?" he says.

"This is my girlfriend, Summer Winters," Liam says, his arm around my shoulder.

When Quinton doesn't let go, Liam clears his throat and holds out his hand, and Quinton shakes his hand, his eyes still on me.

"The body on you. Are you in the entertainment industry?" Quinton says, his eyes dropping to my chest as he puckers his mouth.

"Uh, no?" I say, glancing at Liam who looks livid.

"Tell me she'll be on the set with you," Quinton says.

Is this guy for real?

"Well, I haven't exactly agreed to take this film yet, but if I do, it will be entirely up to her and her body that is off-limits to you," Liam says, looking at me like *is this guy for real?*

"I'll make it worth your while," Quinton says, smirking. He takes another long swig of his drink and reaches for me again. Liam pulls me back and takes my hand, leading me to the rail.

"The fuck was that about?" he says under his breath. "I am so sorry. Are you okay?"

"Oh yeah, I'm fine. He was just a little...much."

He studies me like he's not sure whether to believe me. "I will not be taking the role," he says.

"What? No, Liam. That's—don't do that because of me. I can handle men like that."

"Absolutely not. You shouldn't have to...*ever*...and I refuse to work with a man who treats women like that."

I wrap my arms around him and hug him. I feel the sudden need to hang onto him for dear life.

66

NSFW

OVER THE NEXT COUPLE OF WEEKS, I SETTLE INTO A ROUTINE of going into work three days a week and working from home the other two. I love being in the Lakelyn office. The energy is contagious, and the atmosphere is such a contrast to working on my dad's set where it was stifling and full of friction. Granted, I haven't been on a set with Sophia yet, but if her office is any indication, it will be a completely different experience.

Sven and Ana Claire are the biggest gossips in the place, and the two of them together can make me laugh until I cry.

A couple of days ago, Sven brought lunch back to my office and Ana Claire snuck over while she was supposed to be waiting for an important phone call, to tell us that she thought maybe she had a date by mistake.

When Sven and I grilled her to ask how that was possible, a date by mistake, she said she'd been trying to find a man for her daughter and had *accidentally* gotten into conversation with a very nice gentleman.

"I tried to tell him I was just on the app for my daughter, but he's insisted he wants to meet me instead." Her eyes were huge, and she clasped her Chanel pearl necklace. "What do I do?" Her willowy body draped over my desk. "How could I betray my daughter this way?"

I got the giggles and Sven talked to her as only he could in his no-nonsense way. "I'll tell you what you do. You go out with that fine piece of man and have him work you over, you delicious MILF of all MILFs."

I choked back a laugh as Ana Claire's hand went to her mouth and her shoulders shook as she laughed and looked back to make sure no one else was listening.

"I only know that term because of you, you naughty boy," she tells Sven. She shakes her finger at him, pretending to be stern. "I will do no such thing. But I don't think Sophia can be with him either." She leaned in to whisper, "He sent a photograph over the messages and...well, I will just say this...it reminded me of when that quarterback sent a picture of his you-know-what and it was all over the news." She snapped her fingers trying to remember his name. "Brett...fava beans."

I cackled then and she shot me a stern look, but her eyes were twinkling. "Brett Favre?" I asked.

She pointed at me. "That's the one. Why he ever thought

that was impressive enough to win over that cute young thing he wanted, I will never know."

Sven grabbed his phone and was quiet for a moment, and I knew he was Googling the dick pic even before he laughed. "Oh yeah. No. That's something you only bring out in the dark or with really nice lighting and a glass of whiskey."

Ana Claire nodded like *I told you so*, as I cracked up.

"Dang. Why can't *your* boyfriend get caught sending such scandalous photos, Summer?" Sven cut his eyes over at me and I flushed thinking about what Liam had to work with. Sven's mouth dropped and he laughed. "Look at the face on our girl, Ana Claire! She can't even think about her boyfriend's package without flushing."

"Did you just look for photos of my boyfriend's you-know-what?" I tried to defer.

"Guilty." He raised his hand and Ana Claire tsked.

"Back in my day, you didn't know what you were working with until the wedding night," she said. "Occasionally you'd get a sketchy idea during a nice kiss goodnight, but..." She shook her head primly and smoothed down her black dress. She straightened when we heard footsteps coming down the hall.

"Make sure you tell us if you change your mind about the *mistake date*," Sven mouthed before Sophia walked in and we all tried to act like we were hard at work.

Needless to say, I probably get more done on the days I work from home, but it's too fun to miss out on quality gold like that. And then in the evenings, I look forward to coming back to Liam's and catching up on our days, talking until we fall asleep.

Each day gets easier. I'm grateful I don't have to be in my dad's house or on set. I've made such great friends here, I have a fabulous job...and I've even been writing a ton. The time I spent with Hudson is beginning to feel like a fading snapshot. A blink in time that doesn't feel quite real.

———

Tonight, Liam is working later than usual, and my mom and Autumn FaceTime me while I'm making dinner. I tell them about what happened with Ana Claire and Sven and they're laughing as hard as I did. I have a bottle of wine chilling and the lemon chicken will be done in twenty minutes.

"So, how are you doing about Hudson?" Autumn says carefully. They haven't brought him up in our last handful of conversations, and neither have I. "Are you going to the wrap-up party with Liam?"

The party is tomorrow night and I've told Liam I'd go with him. He wanted me to know he'd understand if I wasn't comfortable going but also that it'd be way more fun if I did.

"I'm doing okay. I try not to think about him at all, and I've been so busy, it's helped. Dad called and asked me to come to the party too, so I'll go."

"Doesn't the fact that he's 'dating' Winslet sort of seem like a sign to you?" Mama asks, ignoring all talk of Dad. I don't blame her. I feel the same way talking about Hudson right now too.

"Well, yeah, it's a sign that I don't want to be with him," I say, dipping the wine bottle in and out of the ice bucket. "But what do you mean?"

"Like more of a sign that you're supposed to be with Liam," she says, grinning.

"Well, there's something that you and Dad agree on."

I hear the garage door opening and Liam walks in a few

minutes later, smiling when he sees my mom and Autumn on the screen.

"Hey," he says, leaning closer to smile at them. He kisses me on the cheek. "Wow, it smells great in here. What are we having?" He rubs his hands together in excitement.

"Lemon chicken. It's almost ready." I glance back at the timer.

"I'll go wash up really quick," he says. "Nice to see you, ladies." He winks at me and goes back to the bedroom.

I look at the screen again and Autumn has both hands on her heart and my mom is grinning from ear to ear.

"What?" I laugh.

"You tell us," Autumn squeals. "Are you guys—"

"No!" I lower my voice, leaning close to the phone. "*No*," I repeat.

But I can't stop flushing and I don't know why.

67

THAT'S A WRAP

LIAM HAS TO RUN ERRANDS THE AFTERNOON OF THE PARTY, SO he rushes in to get ready as I'm finishing up. He comes to a standstill when he sees me in front of the bathroom mirror, where I'm bending close enough to see my mascara as I feather it over my lashes.

"Hey," I say, trying to shut my mouth while I apply mascara, but I'm never able to.

He doesn't say anything, just swallows hard and continues to stare.

I turn to face him. "Are you okay?"

"You look…" He shakes his head and leaves it hanging.

"Am I too dressed up?" I bought this dress hoping it was the perfect mix of casual sexy. The soft black jersey material hugs my figure but is comfortable, and the shoulder and back cutouts give it that edge. My hair is in a thick ponytail of beach waves down my back but showing off the hints of skin through the cutouts.

"Perfect," he whispers. He swipes his hand over his mouth and takes a deep breath, looking like a deer in headlights.

"Are you sure you're okay?" I frown.

He nods reluctantly. "I am."

"*Oh*, I should let you get ready. Sorry, I'm hogging the bathroom. I'm done." I put the lid on the mascara and tuck it away in the drawer he's given me.

As I walk out, I think I hear him say, "*I'm* done."

"What was that?" I ask.

"Have fun," he says weakly.

I laugh. He's in a weird mood.

I, on the other hand, have been sipping a gin and tonic with lime, generous on the gin and lime, while I get ready, trying to override the nerves about this party. It's working. I'm feeling good. Not drunk, but just enough alcohol in my system to be a little happier than usual.

Liam walks out in a grey fitted suit with a white button-up shirt, the black buttons on the shirt a casual, fun touch. His blond hair is just a shade darker than mine, longer on top and messy, his blue-green eyes popping against his tan skin and white shirt. His cushiony lips lift when he sees me.

"You look *amazing*," I gush.

His eyes widen. "Oh. Thank you. You ready?" he asks. His dimples pop out when he sees the gin. "Ah. Yes, you are ready," he answers himself, laughing. "Feeling good?"

"Yes." I grin. "Would you like a drink before we go?"

"I'll have one at the restaurant." He looks around. "Is everyone gone already?"

"Yeah, they left about fifteen minutes ago."

He nods. "All right. Let's do this."

He puts his hand on the small of my back, hitting bare skin through one of the cutouts and I shiver.

"Do you need a jacket?"

"I think I'll be all right," I say, my cheeks getting hot. Must be that gin kicking in.

———

The party is already underway when we get there. My dad comes and kisses my cheeks and Bella stands next to him, smiling wide. She's showing a baby bump and looks much happier than the last time I saw her. She hugs me and plucks a couple glasses of champagne off a tray that passes, handing them to Liam and me.

"I'm apologizing to everyone who enters the party for the scene I created the last time we were all at the house," she says.

"Not necessary. You were going through a stressful time," I say, glancing at my dad who seems to want to be anywhere but here for this conversation.

"That's no excuse. Although it *has* helped for your father and I to have this time together," she says, grinning over at my dad. He grimaces and tries to turn it into a smile, turning around and signaling to the bartender to make him another of whatever he's having.

"That's great," I say. "I'm happy for you guys."

Liam puts his hand on my waist and squeezes and I turn to look at him. He looks worried and leans over to whisper,

"We can go anytime you want. I really just wanted to make an appearance."

"Okay." I turn to see what's caught his attention and Hudson and Winslet are against the back wall of the restaurant. One of his hands is on her hip, the other on her face, as he kisses her hard. I watch long enough to see them finally stop and laugh at something, and Hudson turns and puts his arm around her shoulder, gazing down at her with an intensity I can see from all the way over here. I turn back around and Liam takes my hand.

"Are you okay?" he asks.

I nod briskly. "Fine. Yeah." My voice sounds far away and Liam looks at me with concern. I clutch his arm. "No, really. We're not cutting this short over that. You just finished a movie that you worked really hard on and you deserve a night to celebrate. Don't worry about me."

He clinks our champagne glasses together. "I'd much rather be home with you, talking on the patio or in our bed." I shiver when he says *our bed* in his low, gruff voice. He leans closer. "I'm sick of all these people anyway."

I laugh and it drops when Hudson says, "Hey, Summer. Liam...when did you guys get here?" I turn and Hudson is standing there looking handsome and hopeful like he wasn't just kissing Winslet Barry's face off.

"We've been here a bit," I say, smiling coolly.

"You look gorgeous," he says, leaning down to kiss my cheeks. "I don't know if you saw...anything earlier...the photographers wanted a good shot—" He puts a hand on his neck and looks over his shoulder. Winslet is glaring over here and Liam puts his hand on my waist. Hudson tracks the movement and frowns. "Can I talk to you for a minute, Summer?"

"Sure, go ahead."

"I mean privately."

"No, thank you. I'm good right here," I tell him.

"I just wanted to say that I don't think it'll be much longer," he says quietly. He gives me a meaningful look and goes back to whisper in my ear. "Say you'll give me another chance. Please."

"You know what I've realized tonight, Hudson?" I take a step back and into Liam, whose hands steady me on either side of my hips. "I hope you'll be happy with Winslet. And I mean that. Because you know what? You said some amazing things to me when we were together, things I'm not sure were ever true, but it doesn't even matter. I just saw the truth with my own eyes, I saw how you really feel." I tilt my head toward where he'd been with Winslet. "You've *never* looked at me the way you looked at her just a few minutes ago."

I turn to Liam and his gaze is like molten lava burning through me.

And what I don't say, but it may as well be flashing at me in bright lights: *Hudson has never looked at me the way Liam is looking at me right now.*

I reach out and take his hand. "Take me home," I say.

His smile is all the answer I need.

68

ONBOARD

THE RIDE HOME IS QUIET. I FEEL ALMOST SHY WITH LIAM, which is crazy given how much time we spend together. We've felt like a team, and tonight, when I thought I might be catapulted back into that same weird dynamic that was on my dad's film set, I felt that way more than ever.

"Tanner said he and the girls got most of their stuff out earlier today?" Liam says.

"Yeah. I thought they were staying through the weekend, but Hannah's schedule got bumped up. She starts shooting in Vancouver on Monday. I think she's visiting her family and staying closer to the airport."

"Makes sense," he says.

And then we're back to silence. I start to get antsy, but we pull into his driveway and when he's in the garage, he looks at me tentatively.

"Thanks for going with me tonight. I hope it wasn't too painful," he says.

"I actually feel really good about the night."

"Oh yeah?"

I nod, glancing at him out of the corner of my eye and smiling.

"I'm glad," he says in that deep, intense tone that makes me want to lean in.

My mouth suddenly goes dry and my heart flip-flops in my chest, and he gets out of the car...which makes me think I must have imagined the moment we were having. We walk inside, and he picks up a remote and turns on the music. "Take My Breath" by The Weeknd plays, and he holds out his hand.

"Dance with me?" He moves slightly to the music and when I take his hand, he grins, tugging me close to him.

The beat would have my mom pulling a John Travolta, pointing to the floor and the ceiling as she shakes her hips when she's being silly, but Liam's movements are slow and intentional, and oh, so seductive. My body melds against his as our hips do the slowest sway. I let my body move the way it wants, not holding back, my hands going to his hair and sinking into it. His hands heat my skin as he runs them up and down my back before he clutches my waist and holds me tight against him. My head falls back and his other hand lands on my neck, our faces hovering close and our lips even closer.

"Summer," he whispers.

I close the distance between us, unable to deny this pull a second longer, and when our lips touch, it's different than any kiss I've ever had. Even my kisses with him before haven't been like this.

It's lust and passion and need and comfort and love. I could free-fall into him and he'd be there to catch me.

Is it possible to feel at peace while also practically combusting with excitement? Because that's how I feel and the same thing is radiating back at me through him. I have no doubt that he is totally in, not just for this moment, but he's not going *anywhere*. What we have created together, this relationship that started off as a sham, has become something unshakable.

He kisses me senseless, his tongue and lips dueling with mine. We get lost in each other, his hand tugging on my ponytail as he kisses down my neck. I gasp when his other hand lands on my backside and he groans when he squeezes, dropping his other hand to squeeze the other side.

"I've had a hard time keeping my eyes off of this perfection all night," he says as he kneads my behind and then presses his hardness against me. My mouth falls open. "You in this dress. I can't imagine anything better except maybe you out of it."

I laugh and he kisses it right off of me, his tongue making me weak in the knees. I lean into him, and he picks me up, carrying me to his room. When we get there, I expect him to put me on the bed, but he sets me down in front of it, kissing his way to my ear.

"I want you to know I'm not assuming anything is happening in that bed tonight other than me kissing your face off," he says, his eyes crinkling with his smile. "I just need a minute to convince my dick to get onboard."

I crack up and pull his face toward mine until everything that can touch does. "I love the way you make me laugh. And I'd rather you convince your dick to get onboard *me*."

He laughs at that and especially when I add, "That sounded sexier in my head."

"Are you kidding me? I've never had to shower so much in my life. If you got any sexier, our bed would've gone up in flames the moment you first got in it." His voice is raspy and even though we're being playful, the need for him is all-consuming.

"I love the way you say *our bed*," I whisper.

His hands roam up my sides and when he touches my breasts, palming them before focusing on the nipples, I moan, and he kisses me again until I'm putty in his hands.

"There's no one I ever want in our bed besides you," he says. "Do you believe me yet, Summer? I need you to believe that I am in this. I'm not playing a fucking part. I'm not dicking around to get you to sleep with me or confused about what I'm feeling...I *love* you. I started to love you when you said yes to this crazy plan. And every day since. It grew when you were so brave during the plane crash and getting stung by a freaking box jellyfish. But what has had my heart pounding out of my chest," he puts my hand on his heart and I feel it pounding as hard as mine is right now, "are the moments of perfection we've had since moving in together. It doesn't get any better than laughing with you, talking until we can't keep our eyes open..."

My eyes get blurry with emotion and my heart is so full I can't believe it.

"I do believe you," I say shakily. "I didn't think I could trust my heart, but you've proven that wrong. You show me every day and it's a deep *knowing* right here, that you mean what you say." I put his hand on my heart now and he smiles when it thumps.

"That's some speedy pounding," he agrees. He gets that look in his eye that lets me know he's about to say something ridiculous. "How 'bout you lay back on that bed and I'll show *you* speedy pounding? Damn, *not* speedy... although the first time might be since...fuck, have I ever lost all my smooth..."

I get on the bed and stay on my knees, turning to face him and, as always, laughing. "Come on, Mr. Movie Star, let's see what you've got."

69

LITTLE BUDDY

AND DOES HE EVER PROCEED TO SHOW ME WHAT HE'S GOT.

He's a combination of cocky—because he *is* Liam, after all—and apologetic when I strip his boxer briefs off and send them flying across the room.

It's impossible to look away.

"I mean, holy *hell*." I can't even try to take the awe out of my voice. Sven would be *so* jealous right now.

He shakes his head, grinning, and rubs his hand down his face, his cheeks flushing underneath his tan. "Why am I embarrassed right now? And why are you not naked?"

He lifts my dress up inch by inch, losing all shyness and inhibition as his hands slide up my skin. When he pulls it over my head and I'm in front of him in my pretty black lacy set, he sucks in a breath and stares at me for a long time.

I'm still on my knees as he stands in front of me, and I move back, undoing my bra and letting it drop. His mouth parts and he curses, swelling even harder. He grips his cock as if trying to rein it in and I grin, tugging my panties down. He groans and I hold my hand out, which he takes without hesitation.

He kisses me and I lean into him, gasping when I feel his hardness against my skin.

"Those sounds are gonna be the end of me," he whispers. "Let's see if we can make you sing."

He kisses his way down to my breasts and licks and sucks his way around my cleavage before wrapping his mouth around my nipple. His tongue flicks it and his fingers tease my other side until they trail down my stomach and land on my bud of nerves. He spends time there, watching for every intake of breath, every gasp, as he teases me gently at first, and faster as I rock against him. Just when I feel like I'm about to explode, he dips down and slides a finger inside, in and out, and then two fingers. His mouth moves to my other nipple and his fingers never stop, dipping in deeper each time and coming out all the way to slide over my clit and back inside.

I tremble and reach out to grip him, partly because I need something to hold onto and because I'm dying to touch him, and he backs up.

"Nuh-uh. Not yet. Lie back and spread your legs," he says.

I do what he says, so turned on I can't see straight.

He puts his fingers in his mouth and groans. "Mmm."

I squirm and fist the sheets, as he stares down at me for a few seconds before lowering his face between my legs and adding his tongue to the mix, the same rhythm as his fingers were doing before, only everything is *more*. He slides three fingers inside and I'm so wet, I buck against him, wanting more. I want *him*, but his tongue is amazing and the things it's doing is—

I scream his name, the orgasm catching me off guard even though I've been on the edge of it for a while. It's *mind-blowing*. Liam's hands move around to clutch my ass as he lifts me to his face, his tongue diving inside to catch the aftershocks.

He knows the second it's too much and lifts his head, lowering me back to the bed as he looks up at me. I glance at him incredulously and his expression is blissful.

"I am shooketh," I admit, and he grins, moving up and leaning over me.

"Is that a good thing?"

I nod quickly, my eyes still huge. "Like, the *best* thing."

"Shooketh feels right. I'm there." He nods.

I reach out and wrap my fist around his cock and he takes a deep breath, exhaling through his teeth. "I didn't know if I could handle this guy, but you've got me so worked up, I think I'll inhale you."

He closes his eyes, laughing and thrusting slightly into my fist. "You want this?" When he opens his eyes, the desire is a living, breathing *fire*.

"So much," I whisper.

He grabs a condom out of his drawer and holds up a piece of paper. "For the sake of starting this relationship off with full disclosure, I have to test regularly throughout every role. Here are the negative results, and I haven't had sex with anyone since I met you. I did have to kiss the

Winslet viper on set obviously, but she was also herpes-free."

I make a face. "Since I am still on an orgasm-high, I don't even mind that we're talking about this right now, after the most powerful sexual experience of my life..."

He lifts his eyebrows and grins from ear to ear. "*Really*... and we haven't even done the act. Things are looking good for you, little buddy," he says, looking down.

"Did you just talk to your dick?"

"Uh, yeah."

"There is *nothing* little about our buddy here."

He thrusts harder into my fist and opens the condom. I stop him before he puts it on.

"I tested again a month ago, and the results were negative for me too...and I've been on birth control for a long time. I've never had sex without a condom, and there's no pressure if you're not comfortable with that, but—"

"It'll be the first time for me too." He tosses the condom over his head and kisses me hard. "I love you," he whispers. He pulls out of my fist and lines himself up, easing in so slowly. We both groan with that first contact, skin to skin.

And for all my teasing about inhaling him, he takes his time inching his way in. He pulls out and rubs himself against my clit, making me squirm against him, drunk on the things he makes me feel, and then sliding deeper inside. By the time he does that too many times, I'm practically begging him for more. I whimper and grip his cheeks, tugging him tight against me as I thrust up.

"You want all of me?" he asks. "Is that what you want?" He rocks deeper and faster.

"More," I moan. "Yes. All."

And when he plunges in all the way, as deep as he can

go, we both cry out. I fall apart again and he holds completely still, closing his eyes tight.

"Mmm, you feel too good," he says. "This is...the best."

When he starts moving again, he rests my ankles on his shoulders and we watch him glide in and out. Everything is so sensitive that when he presses his thumb against my bundle of nerves, I think I might pass out. I moan and shudder against him and he twitches inside. He groans and I move my ankles, pulling him back down on top of me.

There's no stopping now. Our movements frantic. Our bodies slapping against each other. Sweaty and resolute focus as we ride it out together.

It's earth-shattering. For me, anyway.

And when he finally drops next to me, panting, and turns to me, grinning, he says, "I never knew sex could be like...that. I'm...speechless." He leans over and kisses me softly, his hands on my face, brushing my hair away. "You're the only one for me, Summer Winters."

70

L-WORD

WE DON'T LEAVE THE HOUSE ALL WEEKEND.

Well, except to venture out to the patio and pool, where he rocks my world in the California breeze.

It's the best weekend of my life.

Every time we're together, something shifts in me, the connection between us transcending into a deeper, more profound bond. And yet, it doesn't feel as strange as I might've expected, that the two of us who have become such best friends, could become *this*.

In the brief downtime, I still try hard not to define what *this* is.

Because I was quick to rush things with Hudson, and I was wrong...about him and the depth of my feelings.

So, I try to just live in the moment and enjoy every second. Because deep down, I know that this is something that would hit me entirely different if *we* went south.

On Sunday night, when Autumn has called a handful of times and is starting to get worried because she still hasn't heard from me after the party, I tell Liam I better call her back. He kisses my shoulder and goes to the kitchen to make us a snack.

As soon as she sees my face, she squeals. "What have *you* been up to?" She shakes her booty and fists and then sticks her mouth as close as it can get to the camera. "So, I guess it's safe to say you're okay?"

She pulls away and is making the goofiest face. I laugh and know that I'm all shades of red.

"You survived seeing Hudson?" she asks, bursting out laughing before she can get it all the way out.

"It went fine. Now that I've seen how much he's like Dad, I can't unsee it. And yeah, just..." I shudder. "He actually grosses me out now. So yeah, I'm glad we got that out of the way, so it won't be awkward next time we run into each other, hopefully "

"And Liam?" she asks.

I look up to the ceiling, trying to tamper down the smile. "Well, let's just put it this way...I just *thought* I'd been ravaged before." I look at her and shake my head, my grin taking over my face. "I-I don't even know what to say. Liam is...I've never felt anything like this."

"Eek," she squeals. "I'm so excited. I *knew* he was the person for you. I knew it. I'm so happy for you, Summer. And...you really are okay about—"

"I am. I really am." I lean in and whisper. "We have had sex in every room in this house and the backyard too." I put my hand over my mouth and giggle. "And each time I can't imagine it being any better than the last time and it *is*."

She puts her hand on her heart. "Awww. I am so jealous right now."

"I'm in love with him." It comes out before I can stop it. I stare at her and my eyes fill with tears. Her eyes go huge. I stare at her in horror. "No, I can't be. I'm crazy. Tell me I'm crazy. I shouldn't be thinking about love anytime soon." I shake my head and shake my hands out too, sniffling and wiping my face. "I'm not going to define it. Things are incredible, and I will just leave it at that. He's said it though. He loves me."

She presses her lips together and her eyes fill before she takes a deep breath, giving her head a quick shake. "Mm-hmm. You wanna know what I think?" She leans in closer to the screen. "I think you've been shoving down feelings for Liam since the day you met him. And you went for what you know—Hudson even has the *same career as Dad*. I'm not saying he didn't care about you—hell, Dad still wants Mom! But you saw through it in time, and you see the difference in what this feels like. It's not too soon when you're feeling the *truth*."

I nod, rolling my eyes to the ceiling when tears stream down my face again. "I don't know why I'm crying. This weekend has been the most perfect thing I've ever—"

"That's why you're crying. You're feeling it all, and it's

normal to be a little scared about it, but I've seen the way Liam feels about you. He's not going anywhere."

I take a deep breath and grab a tissue to wipe my face. "I'm being silly. Why can't I just have a fling with a hot actor and be chill about it?"

"Because that hot actor saw you and wanted you to be *his* from the get-go!" she yells, cackling. "Just make sure you call me the minute he proposes…"

I stare at her and then look around to make sure Liam's not close by, hearing this. "Autumn!" I put my finger over my lips, and she just laughs harder, waving me off. "I might be saying the L-word *to you only*, but stop trying to marry me off already."

She shrugs. "When it's right, it's right. If you love him, tell him. Or just keep doing what you're doing because he looks really happy." She smiles big and my heart drops when she waves and says, "Hi, Liam."

He puts his chin on my shoulder. "Hey, Autumn." His voice sounds on the verge of laughter, and I groan, which makes them both laugh. "Sorry to interrupt, but really, just act like I'm not here." He smiles at me on the screen, and I stick out my tongue. He tickles my side and I squirm against him, which has an immediate effect.

"I'll talk to you later, Autumn," I say, too nervous she'll call me out on my feelings more than she already has. And there's the added fact that I don't want my little sister to see my turned-on face…which is what will happen if he doesn't take a step back with that weapon he wields so well. But oh no, his hand clutches my waist, and he stays *right there*.

Bastard.

Autumn smirks. "Later, you two. Don't do anything I wouldn't do." She blows a kiss and ends the call.

I don't move, staring straight ahead.

It's possible he's orgasmed me into emotional overdrive.

He kisses my neck. "I *am* really happy," he says in my ear.

And even though I could be mortified that he heard that part of our conversation, the way he makes love to me so thoroughly the rest of the night takes away the fear.

He wipes away my inhibition and hope takes root.

Nothing could be better than this.

71

DOMESTICATED

Liam wants me here, there, and everywhere.

I want him just as much.

And the best part? We don't have to hide our relationship from a single soul. We're just catching up to what everyone already thinks of us. So, when we go out to eat or go grocery shopping or to a movie event, it's not as nerve-racking as before since we're just being ourselves. I'm not being careful of his feelings or anyone else's, and the love just deepens.

He keeps being the same amazing person, making it easy for me to trust that I can place my heart in his care.

Summer is long gone, but the weather is still lovely, the evenings cool. I keep thinking I'll be able to wear my boots, but it's almost Thanksgiving and I still haven't.

My job is the next best thing in my life. I love it, and I'm still writing regularly too. Sophia has asked about what I'm working on several times, and when I finally tell her what the story is about, she makes my life.

"Brilliant," she says, eyes bright. "I want to see it as soon as it's complete."

That fills me up with all kinds of fire, and I write every chance I get, letting the words pour out of me.

I hear a rumor about a film Hudson is doing sans my dad, and I'm certain it's my idea, but I'm so far removed from that story now that I'm okay with him taking it.

I've tried to convince my dad to keep working with him, to not let what happened between me and Hudson affect their working relationship, but he swears he's treated Hudson fairly and that it's good for Hudson to spread his wings if he really wants his own career as a filmmaker. My dad also says it's time he puts me first.

I'm so happy with Liam that it's not something I need from my dad regarding Hudson, but I don't belabor the point.

It feels good to be happy.

When I get home around lunchtime, Liam is already home. He's taken a new role and is shooting primarily in L.A., which has been great. Sophia's already made it clear that she'll be fine when I go on set with him, should I choose to do that, because I can still get my work done. We knew today would be a short day for him, so I made sure I got off early too.

He kisses me hello, and whispers against my lips, "Follow me."

I grin, thinking we're going straight for the bed, and I am fine with that. I overslept this morning, and we didn't get our usual lovin' in. But he surprises me by going outside, and on our patio is a beautiful, very fat cat. Grey and white and brown with blue eyes. *Massive.*

I gasp, looking between Liam and the cat. "He's gorgeous."

"I saw him in the front yard the other day and didn't think anything of it, but when I saw him here this afternoon, the dude kept wanting me to pet him, and he hasn't left."

I laugh, petting the cat and melting when he rubs his head all over my hand and then falls over on his side for me to pet him more. "Oh, he's so good."

"Look how domestic we're becoming," he says, grinning as he sits down next to me and pets the cat. "I love our life."

I smile, still looking at the cat. "Me too."

"I'm in love with you, Summer."

He says this often and it still feels like a revelation. I turn to look at him, his blue-green eyes looking even more beautiful in the sunlight.

"I'm in love with you too, Liam."

He swallows hard, his hand moving to my face. "Truly?"

"All my heart," I whisper.

He kisses me hard, and the cat weaves its way between us, plopping down on my lap. I laugh and look down.

"This guy is heavy!"

"Looks like he's found his home and he's not budging." Liam laughs. "Same thing I did when I met you." He smirks and those eyes crinkle up when his smile grows.

"God, you're cute. I will never ever get tired of looking at you...among other things."

"How...uh...would you feel..." He stutters and my eyes narrow.

"What?" My tone is suddenly suspicious.

"You can say no," he says quickly.

"Spit it out, Taylor."

He grimaces and now I'm really worried.

"How would you feel about going to Nantucket to meet my family for the weekend?"

"Oh." I don't hide my surprise. "Of course. Like *this* weekend? Or just sometime?"

"If we don't do it this weekend, I'll talk myself out of it. You know they're...complicated."

I squeeze his hand. "Okay. Sure. It's Friday, so...what does that mean exactly?"

"Well, I tentatively scheduled two different options because I wasn't sure how you'd feel about flying."

I make a face.

"We could take a private plane with a pilot who has taught lessons for twenty years, *or* we could take a commercial flight if you'd feel safer on a bigger plane."

"Can I sleep the whole way?"

"Absolutely. That will ensure you're rested as I ravage you later tonight when we're on solid ground."

I grin. "Okay. Your parents are okay with this?"

"I'll check now."

"This is crazy!" I laugh, and then hold the cat's sweet face in my hands, turning him toward Liam. "But what about him?"

"Let's take him."

"I don't know...I've heard cats take time to acclimate to new places."

"I'm not sure he'll even want to go inside," Liam says, standing up.

I try to shift the cat off of me, but he doesn't budge, so I pick him up and stand.

"But I can see if Troy's wife would want to check on him if we left him here too," he adds.

"Let's see what he does." I move toward the house and then set him down when we go inside. He leans against my legs and goes back and forth, rubbing his head and body against me. I shoot Liam an excited look, and he lifts his eyebrows.

"Told you," he says, his pouty lips puckering as he tries to hold back his laugh. He hurries off to make a few phone calls while the cat entertains me.

Within an hour and a half, Troy's wife, Marla, has the cat we've dubbed Elton, and she's going to check to see if he has a microchip in case his owner is missing him. Otherwise, she'll watch him until we get back. We're on the plane, I'm beginning to feel drowsy, and when I wake up again, we're in Nantucket.

"I've always wanted to come here," I tell him, yawning.

"Welcome. I'll do my best to show you a good time while you're here."

"I have no doubt."

A driver is waiting to take us to Liam's family's restaurant, someone Liam knows named Mal. He's an older local who seems sweet. It's too dark to see much, but when we step out of the car and I hear the waves, I'm already happy. The oval sign for Lancelot's is white with blue letters and turns in circles.

"I know it's later than we usually eat, but this is really the only way we'll see them," he says as we're walking inside.

He's been quiet on the drive over, and it makes my nerves kick up a bit too, thinking about meeting his family.

When we step inside, the restaurant is crowded, despite

it being after ten. The hostess's eyes bulge when she sees Liam, and she grabs two menus, her hand shaking slightly. I've gotten so used to seeing women react to him this way, I'm sympathetic.

"I think Lance and Linda have a table set up for us already," he tells her, smiling.

"Oh," she says, her mouth staying stuck in the O.

Liam nods and that seems to snap her out of it. She starts moving and then tells us to follow her as an afterthought, taking us through the dining room and to a long table toward the back.

No one is sitting there yet, but it looks ready for a party of seven. We sit down and gradually, everyone in the restaurant comes over to say hello to Liam or to introduce themselves to me.

Everyone but his family.

72

WHIPPED

LIAM GOES BACK TO SEE IF THEY'RE HERE AND COMES BACK apologizing.

"This was probably a bad idea," he says. "They work nonstop, so it's never really a good time."

It's after eleven when his mom comes out and then his dad follows, both shaking my hand and saying a brisk hello. And then Lara and her boyfriend, Barrett, come in.

"This was my first night out of the restaurant in ten days straight," Lara says, slouching in the seat across from me.

"Thought you could use one more night here," Liam says, trying to joke, but it falls flat.

His dad, Lance, keeps talking to someone at the bar, and his mom, Linda, instructs the waitress to bring out drinks and clam chowder for everyone.

"Where's Lachlan?" Linda asks Lara.

It's hard not to mention all the L-names, but I am the last one who can talk about anything name-related.

"No clue."

There's an awkward silence, as Liam and I sit waiting for one of them to make eye contact so we can attempt conversation. Once Linda has settled down about the clam chowder taking too long to come out, she turns to me.

"I've been seeing you guys in the magazines," she says. She shakes her head. "Those photographers sure seem to get a kick out of getting celebrities at their worst."

Ow. Yeah.

"You're much prettier than I expected," Lara says, studying me.

"She's breathtaking," Liam says, pulling my hand to his lips.

I flush and look at Lara. "Thank you." I'm not sure if that was the correct response, but my mama taught me to say thank you when anyone even halfway compliments me.

"So, what brought you here this weekend?" Barrett asks. Honestly, he seems to be the nicest one in the bunch. "It's good to see you, man."

"I wanted all of you to meet Summer," Liam says, smiling at me. "And vice versa."

"What was Winslet Barry like?" Lara asks Liam. "*She* is breathtaking. I heard she only eats raw food. Is that true?"

"She's a piece of work," Liam says. "And she's breathtaking in the way that makes you want to stop breathing altogether if you have to be in the same room with her for any length of time." He turns to me and I try not to laugh. "I don't think she eats raw food, but I wasn't paying attention. Does she?"

"No," I say, coughing into my hand.

"Any work for you out there?" Lance seems to finally join the conversation.

"Consistent work, yep," Liam says.

Lance looks away, his eyes on the TV screen over the bar. Does he really not know what a big deal his son is?

Linda gets a text and it's the first time she smiles. "There's Lachlan. Oh...he's not making it. He's taking out that girl who just started working here and didn't want to come back." She glances at Liam when she sets her phone down and crinkles her nose. "Your hair looks blonder. Don't tell me you've started dyeing it now." She turns to Lara and they roll their eyes. "Who knew my son would be more vain than my daughter?"

"Pretty sure it's always done this when I'm in the sun more," Liam says. "Not that I have anything against changing my hair color for roles, but nope, this is what I've got. Baby, I was born this way." He does his best Lady Gaga impression under his breath.

Linda sighs and looks back to catch the waitress's eye, waving her over. "Can you bring our catch of the day and a few sides? We'll finish up what's left..." When the waitress leaves, Linda sighs again, focusing on Liam. "We sure could use your help around here."

"The expansion looks great," he says, his grip on my hand tightening.

"That's not what I meant and you know it. Throwing a little money our way isn't the same as being here for the day in and day out."

Barrett clears his throat. "That expansion was almost half a million dollars, not exactly little," he says, glancing at Liam. "They were pretty stoked when that check came."

"Glad if it helped."

"They were even happier about the other two installments, the one that built a new parking lot and the barrier... it kept us from flooding," Barrett adds.

I definitely like Lara's boyfriend best.

"We are running ourselves ragged here," Linda goes on like no one has said anything since her last statement.

"You seem busy, that's a good thing," Liam says. "I was hoping Summer could try the cheesecake." He turns to me. "My mom makes the best ch—"

"Sold out. You have to get here before ten o'clock if you want to get the cheesecake," she says, sniffing.

My blood has been steadily boiling, but now I'm afraid my brains are going to explode if I keep holding it in.

"Liam has been so excited for me to meet all of you," I say, looking at Linda and then the rest of them. Lance's eyes are the last to meet mine, but he does reluctantly. "He speaks so highly of all of you. And he gets calls from all of the top-tier directors throughout every week...each of them clamoring to work with your son. He never brags about it—I only know because I'm the one answering the phone half the time, or they've started calling *me* hoping they can reach him when he's on set so they can catch him before he says yes to someone else. I'm not sure you realize that he's the highest-grossing movie star, not only of this year, but of *all time*." I look at him and put my hand on his cheek, speaking as if we're the only two people in the room. "And I am so proud of who you are, the way you love, the kindness you show no matter how you're treated. I love you so much," I whisper.

His eyes get shiny and mine do too. "You're the best thing," he whispers. "I love you with everything in me."

He stands and I start to get up, ready to follow him out of here. But then he gets down on one knee, and my heart drops down to the ground next to him. He pulls a ring out of his pocket and holds it up.

"I've been carrying this around since the week after we... danced," he says, his voice husky as he laughs. "You have me whipped, heart and soul, and I want my family to be *you*."

73

SHINE ON ME

"You've got me." My hands land on his cheeks, and I bend closer to him, swallowing hard when I think about how much I mean those words. He does have me...all of me.

"Thank God." His shoulders sag with relief for a second and then he glances at the ring like it's an afterthought. He perks up and grins and my heart turns over. "How would you feel about being my wife?"

I pause for a moment because I'm shocked by how peaceful I feel about all of this. "I'd feel *really great* about it." I laugh and he stands up and kisses me hard.

The restaurant erupts, and I barely glance back at his family when Liam wraps his arm around me and hurries me out the door.

Fortunately, Mal is staring at the water with his hands in his pockets but jumps into action when he sees us walking toward the car. He opens the car door with a flourish, and as we're getting in, says, "Where to next?"

"Give me one second," Liam tells him and then he turns and leans his forehead on mine. "I should have planned all of this out a lot better than I did. And I *did* have an elaborate plan in place for next Friday night, after we're home. The ring has been burning a hole in my pocket for so long." He laughs. "First though...I needed to show you where I was from, give you an out once you'd met my phenomenal family..." He grimaces and I squeeze his hand. "I'm so sorry about them. For the record, my *extended* family truly *is* incredible, and I'll take you to see them in New York and Chicago sometime. I don't get to see them enough, but after tonight with my parents and Lara...I think I'll be more selective about which family I spend time with. But it felt only right to show you what you could be getting into, if you choose me."

"I choose you. Meeting them doesn't change my mind about you." I lower my voice so only Liam will hear me. "If anything, it makes me love you all the more. You're such a good person, Liam, and you're living out your dreams despite opposition from the people who should be cheering you on the loudest. I'm honored that you want to spend your life with me." My voice cracks at the end, but Mal sneezes three times in a row, so loud it makes me jump.

"Sorry. So sorry," Mal says, before sneezing again. He seems mortified, but it's apparent he's incapable of sneezing quietly.

Nothing can affect the moment though. Liam and I laugh and eventually Mal does too.

Liam reaches for his phone. "Let me shoot a quick text and if I don't hear something right back, I'll go with another plan," he says, fingers flying.

Mal nods. "Whatever you say, boss." He lifts a finger and then sneezes again.

Liam's phone rings and he answers right away.

I can hear a guy's voice through the phone and Liam glances at me, grinning. "I should've known you'd have conditions. It's a deal. Gladly. Hell, you can come to every single one of my premieres if you want, bring a date, you name it." He laughs and lifts my hand up to his lips, kissing it twice. "Thanks, man. I'm the lucky one. Can't wait for you to meet her. Kind of glad it won't be tonight though." I can hear the guy laughing, and Liam winks at me before hanging up. He leans forward and gives an address to Mal.

Mal pulls out of the parking lot and Liam leans back in the seat, more relaxed.

"This is turning out way better than I'd hoped," he says. "I mean, it can't get any better because you said yes. But...I'm really glad we aren't going back to my parents' house tonight."

I am too, but I keep that to myself. We drive for a while and my curiosity gets the best of me. "Where *are* we going?"

"Well, I hope it's as cool as Zac made it sound."

"Zac?"

"Zac Ledger..."

"As in the quarterback for—I have no idea who..." I laugh and try to come up with a team, but nope. Sports aren't my specialty.

"The Patriots." He grins. "Yeah, we were seated at an award show together and when he found out I'd grown up in Nantucket, he mentioned he'd renovated this place...and he offered it to me whenever I came through."

We eventually pull down a long driveway and I see a house surrounding a lighthouse ahead, overlooking the water.

"We're just a night earlier than planned," he says, bumping my shoulder with his.

My eyes grow wide. "We're staying in that?" I don't see another soul—maybe in the light of day, I'll see other houses, but for now, it's like we're on our own private beach. "It's gorgeous! I've been obsessed with lighthouses since seeing that movie with all the kids—"

"*Yours, Mine & Ours*," he says, stepping out of the car and holding out his hand for me. "That's exactly what I said when Zac told me about this place."

My face hurts from smiling so hard. "I can't believe we've never talked about this. My dad hated that movie so much... which just made me love it more."

He laughs and then turns around, remembering Mal. He reaches out to shake his hand and Mal beams up at Liam. "Thank you for your help tonight."

"It was my pleasure," Mal says. "I'll be here in two shakes if you need me again." He mimes zipping his lips and throwing away the key. "And I won't breathe a word of your news or your location," he whispers.

"We appreciate that," Liam says.

Mal gets in the car and waits until Liam unlocks the door before pulling away. And then I'm lifted off my feet as Liam carries me inside, flipping on the closest light. We both stare up at the amazing circular staircase that seems endless from this angle.

"It's so beautiful," I whisper.

Liam moves toward the stairs and not taking his time

either—he bolts up the stairs, still carrying me. I jostle around, laughing.

"What are you doing?"

He barely even sounds out of breath as he says, "I'm getting you naked at the top of this lighthouse as fast as I possibly can. I can't wait another second."

74

EPILOGUE, SUMMER

WE GET MARRIED TWO SUMMERS LATER ON THE PRIVATE BEACH surrounding the lighthouse with our close friends and family. Yes, even Liam's family. And I have to hand it to them —they've made an attempt to be pleasant since the night we met. I think my little speech and then Liam's proposal might have stunned them speechless...or maybe it was the fact that Barrett broke up with Lara after our visit and told her it was because of how awful all of them are to Liam. I don't know if they eventually got back together because he's the best chef they have at Lancelot's or if Lara realized she can't live without him, but I guess they've figured it out because they're engaged.

Sven cannot stop beaming the whole day. He also can't stop trying to sneak in selfies next to Liam. I finally step aside and let him snap away until Liam pulls me back in, and the three of us get some great shots.

I can't tell if Zac Ledger and my sister hit it off or clash at the wedding, but every time I turn around, they're near each other. Autumn looks gorgeous, and Zac was just on the cover as *People's* Sexiest Man Alive, so he's clearly not struggling in the beauty department either. But my sister is wearing an expression I've never seen on her—a mix of bashful and furious—while Zac looks amused, and I can tell the photographers are dying to go snap happy on the two of them when they're not taking pictures of Liam and me.

We give *People* an exclusive photo shoot and hold off on an exotic honeymoon, choosing instead to drive along Highway 1. We stop at exquisite Airbnbs along the way, taking our time getting home. We have the best time but are so happy to get back to Elton, who is officially ours now. He is the cuddliest, neediest cat in the universe, and we're mad about him.

———

My first film comes out just after our second anniversary. Liam's in it, which automatically makes it a huge hit, but with Sophia's help along the way and my dad throwing in his two cents too, it can't help but be a success. I pinch myself every day that this is my life. I'm living my dream and it's far exceeded anything I could have expected. But it's Liam who makes all of it feel meaningful.

I've seen Winslet a few times and her career isn't faring

so well these days. Her reputation for being difficult to work with has gotten out, and the last time I saw her, I kind of felt sorry for her. Not enough to have her in my movies, but I wish her well. Maybe she'll try being nice.

Hudson has been linked with various actresses since Winslet, who I think might've broken his heart when she dumped him to date Quinton Rivers for a hot minute. Yes, that gross director. The rumor going around now is that Hudson is involved with director Joanna DeGenali's daughter, and his screenplay has been optioned. I wish him well too, and the last time I saw him, we had a nice conversation.

"How does it feel to be at the top of your game?" he asked.

"I don't know that I'm at the top of my game, but I'm really happy," I told him.

"Still can't believe you married that fool," he said, laughing.

"Sure did," I said. "He's the real deal."

He nodded, his laugh dying down. "You made the right call."

"Be happy, Hudson. And you never know, the next time I see you, maybe both of our films will be competing for an Oscar."

"May the best person win," he said, smiling. "It'll be you, Summer. You deserve it, you really do."

It was a sweet moment. He was never a bad person. My dad either. Consumed by careers and the heady feeling of power? No question. But Dad has even matured. He's been a good dad to little Augusta. (Bella put her foot down when my dad tried to fight for Winter Winters.) I think he might get it right with this one.

What Liam and I have is unique for Hollywood, and really, for most couples we know, period. We work hard to stay grounded and to put each other first.

"What are you doing?" he asks, coming out to sit next to me on the patio.

I point to Elton, who is taking a bath under the lemon

tree. "I'm thinking he's got it made, and so do I." I turn to face him, leaning my knees against him. He turns and props his arm on top of my knees.

"Should we complicate his life by giving him a baby to cuddle next to?" he asks.

We've been talking about it more and more, both of us wanting to be young when we have our kids.

I bend down and pick up the wrapped box I hid under the couch, handing it to him with a smile. "I was going to ask you the same question."

His eyes light up and he tears open the package, yelling when he sees the positive pregnancy test. "I can't wait," he says, kissing me. "You're having my baby, Sweet Lips?"

"You're in this now, no backing out of the contract," I tease.

"I've got you right where I want you, Mrs. Taylor." He lifts his hand and tilts his head. "One second." He picks me up and moves me until I'm straddling him. "*Now*, I've got you right where I want you," he whispers.

75

EPILOGUE, LIAM

I HEAR THE WHIMPERS FROM THE BABY MONITOR AND GET OUT of bed, staring down at Summer sleeping. The woman is beautiful in any setting, from any angle, no matter if she hasn't slept in days or if she's sick or...well, you name it, she guts me on a daily basis, and has since the day I first saw her. It's been eight years since she moved in with me and I'll never get tired of seeing her in my bed.

I hear the sounds again and turn the monitor off, rushing to the baby's room before she starts wailing.

I pick up Scarlet and she nestles into my arms trying to

suck my neck the hilarious way babies do before I place her on the changing table and change her diaper. When I'm done, we walk down the hall, pausing outside Evan and Elijah's rooms and then across the hall to Dylan's, before I take Scarlet to her mama.

We added a few bedrooms on the main floor once we knew we were pregnant with the twins and it's a good thing because they were just the beginning. We're having so much fun having babies, I'll build another wing if I have to. Summer swears this is our last baby though.

"Hey, little angel," I say, looking down at Scarlet. "Your brothers are sleeping soundly like you'll be doing in no time. *Please* be sleeping soundly in no time." I laugh when her mouth moves in a sucking motion. "Your mama needs a few more minutes of sleep. She's had a long stretch, winning an Oscar in the middle of filming just four weeks after giving birth and whatnot. Think you can go gentle on her and make this meal speedy-quick and then get right back to sleep?"

She squeaks and I grin, my heart fuller than I ever thought possible.

"Good girl," I whisper.

"Are you gonna chat her ear off or let me feed her?" Summer laughs when I jump and I turn, grinning when I see her leaning against the wall.

"I was trying to give you a few more minutes of sleep, but yeah, we got to talking and...she said she's gonna make this quick," I tell her.

Summer leans up and kisses my cheek before taking Scarlet from me. I follow her to the bedroom and crawl into bed next to them as Scarlet starts nursing.

"It was sweet of you," Summer says, turning her sleepy smile on me. "But these milk jugs woke me up."

"I don't know how you do it, but you even make milk jugs sound enticing." She snorts and then her eyes get wide when I palm my dick. Yep, it's hard. I wasn't kidding.

"Poor guy. Hang in there a few more minutes and I'll take care of that."

"What? No. Really?" I ask hopefully and then shake my head, trying to declutter the raunchy. "Nope. It's too soon. You've gotta heal up. *If you can't get any, I don't get any*," I quote the line I say every time she's healing from a pregnancy. She tries to argue with me every time, and my dick tries to join in on the argument often, but fair is fair.

She bumps her shoulder into mine. "I'm healed up and I am getting some *to*-night," she sings.

"You didn't tell me you had your checkup," I say.

"They had a cancellation. It was this afternoon. It was going to be a surprise, but the surprise was on me when I fell asleep tonight before I could rock your world."

"Hurry up, Scarlet," I whisper urgently to the baby and Summer giggles.

It's only fifteen or twenty minutes later but feels like an eternity before I'm taking Scarlet back to her bed, while Summer turns the baby monitor back on. I wait until the little angel's eyes are heavy and closing before I place her in her crib. And then I hold my breath as she wiggles around, exhaling with relief when she settles into a deeper sleep.

I sneak out of the room and hustle back to Summer, half expecting her to be sleeping when I get back. I wouldn't blame her, the first three months are exhausting with a baby; hell, it's all exhausting. But my face nearly breaks with how hard I smile when I see my wife stripped bare on our bed.

"Fuck me," I whisper.

"I plan on it," she whispers, leaning up on her knees,

and I'm reminded of our very first time, right here in this bed.

I get on my knees too, but on the floor, where it's just the right angle to get my mouth where I want it. I take my time worshiping her completely, until she's fluttering against my tongue, her fists in my hair as she chants my name over and over and over. And then she's begging for more.

"I love it when you beg," I tell her, coming up for air. "You know I will never deny you, Sweet Lips." I give her one more long swipe with my tongue and she shudders against me. "Lie back and spread your legs."

"I love it when you're bossy," she moans, doing as I ask.

I move over her and lower my face back down between her legs and she gives my hair a hard yank.

"Get in me now," she says.

"Who's the bossy one?" I tease.

"So help me, if one of the kids wakes up and we haven't done this at least twice, I will never forgive you."

"So greedy." I laugh, but I give her what she wants, my eyes rolling back in my head when I thrust in deep. Her head shakes back and forth as she clenches around me, coming hard again.

"I've missed you so much," she whimpers.

"Mmm, not as much as I've missed you," I groan.

"We can argue about that later. Get busy," she says, her eyes opening as she looks up at me with those fuck-me eyes and rocks against me. I get distracted by her tits and the way they sway with every thrust. "Eyes up here," she teases.

It's one of the first things she ever said to me. I couldn't take my eyes off of her then and I can't now.

"You don't mean it," I whisper, leaning down to kiss her hard.

"I love you, Liam," she says when we break apart, her breaths jagged as we get close.

I'll have to take my time with her the next round because she's greedy all right, she's on a mission to milk me dry.

"Best thing I've ever done, loving you," I tell her. And I mean it with everything in me.

Once a player, always a player—I never bought that nonsense. I was just waiting for her.

For Zac and Autumn's story, click here for Autumn Nights!

ACKNOWLEDGMENTS

Thank you to those of you who read *Summertime* on Kindle Vella. I hope you like the changes/additions. Kalie Phillips and Layne Deemer, your messages during the Vella version of this story motivated and inspired me. Thank you!

Nina Grinstead, I just love you...did from the first time we met and it only grows! Thank you for EVERYTHING.

Thank you, Valentine PR! And huge thanks to Kim Cermak, Sarah Norris, and Christine Miller for doing SO MUCH for me this year and for your kindness all along the way!

Emily Wittig, you've got a friend and fan for life. I heart you big-time. And your covers are amazing. Thank you for making this one so special!

Christine Estevez, thank you for your help (!) and your friendship and for still saying you love my books after all these years. :) I love you and I'm so grateful for you.

The Love Chain, Laura Pavlov and Catherine Cowles— thank you just doesn't seem big enough for what the two of you are to me on a daily basis. I love you always.

Tosha Khoury, my sister bff, I love you. Thank you for finding the things no one else finds in my books. I like your questions and I like everything about you.

Christine Bowden, I feel your love across the WORLD and am grateful that books brought us together. Love you so much.

Courtney Nuness, Claire Contreras, Tarryn Fisher, Troi and Phyllis Atkinson, Terrijo Montgomery, Anna Gomez, Kell Donaldson, Korrie Kelley, Savita Naik, Darla Williams, and Priscilla Perez, and those I'm forgetting eek, thank you for your encouragement and the love. I love you all.

For those who are part of my Asters group on a regular basis —you're the best!

Dad, I love you so much. And even though I hope you're not reading my books still, I love that you're a hardcore reader like me and that Mama was too.

One more thanks to my family. I can't say enough good things about you.

And special mention goes to my writing partner through every circumstance, rain or shine, no matter what—Sir Winston of Inver, my true puppy love, thank you for being the best companion ever.

Elton, I love you. You're the best grandcat I could ever ask for. :)

And thank you to every reader, every blogger, every author who took the time to share posts about this book and to review it! I'm so grateful for each one of you.

XO,
   Willow

ABOUT THE AUTHOR

Willow Aster is a USA Today Bestselling author and lover of anything book-related. She lives in St. Paul, MN with her husband, kids, rescue dog, and grandcat.

For ARCs, please join my master list: https://bit.ly/3CMKz5y

For behind-the-scenes of my books and freebies every month, sign up for my newsletter: http://www.willowaster.com/newsletter

www.willowaster.com

ALSO BY WILLOW ASTER

Standalones

True Love Story

Fade to Red

In the Fields

Maybe Maby (also available on all retailer sites)

Lilith (also available on all retailer sites)

Miles Apart (also available on all retailer sites)

Falling in Eden

Summertime

Autumn Nights

Kingdoms of Sin Series

Downfall

Exposed

Ruin

Pride

The End of Men Series with Tarryn Fisher

Folsom

Jackal

The G.D. Taylors Series with Laura Pavlov

Wanted Wed or Alive

The Bold and the Bullheaded

Another Motherfaker

Don't Cry Over Spilled MILF

Friends with Benefactors

Printed in Great Britain
by Amazon